"Well, well, well, what have we here? Bea in my bedchamber, looking very beddable."

Ranulf leaned forward as if he was about to kiss her and gave her a sodden grin. "If you only knew the thoughts I have about you sometimes, my dear, you'd steer very clear of me. I may not be the devil, but I'm certainly no saint."

No doubt he thought he was warning Beatrice, telling her to beware his animal lust.

His lust didn't frighten her. Indeed, she wished they could be this close, in this chamber, when he was sober.

Why not show him how she felt now?

Determined, excited, yet hardly believing that she was about to be so bold, Beatrice rose on her toes and whispered, "And if you, my lord, only knew some of the dreams I've had about you."

And then she kissed him...

MARGARET MOORE

Hers To Desire

HQN™

ISBN-13: 978-0-373-77124-0
ISBN-10:   0-373-77124-X

HERS TO DESIRE

Also by MARGARET MOORE

With special thanks to Nicole Hulst and Taline Jansezian for suggesting Titan for the name of Ranulf's horse.

HERS To DESIRE

PROLOGUE

The Midlands, 1228

IT WAS A MISTAKE to show fear.

If the boy had learned anything from the harsh, mocking tongue of his father and the fists of his older brothers, it was that. It was also a mistake to show joy. Or pity. Or indeed, any emotion at all. His home, if it could be called such, had been a cold brutal place after his mother had died.

So when Ranulf was forced to leave it, the twelve-year-old didn't mourn as most boys would. He didn't shed a single tear as his father chased him away with a whip, cursing and swearing and calling him terrible names. Nor did he run to avoid the blows. He ran because he was free. Free of the father who'd never cared for him. Free of his older brothers who beat and teased and tormented him. Free to go where he would, and do what he liked.

He knew exactly what that would be. No matter how difficult or long the journey, he was going to the castle of Sir Leonard de Brissy. He was going to learn to fight and eventually become a knight.

It was indeed a long and difficult journey—more so than he'd imagined—yet when Ranulf finally reached the gates of Sir Leonard's castle, he walked with his head high, his shoulders back, as if he feared nothing, his determined pride as fierce as his desire.

"Take me to Sir Leonard de Brissy," he ordered the startled soldiers standing in front of the massive wooden portcullis.

"Who are you and what do you want with Sir Leonard?" the older of the two men asked, his heavy dark brows furrowing as he studied the boy with the mop of matted red hair and torn, dirty clothing. The lad looked like a penniless urchin, but he carried himself as if he were a prince of the blood and spoke like one of the many noblemen's sons who came to be fostered and trained by Sir Leonard de Brissy in chivalry and the arts of war.

"I am Ranulf, son of Lord Faulk de Beauvieux. I have come to train with Sir Leonard," the boy declared, his slender hands balled into fists at his sides. Beneath the dirt, his sharp-featured face was pale and there were dark circles of fatigue under his hazel eyes.

"Well, Ranulf of Beauvieux," the older guard said, "it's not so simple as that. Sir Leonard chooses the boys he trains. Nobody—least of all a stripling lad—just arrives and demands to stay."

"I am the exception."

The younger soldier whistled under his breath. "Ain't you the cocky one?"

The lad raised one tawny brow. "I told you, I am Ranulf, son of Lord Faulk de Beauvieux, and I must see Sir Leonard. I have walked…I have come a long way to do so."

After the boy faltered, he fought all the harder to maintain his mask of haughty self-confidence, even though he began to despair that he might have come so far—walking alone in the dark of the night, stealing to eat and sleeping anywhere he could—for nothing.

"Walked here, eh?" the younger guard asked, his expression relaxing into a grudging respect. "Come from a long ways off, have you?"

"I will explain to Sir Leonard, not to you," Ranulf replied.

"What will you explain to me?" a deep, gruff voice demanded.

The guards immediately straightened, stiff as planks. They continued to face the road leading into the castle and didn't turn around to look at the man who'd spoken. Ranulf, however, could easily see the tall, gray-haired man dressed in chain mail and a black surcoat striding toward them with the easy gait of a man half his age. His long, narrow face was brown as oak from days in the saddle and marked with several small scars. Yet it was not the sun-browned skin that drew Ranulf's attention, or the scars, or the shoulder-length iron-gray hair. It was the man's piercing ice-blue eyes, eyes that sought the truth.

This man had to be Sir Leonard de Brissy and Ranulf knew, with absolute certainty, that if he lied or exaggerated, he would be turned away. He would never learn how to fight and use weapons with skill. He would never be a knight.

When Sir Leonard came to halt, Ranulf met that stern gaze as he bowed. "Sir Leonard, I am Ranulf, son of Lord Faulk de Beauvieux. I wish to join your household and learn to be a knight."

"I have heard of Faulk de Beauvieux," Sir Leonard coolly replied as he studied the son of a man known to be viciously cruel, who drank hard and fought harder. He saw Faulk's foxlike features repeated in his offspring. The lad had also inherited his father's slim, wiry build, broad shoulders and straight back, as well as the proud bearing of his arrogant sire.

Yet the sight of that red hair and those green-brown eyes tugged at Sir Leonard's stern heart. They were not from Faulk; they came from the lad's mother, a woman Sir Leonard had not seen for twenty years. Yet the eyes Sir Leonard remembered had been soft and gentle; the ones gazing back at him now had a strength and determination his mother had never possessed, or she might have been able to avoid the marriage her parents arranged for her.

And there was still more. That the boy was anxious was obvious to Sir Leonard's seasoned eye, for he'd been training noblemen's sons for thirty years and had seen more than his share of youthful bluster. Still, this boy stood with a self-controlled fortitude Sir Leonard had rarely seen, except in the most well-trained, seasoned knights.

This was no ordinary lad. One day, he could either be a valued ally, or an implacable enemy.

He would prefer the ally.

So Sir Leonard gave the boy one of his very rare smiles and said, "I knew your mother when she was a girl. For her sake, you are welcome here, Ranulf de Beauvieux."

Although relief flooded through Ranulf like a river breaking its banks, he hastened to set Sir Leonard straight on one important thing. "I am not of Beauvieux, and I never will be. My father has cast me out, and I want nothing more to do with him, or my brothers."

"Why did your father do that?"

Ranulf had known this question would be asked and, as before, he could not lie. "That I will tell you in private," he said, sliding a glance at the sentries still standing stiffly nearby. "My family's business is not fodder for gossip."

Instead of taking offense or—worse—laughing, Sir Leonard gravely nodded. "Then come, Ranulf. I believe we have much to talk about."

CHAPTER ONE

Cornwall, 1244

THE LORD OF TREGELLAS fidgeted on his carved oaken chair on the dais of his great hall. "God's wounds, does it always take so long?" he muttered under his breath.

Normally Lord Merrick was the most stoic of men, and the hall of Tregellas a place of ease and comfort. Today, however, his lordship's beloved wife was struggling to bring forth their first child in the lord's bedchamber above, so everyone was anxious. The servants moved with silent caution, and even the hounds lay still and quiet in the rushes that covered the floor.

Only Lord Merrick's bearded, red-haired friend seemed at ease as he sat on that same dais and took a sip of wine. "I've heard that two or even three days are not uncommon for a first birthing," Sir Ranulf remarked.

Merrick's eyes narrowed. "Is that supposed to comfort me?"

Ranulf's full lips curved up in a slightly sardonic smile. "Actually, yes."

As Merrick sniffed with derision, Ranulf set down his goblet. "It seems an age to us, and no doubt longer to your Constance, but I gather a lengthy labor is not unusual the first time, nor does it indicate any special danger for the mother or child."

"I didn't know you were an expert."

"I'm not," Ranulf said, refusing to let his friend's brusque manner disturb him. Merrick had never been known for his charm. "I truly don't think there's any cause for worry. If your wife or the babe were at risk, the midwife would have summoned both you and the priest, and Lady Beatrice would have been sent from the chamber."

In fact, and although he didn't say so, Ranulf thought it rather odd that Beatrice was still in Constance's bedchamber, regardless of what was transpiring. He didn't think Beatrice should be witnessing the travails of childbirth, or inflicting her rather too bubbly presence on a woman at such a time. If he were in pain, the last thing he'd want would be lively Lady Bea buzzing about, telling him the latest gossip or regaling him with yet another tale of King Arthur and his knights.

"Constance wanted her," Merrick said with a shrug. "They are more like sisters than cousins, you know."

Ranulf was well aware of the close bond between his best friend's wife and her cousin. That was why

Beatrice had a home here in Tregellas although she had nothing to her name but her title, and that was due to Merrick's influence with the earl of Cornwall. Otherwise, Beatrice would have lost that, too, when her father was executed for treason.

Merrick started to rise. "I cannot abide this waiting. I'm going to—"

The door to the hall banged open, aided by a gust of wind. Both men turned to see a vaguely familiar man on the threshold, his cloak damp with rain, his chest heaving as he panted.

"My lord!" the round-faced young man called out as he rushed toward the dais.

"It's Myghal, the undersheriff of Penterwell," Merrick said.

That was one of the smaller estates that made up Merrick's demesne on the southern coast, and as they hurried to meet the man halfway, Ranulf was unfortunately certain this fellow's breathless advent could herald nothing good.

"My lord!" Myghal repeated as he bowed, his Cornish accent apparent in his address. "I regret I bring bad tidings from Penterwell, my lord." He bluntly delivered the rest of his news. "Sir Frioc is dead."

Sir Frioc was—or had been—the castellan of Penterwell. The portly, good-tempered Frioc had also been a just man, or Merrick would have chosen another for that post when he assumed lordship of Tregellas after his late father's demise.

"How did he die?" Merrick asked, his face its usual grim mask.

Ranulf could hear his friend's underlying concern, although there was no trouble at Penterwell that Ranulf could recall, other than the usual smuggling to which Merrick and his castellan generally turned a blind eye.

"A fall from his horse while hunting, my lord," Myghal answered. "Sir Frioc went chasing after a hare. We lost sight of him and when we finally found him, he was lying on the moor, his neck broken. His horse was close by, lame. Hedyn thinks it stumbled and threw him."

Hedyn was the sheriff of Penterwell, and a man Merrick had likewise considered trustworthy enough to remain in that post. Ranulf hadn't disagreed. He, too, had been impressed by the middle-aged man when Merrick had visited his recently inherited estates.

Myghal reached into his tunic and withdrew a leather pouch. "Hedyn wrote it all down here, my lord."

Merrick took the pouch and pulled open the drawstring. "Go to the kitchen and get some food and drink." he said to Myghal. "One of my servants will see that you have bedding for the night and a place at table."

After Myghal bowed and headed toward the kitchen, Merrick's gaze flicked once more to the steps leading up to his bedchamber, and his wife, before he walked back to his chair, drew out the letter, broke the heavy wax seal and began to read.

Trying not to betray any impatience, Ranulf finished his wine and waited for Merrick to speak. Yet after Merrick had finished reading and had folded the letter, he remained silent and stared, unseeing, at the tapestry behind Ranulf, tapping the parchment against his chin.

"I'm sorry to hear about Sir Frioc," Ranulf ventured. "I liked him."

Merrick nodded and again he glanced toward the stairs, telling Ranulf that whatever else occupied his friend's mind, he was still worried about his wife.

"At least there's no widow to consider," Ranulf noted, "since Frioc's wife died years ago—or daughters, either, for that matter. Nor are there sons who might expect to inherit a father's position, although that privilege is yours to bestow or withhold."

Merrick put the letter into the pouch and shoved it into his tunic.

"You'll need a new castellan, though."

"Yes," Merrick replied.

"Who do you have in mind?"

His dark-eyed friend regarded Ranulf steadily. "You."

Ranulf nearly gasped aloud. He wanted no such responsibility—no ties, no duty beyond that of the oath of loyalty he'd sworn to his friends, and Sir Leonard, and the king.

He quickly covered his dismay, however, and managed a laugh. "Me? I thank you for the compliment, my friend, but I have no wish to be a castellan on the coast of Cornwall. Even my position here as garrison commander was to be temporary, remember?"

"You deserve to be in charge of a castle."

Ranulf couldn't help being pleased and flattered by his friend's answer, but this was still a gift, and a gift could be taken away. He would have no man— or woman—know that he mourned the loss of anything, or anyone.

He inclined his head in a polite bow. "Again, my friend, I thank you. However, a castle so near the coast would be far too damp for me. I already feel it in my right elbow when it's about to rain."

Merrick's dark brows rose as he scrutinized Ranulf in a way that would have done credit to Sir Leonard himself. "You would have me believe you're too old and decrepit to command one of my castles?"

"I am still fit to fight, thank God," Ranulf immediately replied, "but truly, I have no desire to spend my days collecting tithes and taxes."

Merrick frowned. "The castellan of Penterwell will have much more to do than that, and I would have someone I trust overseeing that part of the coast. There has been some trouble and I—"

A woman's piercing cry rent the air. His face pale, his eyes wide with horror, Merrick jumped to his feet as a serving woman came flying down the steps from the bedchamber.

Merrick was in front of the plump, normally cheerful

Demelza in an instant, with Ranulf right behind him. "What's wrong?" the lord of Tregellas demanded.

"Nothing, my lord, nothing," the maidservant hastened to assure him as she chewed her lip and smoothed down her homespun skirt. "It's just the end, i'n't? The babe's coming fast now. If you please, my lord, the midwife sent me to fetch more hot water."

When Merrick looked about to ask another question, Ranulf put his hand on her friend's arm. "Let her go."

Merrick nodded like one half-dead, and Ranulf's heart, even walled off as it was, felt pity for him. He knew what Merrick feared, just as he knew all too well what it was to lose a woman you loved.

"Tell me what's going on at Penterwell," he prompted as he led his friend back to the dais and thought about Merrick's offer.

Merrick was one of his best and oldest friends. Together with their other trusted comrade, Henry, they had pledged their loyalty to each other and to be brothers-in-arms for life.

What was Merrick really asking of him except his help? Did he not owe it to Merrick to respond to that request when Merrick was in need, as he'd implied?

Besides, if he went to Penterwell, he would be well away from Beatrice. "I should know everything you can tell me if I'm to be castellan."

"You'll do it?" Merrick asked as he sank onto his cushioned chair.

"It has occurred to me, my friend, that as castellan I shall also have control over the kitchen," Ranulf replied with his usual cool composure. "I can have my meat cooked however I like, and all the bread I want. That's not an entitlement to be taken lightly, I assure you."

Because he knew his friend wasn't serious when he named culinary benefits as his primary reason for accepting the post, a genuine, if very small, smile appeared on Merrick's face. "I didn't realize you considered yourself ill-fed here."

"Oh, I don't. It's the power that appeals to me."

Merrick's smile grew a little more. "Whatever reason you give me, I am glad you've agreed."

"So, my friend, what exactly is going on in Penterwell?"

Becoming serious, Merrick leaned forward, his forearms on his thighs, his hands clasped. "There's something amiss among the villagers. Frioc didn't know exactly what. He thought it might be rivalry over a woman, or perhaps an accusation of cheating in a game of chance. Either way, he didn't consider it serious enough to merit a visit from me."

Merrick stared at his boots and shook his head. "I should have gone there myself anyway."

"You had other things on your mind."

Merrick raised his eyes to regard his friend. "That's no excuse, and if Frioc is dead because I was remiss…"

"You're worrying like an old woman," Ranulf

chided. "It could well be that Frioc was right, and he was simply noticing some minor enmity among the villagers. We both know there can be a hundred causes for that, none of them worthy of investigation. As to his death, I wouldn't be surprised if the man simply fell. He was no great rider, if memory serves."

Another clatter of footsteps came from the stairwell and again, Ranulf and Merrick leapt to their feet.

"It's a boy!" Lady Beatrice cried as she appeared at the bottom of the steps. Her bright blue eyes were shining with happiness, her beautiful features were full of delight, and with her blond hair unbound about her slender shoulders, she looked like an angel bringing glory. "Merrick has a son! A beautiful baby boy!"

Merrick nearly tripped over his chair as he rushed to her. Then the normally restrained and dignified lord of Tregellas grabbed his wife's cousin around the waist and spun her, giggling like a child, in a circle.

Ranulf stood rooted to the spot while envy—sharp as a dagger, bitter as poison—stabbed his heart.

Merrick set the laughing Beatrice down and worry returned to his features. "Constance? How is—?"

"Very well indeed," Beatrice answered, smiling and excitedly clutching Merrick's forearm. "Oh, Merrick, she was wonderful! The midwife said she'd never seen a braver lady. You should be so proud. She hardly cried out at all, and only right at the end. She did everything just as the midwife said—and that's a very good midwife, too, I must say. Aeda was very competent and encouraging, and never once gave Constance any cause to fear. She assured her all would be well—as, indeed, it was.

"And oh, Merrick! You should see your boy! He has dark hair like you, and he started to cry right away and kicked so strongly! Aeda says he would have come faster except for his broad shoulders. It seems ridiculous to think of a baby with broad shoulders, doesn't it, but I suppose she ought to know, having seen so many. She says he's going to break hearts when he's older, too, because he's so handsome."

Beatrice finally let go of Merrick's arm. "I mustn't keep you here. Constance is very anxious to see you and show you your little boy."

Once released, Merrick ran to the steps and took them three at a time. Meanwhile, Ranulf decided he had no more reason to remain in the hall. He was beginning to turn away when Beatrice suddenly enveloped him in a crushing embrace.

"Oh, this is a joyous day, is it not?" she cried, her breath warm on his neck as she held him close.

Ranulf stood absolutely still. His arms stayed stiffly at his sides and he made no effort at all to return her embrace, although she fit against him perfectly.

Too perfectly.

He ordered himself to feel nothing, even when her lips were so close to his skin. He would pay no heed to the softness of her womanly curves against him. He would not think about her bright eyes and lovely features, or the way her mouth opened when she smiled, or notice the delicate scent of lavender that lingered about her. He would remember that she was sweet and innocent and pure—and he was not.

"Yes, it is a momentous occasion," he replied evenly. He gently disengaged her arms. She was surely too naive to realize the effect that sort of physical act could have on a man. "But alas, my duties remain. If you'll excuse me, my lady, I should give the men the watchword for tonight. I think it will be 'son and heir.'"

"That's wonderful!" she cried, apparently not at all nonplused by his lack of response to her embrace. "And you're quite right. We mustn't let everything come to a complete halt."

She turned to the equally pleased servants, some of whom had been in the hall, and others who had heard the news and hurried there. "Back to work, all of you," she ordered, the force of her command somewhat diminished by her merry eyes and dimpled cheeks.

Then she put her slender hands on Ranulf's forearm and smiled up into his face. "Oh, Ranulf," she said with the same happy enthusiasm, "he has the sweetest blue eyes, just like his mother's. Aeda says all babies have blue eyes, but I think they'll always be blue. And the way they crinkle when he cries! It's so adorable!"

Ranulf was tempted to lift her slender hands from his arm to stop the torment of her touch, but he didn't want to draw any attention to his discomfort. "I daresay the crying will become less adorable in the next few weeks."

"It means his lungs are strong and healthy," Beatrice replied, her tone cheerfully chastising. "He started to whimper right away and then he let out such a cry, the midwife said, 'There's nothing wrong with this boy's lungs, that's for certain.'"

Beatrice leaned against Ranulf, bringing her breasts into contact with his arm. "That's how we learned it was a boy. You should have seen Constance's face!"

Beatrice gripped him a little harder and he was uncomfortably reminded of the sort of force a woman sometimes exerted in the throes of passion.

Sweet heaven, how long was this torture going to last?

"Constance started to cry and then she laughed and said Merrick claimed he didn't care if it was a boy or a girl, but she had prayed and prayed for a boy. I think it would have been too mean of God to deny her prayers after all she went through with Merrick's father, don't you?"

"I think God moves in mysterious ways," Ranulf replied as he finally pulled away and reached for Merrick's goblet and offered it to the breathless Beatrice. It was one way to part from her, and he was very careful to ensure that his hand did not touch hers when she gratefully accepted it.

As she drank, he noticed the dark circles of fatigue beneath her eyes, and that she was far too pale. "You should rest," he said with a displeased frown.

"Oh, I'm not at all tired!" she exclaimed. "And it's such a wonderful day—although now I confess I was very worried and afraid some of the time, not like Constance, who didn't seem frightened at all. She asked me quite calmly to tell her all the gossip and when I'd told her everything I could think of, she suggested I tell her the stories of King Arthur she likes best." Beatrice beamed proudly. "She told me I was a great help—and Aeda only asked me to be quiet once!"

The midwife must be a model of patience, and Constance was kind. If he was lying in pain, he wouldn't want Beatrice hovering near the bed, bathing his heated brow, or offering him food and drink, perhaps whispering a few soothing words in his ear…

He mentally shook his head. He must be fatigued himself if he was envisioning Beatrice nursing him and thinking it might be pleasant. For one thing, she'd never be able to sit still.

"If you'll excuse me, Lady Beatrice," he said, "I really must go. I've wasted enough of the day already."

"I wouldn't call sitting with your friend at such a time a waste. I'm sure Merrick was very grateful for your company."

"Be that as it may," Ranulf replied, "I really must be about my duties. Until this evening, my lady," he finished with another bow. "After you've had a nap, I hope."

She put her hands on her slender hips, reminding him—as if he needed it!—that she had a very shapely figure. "I'm not an infant to be taking naps. You seem to forget, Sir Ranulf, that I'm old enough to be married and have children myself."

"Rest assured, my lady, I'm very aware of your age," Ranulf said before he made another bow, turned and strode out of the hall.

"What's that devil's spawn been saying to you?"

CHAPTER TWO

SUBDUING A GRIMACE, Beatrice turned to find her former nurse behind her. There were times Beatrice found Maloren trying, even though Maloren had been like a second mother to her after her own had died when she was very young.

For one thing, Maloren hated men, and red-haired ones most of all. Right now she was scowling as fiercely as an irate fishmonger with a basket full of spoiled salmon, and Beatrice prepared for a tirade before she answered. "He was telling me I look tired and ought to take a nap."

Maloren shook her finger at Beatrice. "I knew it! He was trying to get you into his bed, that rogue! Haven't I warned you a hundred times, my lamb, my dear? Stay away from that scoundrel with his red hair and those devil eyes. He'll ruin you if you're not careful."

Beatrice subdued a mournful sigh. Little did Maloren know—for Beatrice was certainly not going to tell her—but that was exactly what Beatrice wanted: to share Ranulf's bed.

If her father hadn't been a traitor, she could have

hoped to become Ranulf's wife. Unfortunately, thanks to her father's treacherous ambition, she no longer had any chance for that. Even though her cousin and her husband had seen to it she'd kept her title and even offered to provide a dowry, she was still no bridal prize. Ranulf could—and should—aim higher when it came to taking a wife.

That meant the best Beatrice could hope for was to be his lover. And how she did hope! With his lean, angular features, powerful warrior's body, and intelligent hazel eyes, Ranulf was the most attractive man she'd ever met. He also moved with a graceful, athletic gait no other man possessed. Moreover, he was Lord Merrick's trusted friend and a chivalrous, honorable knight.

Yet therein lay the problem. Because he was such an honorable man, Ranulf would never attempt to seduce a friend's relative, not even if she wanted him to, or if he shared her desire.

"I've seen the way that Ranulf watches you sometimes," Maloren grumbled, her features twisting as if she'd eaten something sour. "I know what's on *his* mind."

Beatrice nearly gasped aloud. Maloren hadn't meant to be encouraging, but Beatrice's heart seemed to take wing. Perhaps she wasn't wrong to hope, after all, and her dearest dream could come true.

Although Ranulf treated her with an aloof courtesy most of the time, there had been times when

Beatrice, too, thought he looked at her as if he felt
the same strong longing she did and might even act
upon it. Last Christmas, after they had danced a
round dance together, they had somehow, by mutual
unspoken consent, moved away from the other
dancers until they were in a shadowed corner out of
sight. She had turned to him to say something—she
couldn't remember what—and found him regarding
her with a look of such…such…*implication,* she had
immediately been struck speechless, silently thrilled
beyond anything she had ever known.

Her body had responded, too, warming beneath his
gaze. Softening. Her heartbeat quickened and her lips
parted, ready for his kiss. She craved his lips upon hers,
as if there was nothing more important in all the world.

But then he'd drawn back and that indifferent
mask had returned, and he had offered, in a cool,
offhand way, to fetch her some mulled wine.

She feared she'd imagined his look of longing. She
found it easy to imagine him raising one quizzical brow
and rejecting her with cutting sarcasm or laughing at
her for thinking she could ever be attractive to a man
like him. Maybe, she'd feared, he was only tolerating
her because she was Constance's cousin and she was
being vain to think he could ever want her.

Yet she had also wondered if he'd withdrawn
because he would never give in to his desire for a
friend's relative unless they were honorably married.

Whatever her hopes and fears regarding Ranulf,

she didn't dare betray them to Maloren. She didn't want everyone in the castle to hear Maloren's cries of dismay, followed by curses, accusations and denunciations. She wanted to be able to retain some shred of dignity if Ranulf didn't want her after all.

Nevertheless, Beatrice couldn't help smiling when she said, "*Sir* Ranulf's mind is on his duties. He's rightly gone about them, and so should I. I should ensure Gaston has made suitable dishes to build up Constance's strength. Aeda says Constance should have some ale, as well. You may come with me to the kitchen or not, as you choose."

"That Gaston puts far too many spices in his sauces," Maloren complained as she followed. "Does he think Lord Merrick richer than the king? I'm surprised we don't all have bellyaches every day."

Since Maloren ate most of the sauces she was complaining about, Beatrice made no reply. Instead, she wondered what she should wear to the evening meal, when she would be sitting beside Ranulf.

BEATRICE DISCOVERED it didn't matter what she wore. Ranulf barely looked at her at all; his attention was focused mainly on the food. To be fair, Gaston, who'd been as happy as everyone in Tregellas about the birth, had outdone himself. There were cunning puddings and savory stews of leeks and mutton, rich pastries and venison roasted to perfection, along with several kinds of fish and a dish made of eggs and breadcrumbs so deliciously and delicately spiced, not even Maloren could find fault with it.

Beatrice tried not to be hurt by Ranulf's lack of attendance on her. After all, he never made much conversation during a meal. But surely tonight, when they had such a wonderful thing to talk about, he could make more of an effort instead of leaving her to carry on the conversation all by herself.

Eventually, worried that she was irritating him with her chatter, she fell silent.

Ranulf didn't seem to notice that, either.

A short time later, Merrick arrived in the hall, bringing with him his grandfather Peder, for whom the heir of Tregellas was to be named. Beatrice retired shortly after that and left the three men drinking toasts to the future lord. Merrick bid her a jovial goodnight, and Peder told her to sleep well. Ranulf merely sipped his wine and watched her turn away, as if he didn't care one way or another if she stayed or went.

Perhaps she was wrong after all to think that Ranulf felt any kind of affection or desire for her. Maybe what she thought she saw didn't exist outside her own hopeful imagination.

No doubt she would do better to try not to want him. Surely there were other men…there *must* be other men who could stir her heart. Somewhere.

Disturbed and dismayed, and although she'd been summoned to Constance's bedchamber very early that morning, she couldn't fall asleep.

When Maloren, lying on the pallet near her door, began to snore, Beatrice quietly got out of bed. She drew her bed robe on over her shift and shoved her feet into her fur-lined slippers.

What would happen if she went to Ranulf now? she wondered. Would he welcome her or regard her with horror? Take what she offered or send her away and, in the morning, tell Merrick that his ward was a wanton who ought to be sent to a convent?

A thud, followed by a muffled curse, interrupted her turbulent thoughts. She immediately glanced at Maloren, who was mercifully still asleep, in part because she had always slept soundly and also because she was lying on her good ear.

There was another muttered curse, followed by a low groan. Beatrice was sure she recognized that voice, and that Ranulf was in some pain. She hurried to the door and eased it open, holding her breath as Maloren shifted and began to snore louder.

Moonlight streamed in through the narrow arched windows, lighting the corridor and Ranulf, sitting with his back against the wall, his legs outstretched and a rather baffled look on his face. At the evening meal he'd been wearing a black woolen tunic over a white linen shirt, black breeches and boots. After she'd retired, he'd obviously taken off the black tunic and loosened the ties at the neck of his shirt. Now it gaped open to reveal his muscular chest and the reddish-brown hairs growing there.

"Can you help me to my feet, my angel?" he asked with a decidedly drunken grin, his words slurred as he slackly held out his hand.

Beatrice had never seen Ranulf in his cups before, and she didn't doubt celebrating with Merrick explained his state now. Even so, if he didn't get into his chamber soon, he might wake Maloren, and her annoyed reaction would surely rouse the household.

Beatrice hurried to put her shoulder beneath his arm to help him rise. Unfortunately, he made no effort to move except to shake his head and say, "I don't think this's quite right. You ought to be in bed."

"I'm not going to leave you here in the corridor. And please be quiet, or Maloren might hear you."

"That old witch," Ranulf muttered with a frown. "Keeps calling me the devil's spawn. As if I could help who my father was." He began to get to his feet, leaning heavily on her. "But no, we don't want to wake her, Bea, my beauty."

He had called her an angel and "his" beauty, and Bea. Not even Constance used that diminutive of her name. Perhaps he really did like her, after all.

As they started toward his chamber, which was at the far end of the corridor, he mumbled, "D'you suppose she's met my father? Or my brothers? They used to beat me to see who could make me cry first, you know. Sort of a contest."

Beatrice knew almost nothing about Ranulf's past, except that he had trained with Merrick under the tutelage of Sir Leonard de Brissy, and that he, Merrick and their other friend, Henry, had sworn to be brothers-in-arms for life. That was why Ranulf had come with Merrick to Tregellas, why he'd accepted the post of garrison commander at his friend's request, and why he was still there.

"No pity, my little Lady Bea," he warned as he waggled a finger at her. "I won't have it. Don't need it. They made me strong, you see."

What was there to say to that, especially when she had to get him to his chamber undetected? Although she didn't have to support his full weight, he was no light burden.

Ranulf suddenly came to a halt and tried to push her away. "You should be in bed. Sleeping."

"I'll sleep later."

He leaned dizzily against the wall. "All by yourself."

"Yes. Now come, Ranulf, and let me help you to your chamber."

She tried to take his arm, but he slid away. "My bed. Where I'll be all by myself, too. Where I'm always by myself. No mistresses for me. No lovers. Just the occasional whore in town, because a man has needs, my lady."

"I really have no wish to stand here in the middle of the night and hear about your women," Beatrice said with a hint of frustration. "Now come along, or I may be forced to leave you."

He lurched forward and threw his arm around her

shoulder, making her stagger. "In that case, lead on, my lovely lady. Don't want to be left again. No, never again."

When had he been "left"? She longed to ask him, but his words were coming more slowly and were harder to make out. If she didn't get him to bed soon, she might have no choice but to leave him in the corridor.

Fortunately, they made it to his chamber without further interruptions. She shoved open the door with her shoulder and together they staggered into the room.

He tilted backward and she grabbed him about the waist to keep him upright. As he regained his balance, she was acutely aware that if anybody saw them, it would look as if they were in a lover's embrace. Unfortunately, she couldn't reach the door, not even to kick it shut with her foot.

Ranulf looked down at her, his eyes not quite focused. "Well, well, well," he murmured, and she could smell the wine on his breath, "what have we here? Bea in my bedchamber, looking very bedable."

He leaned forward as if he was about to kiss her and gave her a sodden grin. "If you only knew the thoughts I have about you sometimes, my dear, you'd steer very clear of me. I may not be the devil, but I'm certainly no saint."

No doubt he thought he was warning her, telling her to beware his animal lust.

His lust didn't frighten her. Indeed, she wished

they could be this close, in this chamber, when he was sober.

Who could say when she would ever be alone with him again, when there would be no irate Maloren watching, or other servants wandering by? Why not show him how she felt now?

Determined, excited, yet hardly believing that she was about to be so bold, Beatrice raised herself on her toes and whispered, "And if you, my lord, only knew some of the dreams I've had about you."

And then she kissed him, brushing her lips against his as she had dreamed of doing so many times. For an instant, he stiffened and then, with a low moan that seemed to come from the depths of his soul, he gathered her into his arms. Holding her close, his lips moved over hers with a yearning, passionate hunger, while his hands pressed her closer. They were like two lovers alone at last, and she eagerly surrendered to the burning desire coursing through her body.

This was what she'd hoped for, dreamed of—this touch, this taste, this kiss, these caresses. This was the embrace, the imagined feelings, that had haunted her dreams, both sleeping and waking. This was what she'd imagined since even before Christmas, when she wanted Ranulf to take her in his strong arms and kiss her until morning.

Very much in the present, the tip of his tongue pushed against her lips. She willingly parted them to allow him to deepen the kiss in a way that made her passion flare.

She moaned with sheer pleasure. She had never been happier, or more excited.

He suddenly reared as if she'd struck him. "Stop it," he cried as he reeled toward the bed. "Leave me alone!"

He was so angry, when before he'd been so passionate. Why had he changed? Had he suddenly remembered who she was? Was he appalled because she was Constance's cousin and his friend's ward—or because she was Beatrice? "Ranulf, please! What is it?"

He sat heavily on the bed and put his head in his hands. "Just go!"

Tears starting in her eyes, Beatrice turned and fled without another word.

"I KNEW THERE'D BE trouble, the three of them drinking like farmhands at a feast day," Maloren said as she came bustling into Beatrice's chamber the next morning, a bucket of steaming water in her hands.

"Trouble? What sort of trouble?" Beatrice demanded, instantly wide-awake and worried that Maloren had somehow learned about her disastrous, humiliating encounter with Ranulf.

After leaving his chamber, she'd run back to her own and climbed into her bed, where she'd silently cried herself to sleep, all her lovely dreams like ashes in a dust heap and the memory of that incredible kiss ruined forever by her shame.

As Maloren set down the bucket and proceeded to straighten the combs and ribbons lying on her dressing table, Beatrice relaxed a little. Maloren couldn't have found out that she'd been with Ranulf, or she'd be berating her.

"Lord Merrick took a tumble getting his grandfather home last night—the two of them drunk and singing songs at the top of their lungs, or so I hear," Maloren announced. "Lady Constance had to send for the apothecary."

Sending for the apothecary meant that Merrick's injury might be serious. Her own troubles momentarily forgotten, Beatrice threw back the covers and got out of bed. "I hope he's not badly hurt."

"It's a clean break, the apothecary says, and should mend nicely if Lord Merrick keeps off his leg. Maybe now old Peder will come to live here as he should, instead of in that cottage of his. Many's the time I've said—"

"The apothecary's been and gone?" Beatrice interrupted as she went to the chest holding her gowns.

Maloren gave her an indulgent smile. "Lord love you, my lamb, it's nearly the noon. You needed your rest, so I let you sleep."

Perhaps that was just as well. She wasn't sure what she would have said or done if she'd met Ranulf at mass, Beatrice thought as she lifted the chest's lid. "Constance must have been upset. I should go to her at once."

"She'll be glad of your company, I'm sure, and she's going to have her hands full keeping Lord Merrick still, I don't doubt. I wouldn't be surprised if he's grumbling already. That's menfolk for you—big babies the lot of them when they get hurt or take sick. If they had to bear children, they'd be whining forever. But first you ought to get something to eat, my lamb. Gaston should have a nice porridge waiting. I told him to keep it warm."

"At least Ranulf is here to command the garrison," Beatrice noted as she pulled out the uppermost gown made of a soft, leaf-green wool. "We need have no fear that anyone would dare attack, even if they hear Merrick's injured."

Maloren sniffed. "That devil of a Sir Ranulf rode out at first light, and good riddance."

Beatrice couldn't hide her shock as she turned to stare at Maloren. Fear and shame shot through her, combining with her guilt. She didn't think anyone had seen her, but she'd been distraught when she'd left Ranulf's chamber. Perhaps a wakeful servant or a guard on the wall walk had noticed her and told Constance or Merrick.

If that was so and they had sent Ranulf away because of what had happened last night, she must explain that Ranulf was innocent of any immoral intentions and ask them to summon him home. Anything improper that had happened between her and Ranulf had been all her doing, and she would tell them so, no matter how humiliating that would be. "Why did he go?"

"Didn't you hear? Lord Merrick's made him the castellan of Penterwell," Maloren answered as she helped Beatrice into her gown.

Beatrice nearly sank to the floor with relief. That wasn't a punishment. That was a reward. So why hadn't he told her during the evening meal, instead of sitting so silently beside her?

Perhaps Ranulf thought she already knew. Demelza and the other servants had probably assumed the same.

What must Ranulf have thought as she babbled away about Constance and the baby without ever once mentioning his well-deserved reward and subsequent departure? That she didn't care?

"Although why Lord Merrick did that, I don't know," Maloren muttered as she tied the laces of Beatrice's gown. "That fall must have addled his wits. Everybody knows you can't trust people with red hair. And him with those sly, foxy eyes, too. Next thing you know, that Ranulf'll be stealing this castle out from under Lord Merrick's very nose."

Beatrice whirled around to face Maloren. Whether Maloren was her treasured almost-mother or not, Beatrice couldn't allow such an accusation, unfounded as it was, to pass unremarked. "You know Ranulf would never do such a thing, or even think it. He's a good and loyal friend to Merrick."

Maloren flushed. It wasn't often Beatrice spoke or acted like the titled lady and daughter of an imperious father she was, but when she did, Maloren dutifully deferred to her mistress. "Forgive me, my lamb. I'm only worried for Lord Merrick's sake."

"Lord Merrick is more than capable of managing his estate without your assistance and if he sees fit to make Ranulf a castellan, that should be more than enough for you—or anyone."

Maloren suddenly looked every one of her years. "Don't be angry with me, my lamb, my own," she pleaded, wringing her work-worn hands. "You can't see it, I suppose, but he's just like your father when he was young. Handsome as the devil, and witty and clever. Slick as lamp oil in a puddle."

She took Beatrice's hands in her callused ones and regarded her charge with loving concern. "He had your mother in love with him in a week and made her his wife in a fortnight." Maloren's hands squeezed tighter as her voice grew full of sorrow. "But oh, the pain he brought her! First he killed her joy, and finally her spirit, till even her love for her baby couldn't give her strength against illness."

Maloren let go of Beatrice as a fiercely protective gleam came into her eyes. "I won't let any man hurt you as your father did your mother."

This was the first time Maloren had ever spoken of her mother's fate, and it hurt Beatrice to hear how her mother had suffered. Yet she had always supposed her mother's life hadn't been a happy one. Her father had loved no one but himself. He cared only about wealth and power. He'd been pleased his daughter was pretty, because that made her a more valuable prize to offer. She had been a thing to be traded, sold or bartered.

How much worse her life would have been if she'd not had Maloren to love and comfort her in her poor mother's place!

Overwhelmed with gratitude, she hugged Maloren tightly. "I'm sorry I lost my temper with you, Maloren. I love you as if you were my own mother." She drew back and looked up into the beloved, wrinkled face and pale gray eyes. "You know that, don't you?"

"Bless you, my lamb, I do, and I love you as if you were my own daughter."

Beatrice once again embraced her former nurse, feeling as she had when she was a little girl and her father had shooed her away as if she were nothing more to him than one of his hounds. Maloren's arms had brought comfort and security then, while her father had brought her only sorrow, heartache and, eventually, disgrace.

What honorable knight would want such a man's daughter? No wonder Ranulf had left without even saying goodbye.

CHAPTER THREE

HIS ACHING HEAD WAS a just punishment for too much celebrating, Ranulf thought as he rode wearily along the coast of Cornwall over a very rocky road, doing his best to keep his destrier firmly in check. Titan was a lively beast, which usually suited Ranulf. Not for him a stolid warhorse, although there were those who preferred a calmer animal. Ranulf wanted a horse with spirit, one that was ready to fight and willing to attack with the lightest touch of his master's heels.

Today, however, a less frisky mount would have been welcome.

Ranulf knew he should have retired long before he did, even if Merrick had been in a rare and boisterous mood last night. Henry would never believe the way their usually grim and silent friend had laughed and joked, especially once his grandfather— a fine old fellow—began to toast his great-grandson, the future lord of Tregellas, as well as his namesake. Peder had been justly proud and insisted they salute everyone from the king down to the maid who kept their goblets full, until they'd finally parted, Merrick helping his grandfather back to his cottage while Ranulf staggered up to his spartan bedchamber.

Not that he could remember actually getting to his bedchamber.

Once asleep, he'd had the most devilishly disturbing dreams, too, all featuring Bea. Sometimes she was making merry with him, toasting and eating and dancing, and it was Christmas. Sometimes she was undressed and in his bed, and they were making love. The most vivid dream of all, however, had taken place in his bedchamber. She'd been dressed as she'd been at the evening meal, in a lovely blue gown that clung to her shapely body, and she'd been kissing him. He'd returned her kiss with all the passion she aroused in him.

That one had seemed particularly vivid…

He wouldn't think about Bea, or what she might have said if he'd gone to bid her farewell that morning, just as he must not think of her as anything other than his friend's wife's lively and pretty cousin. To believe otherwise, despite what he thought he saw in her eyes sometimes, was surely only vanity and pride. He was a knight, but a poor one, with no estate and little money. Anything he had he owed to his prowess with a sword and his friends' generosity. What had he to offer a vibrant, beautiful woman like Bea, who could hope to win the heart of many a better, richer man?

With such disgruntled thoughts to plague him, Ranulf surveyed the windswept moor around him. Over a low ridge, the sea was just out of sight, if not quite beyond smell. In the distance, gulls whirled slowly, white and gray against the blue sky, telling him where the frothy, roiling water surged and beat against the helpless shore.

His thoughts fled from the awful open water back to Tregellas. He hoped Merrick's injury wasn't serious. Merrick had assured him before he'd departed that it was just a bad sprain and Constance, being a woman, had overreacted when she sent for the apothecary. No doubt the apothecary would agree when he arrived and examined Merrick's swollen limb.

Since all the men trained by Sir Leonard had learned something about wounds, sprains and breaks, Ranulf accepted his friend's opinion and, instead of worrying about Merrick's leg, envisioned Bea telling everyone about the accident and pestering the apothecary with questions.

Scowling and determined to stop thinking about Bea, Ranulf drew Titan to a halt and twisted in the saddle, gesturing for Myghal to come beside him. Maybe talking about the situation at his new command would help him concentrate on what lay ahead and not what he'd left behind.

"Tell me about Sir Frioc's accident," he said as he nudged Titan into a walk after the undersheriff arrived beside him.

"It's like I told Lord Merrick," Myghal replied with obvious reluctance. "He was out hunting—"

"With whom?"

Myghal's brow furrowed. "There was Hedyn, and me, and Yestin and Terithien—men of his household. We often went hunting with him, my lord. Penterwell's a peaceful sort of place, so there wasn't a lot for us to do otherwise. 'Twas no different that day—except for Sir Frioc dying, of course."

Ranulf heard the sorrow and dismay in the younger man's voice. "It's never easy to lose a friend, or someone we respect. We all need time to mourn such a loss, but at least we have our memories of better days to sustain us."

With a heavy sigh, Myghal nodded.

"Sir Frioc must have liked and trusted you, to have you in his hunting party."

That brought a smile to Myghal's face. "Aye, sir, he did. He was a kind man, and after my father died, he treated me…well, not like a son, exactly, but very well indeed."

"I'm sorry I didn't know him better myself," Ranulf answered honestly, thinking of his own youth and the man who'd been a better, second father to him.

Myghal's face resumed its grim expression. "And all because of a rabbit."

"That does seem a small beast for such a chase."

"Aye, sir, 'twas. But we'd had no luck that day finding anything bigger, and we were on our way home when the dogs started fussing and Sir Frioc spotted this big rabbit. And he *was* big! So my lord laughed and said he'd be damned if he'd have fish again for his dinner and spurred his horse to give chase. The rabbit took off like a shot from a bow. By the time the dogs were loosed, we'd lost sight of Sir Frioc. His tracks were easy enough to follow, though, and we come to a dip in the hill, and there he was." Myghal swallowed hard. "He was just lying there on the ground, his eyes wide open and he looked so surprised…."

Ranulf took pity on the man and changed the subject. "It's been a while since I've been to Penterwell. I assume little else has changed in the past few months."

Rather unexpectedly, Myghal flushed. "Some things have, my lord."

"Such as?"

"Well, sir, Gwenbritha went home to her mother."

Myghal seemed to think Ranulf would know who this was, but no one came immediately to mind.

"Sir Frioc's leman, sir," Myghal clarified. "They quarreled and she left him."

Ranulf didn't want gossip. On the other hand, a lover scorned could mean trouble. He knew full well that honor and wisdom could be subverted by the need to regain one's wounded pride. "What did they argue about?"

"I heard she wanted him to marry her, and he wouldn't, so she left him. She said she wasn't never coming back, neither."

"Has she been seen around the village since?"

"No, sir, she's been true to that. Sir Frioc, well, he, um, didn't take it too well. He tried to pretend he wasn't upset, but he spent a lot of time hunting, or sitting in the hall…thinking."

"Thinking, or drinking?" Ranulf asked. A man in sorrow often imbibed more than he should, as he also knew from personal experience.

"Well, sir, drinking," Myghal admitted.

"The day he died—had he been drinking then?"

Myghal shook his head. "No, sir, not so's you'd notice. He'd had some ale when he broke the fast and a few tugs at the wineskin while we tried to find some game, but he wasn't drunk, if that's what you mean. He could hold his drink, too. Why, many's the night I saw him…well, sir, he could hold his drink."

Which didn't mean Frioc wasn't the worse for wine or ale when he died, Ranulf thought. But he would say no more about Frioc now. He would ask the sheriff later.

They rode over a small rise, and there in the distance, close to the turbulent sea, was the castle of Penterwell. Its gray stone walls rose up from the cliff upon which it sat as if they'd grown there, and gulls wheeled in the sky above like pale vultures. Ranulf knew that there was a village on the other side of the castle, where its great walls afforded some protection from the winds that blew off the sea and churned the white-capped waves.

Even from here he could hear those waves crashing on the rocks at the foot of the cliff.

Of all the places he could have been given as castellan! This must be God's idea of a jest—or perhaps a punishment—to have Penterwell so close to the sea.

Realizing Myghal was eyeing him curiously, Ranulf gave the fellow a genial smile. "I'm in need of a warm fire and a good meal."

A flicker of dread flashed across Myghal's face.

"You think I'll not be welcome in Penterwell?" Ranulf asked, his tone deceptively mild, "or do you fear someone might try to prevent my arrival?"

"Oh, no, sir, no, it's nothing like that," Myghal hastened to reply. "It's just that, like I said, after Gwenbritha left, things aren't what they were. Penterwell might not be as comfortable as you're used to."

Myghal could have no idea of some of the places Ranulf had laid his head in days gone by.

"I daresay I'll manage," the new castellan of Penterwell replied, and as he did, something on the shore at the bottom of the cliff caught his eye.

"What are those men doing?" he asked, nodding at the group.

His expression puzzled, Myghal half rose in his stirrups. "I don't know, sir."

"Can you tell who they are?"

"No, sir."

"Then I suppose we had better find out," Ranulf said.

He kicked Titan into a gallop and headed toward the shore.

And the cruel, unforgiving sea.

THE SHERIFF spotted Ranulf, Myghal and the rest of the castellan's escort as they drew near, recognizing Lord Merrick's friend at once. Like their overlord, Sir Ranulf was very well trained and a fierce fighter, and his ruddy hair made him easy to distinguish. Hedyn also knew that Sir Ranulf had been made garrison commander of Tregellas and, in the few months he'd been in that position, had wrought an amazing change in the men under his command. They were now said to be the equal of any army in England, and if the lord of Tregellas had any enemies, they would surely think twice before attacking his fortress.

Even so, the sheriff had expected Lord Merrick himself to come in answer to his laboriously written letter, not his garrison commander, so it was with a mixture of respect, disappointment and curiosity that Hedyn approached Sir Ranulf and his party.

"Greetings, Sir Ranulf," he said, his black cloak fluttering about him in the wind as he bowed. "As pleased as I am to see you again, I wish we were meeting under happier circumstances."

"As do I," Ranulf returned as he swung down from his horse.

"Begging your pardon and meaning no offense, I expected Lord Merrick to come."

"If I were in your place, I would expect him, too," Ranulf replied. "Unfortunately, Lord Merrick was a little overzealous celebrating the birth of his son and injured his leg. Since I'm to be the new castellan, I've come in his place."

Hedyn's eyes widened. "Well, it's a pity he hurt his leg, but it's good news about a son." He bowed again. "Welcome to Penterwell, my lord. It's too bad you've got to take command when we're having some trouble. How's Lady Constance?"

"I'm happy to report that Lady Constance came through the experience very well indeed." As Bea had made vivaciously clear before, during and after the evening meal when she made no mention of his imminent departure. Either she hadn't known—which he didn't think likely—or she hadn't cared as much as he thought she might. God help him, it would be vanity of the most deluded kind to hope such a woman would ever consider him for a husband!

Turning his attention to more important matters than his own foolish dreams, Ranulf nodded at the group of men now facing him, their bodies shielding something on the ground. "What have you been looking at?"

All trace of good humor left the sheriff's face. "It's

Gawan, my lord, a fisherman from Penterwell. One of the lads found him this morning. He's drowned."

Drowned.

Ranulf closed his eyes as he fought the pure terror that word invoked. He pushed away the memory of strong hands holding him down while salt water filled his nostrils, his mouth, his throat. The panic, the struggle, the sudden surge of strength as he fought to get away…

Hedyn continued matter-of-factly, not realizing he was addressing a man with the sweat of fear chilling upon his back. "Two days ago he put out like always and when he didn't come back, nobody 'cept his wife was too worried. And then a boy found his body washed up here this morning."

"Why didn't anybody else wonder about his well-being?"

The sheriff hesitated, glancing first at Myghal, who was still sitting on his horse, then toward the silent group of men in simple fisherman's smocks and breeches.

Ranulf could guess why Hedyn didn't have a ready answer. The man had probably been a smuggler as well as a fisherman. Smuggling tin out of Cornwall had a long history here on the coast.

Ranulf clapped a hand on Hedyn's shoulder and led him away from the group of men, the corpse and the sea. "I'm well aware that most of the fishermen are also smugglers," he said quietly. "Lord Merrick is aware of it, too, as was Frioc. So if you're reluctant to tell me you think this Gawan was meeting someone to exchange tin for money or other goods, you need not be."

The sheriff nodded. "Aye, sir, that's what we thought—that he'd gone to make an exchange and been delayed. Like I said, one night didn't trouble anyone except his wife, who's heavy with their first child and prone to worry like all women in such a state. In truth, I was more concerned about Sir Frioc's death and my letter to Lord Merrick. But when Gawan didn't return after another night, we all began to wonder if something'd gone amiss. He was out alone, too."

Alone in a boat at sea. Ranulf subdued a shiver, and it was not from the breeze.

"But the weather was clear and there's no sign of his boat. It's strange to find his body but not so much as a board or rope from his boat."

"Are you saying you think his death was the result of foul play?"

Hedyn rubbed his grizzled chin. "Aye, sir. Two other men have gone missing, as well."

Perhaps this was the "trouble" Frioc had alluded to, but if so, Frioc should certainly have informed Merrick.

"Nobody thought too much about that at the time, sir," Hedyn said as if in answer to Ranulf's unspoken question. "Rob and Sam weren't from Penterwell, you see, and only came to stay in the winter months."

He gave Ranulf a look, as one worldly-wise man to another. "They weren't the kind to stay close to hearth and home, or their wives, if you follow me. And there'd been some trouble between them and some of the other fishermen. Most of the villagers thought they'd just sailed off before they were forced to go—and good riddance to 'em. Their wives were as relieved as anybody."

That might explain why Frioc had not considered their absence important, but taken with this new death… "Gawan was not of that sort?"

"Lord bless you, no," Hedyn replied, shaking his head. "He loved his wife dear, and she him. They've been sweethearts since they were little, and he was looking forward to the child."

Which didn't mean he couldn't have left her, no matter how he acted in public, or what vows of love he swore.

"It may be Gawan took a risk because he thought they'd need more money with a babe on the way." The sheriff sighed. "Poor lad. It wouldn't be the first time one of those French pirates has done murder for a man's tin."

"I suppose we should be grateful his body washed ashore," Ranulf mused as they started back toward the men. "Otherwise, we might never have known what happened to him."

"It's damned odd," Hedyn retorted.

Ranulf halted and regarded Hedyn quizzically, taken aback by the force of the sheriff's words. "How so?"

"Well, sir, when a man drowns in the sea, his body

sinks like a stone. It can take days for it to bloat and come up again, and when it's in the sea…well, it can drift for miles before it washes up, if there's anything left *to* wash up by then. This is more like he was killed first and then thrown over the side. But there's not a mark on him. Come see for yourself."

Ranulf's stomach twisted. He'd seen men killed, their faces ruined, limbs torn and bloody. He could deal with that. But to look at a drowned man's corpse…

Ranulf would not show any weakness. He would give no sign that he would rather face fifty mounted knights while armed with only a dagger than follow the sheriff to the body that lay upon the shore.

A SENNIGHT LATER, Beatrice watched Gaston sprinkle thyme over meat, gravy and leeks in an open pastry shell.

"The secret, my lady, is in the spices," Gaston explained as he added a pinch of rosemary. "Too much, and you lose the taste of the pheasant, too little and it's too much pheasant, if you understand me."

Beatrice nodded as she studied Gaston's technique. The slim middle-aged man had been the cook for Lord Merrick's father, too, and had the worry lines in his face to prove it. These days, though, Gaston smiled far more than he frowned. Lord Merrick was a generous master who appreciated good food, and he never once accused the cook of trying to poison him.

As for a lady's presence in the castle kitchen, Beatrice enjoyed being in the warm room, with its bustling servants and pleasant aromas. In the days since Ranulf had gone, she'd spent plenty of time with Gaston and the servants there. She had also whiled away several hours sitting with Constance, making clothes for the baby and retelling the stories of King Arthur and his knights that she loved, even though they made her think of the absent Ranulf. He claimed he didn't enjoy those tales one bit. He called Lancelot an immoral, disloyal dolt whose battle prowess had gone to his head, and he thought Arthur much too generous to his traitorous son.

Ranulf had no sympathy for traitors. As for a traitor's daughter…

Demelza, middle-aged and amiable, and a servant who could always be counted on to have the latest gossip, appeared at the door to the courtyard. She grinned when she spotted Beatrice.

She also noticed Maloren, slumbering in the warm corner near the hearth. Like everyone in Tregellas, Demelza knew that the very mention of Ranulf's name could cause Maloren to launch into one of her tirades against men, so she approached Beatrice as stealthily as a spy and addressed her in a hushed whisper. "A messenger's arrived, my lady. From Penterwell. I come the moment I heard, my lady, just like you asked."

"Thank you," Beatrice said, trying not to sound

overly excited or wake Maloren as she wiped her floury hands on a cloth. "It's so difficult for Lord Merrick to have to sit all day. Tidings from Penterwell should cheer him up. And I daresay Constance will want to hear the news. I'll look after little Peder for her, and then they can have some time alone, too."

She gave Demelza and the other servants a knowing smile. "I'm sure they'll like that."

The servants shared a quiet, companionable chuckle. Rarely had anyone seen a couple more in love than the lord and lady of Tregellas.

Beatrice, meanwhile, hurried on her way, glad that Maloren was still sleeping and hadn't awakened and offered to go with her.

Merrick and Constance would indeed be glad to have news of Penterwell and Ranulf, but not so much as she. In the days since Ranulf had departed, Beatrice had had plenty of time to mull over what had happened the night they'd kissed, and her hopes had started to revive. In spite of what had happened just before they parted, Ranulf had certainly been passionate when they began. He'd surrendered to his desire just as she had. Unfortunately for her, as the yearning flared and the need grew, he must have remembered that honorable men didn't make love with ladies to whom they weren't at least betrothed. It could be that, as she'd felt ashamed and humiliated afterward, so had he when he broke the kiss.

If he were still here, she would be able to tell him

that he had no need to condemn himself for what she had initiated. She could say she was sorry if he'd been upset, but she couldn't regret their kiss, not when she cared about him as she did. She would finally be able to tell him how she felt.

But he wasn't here, and until she could speak to him again, she must keep her desire and her hopes to herself as she had before.

When Beatrice arrived at the lord's bedchamber, Merrick was seated with his left leg propped on a stool as he perused a scroll in his hand. Constance sat on a cushioned chair beside him, holding their son in her arms. There was concern on her features, and Merrick was scowling.

But then, he'd been scowling nearly continuously since he'd broken his leg.

Beatrice put a smile on her face and tried to act as if she'd just happened to come by because she hadn't confided her greatest hope to Constance yet, either. Although Ranulf was Merrick's trusted friend, Constance might not entirely welcome a marriage between her cousin and her husband's brother-in-arms. Ranulf was more than ten years older than she, for one thing, and, worse, landless. Constance might think she should aim for a richer or more powerful husband, unwilling to accept that her cousin was not the matrimonial prize Constance, with her sisterly love, believed her to be.

"Good morning, Constance. Merrick," Beatrice said brightly after knocking on the frame of the door to announce her arrival. "A fine day, isn't it? Spring is surely on its way. I believe I could find some early blooms if I went out walking today, and the air smells so fresh and lovely—well, except if you wander too close to the pigsty." She held out her hands for little Peder. "May I hold him?"

Constance nodded and Beatrice took the infant in her arms. "And good morning to you, little man," she murmured as she tickled the baby under his dimpled chin.

"We've had another letter from Ranulf," Constance said, nodding at her husband, who was still reading and still scowling.

"Oh, indeed?" Beatrice replied as if this was news to her, loosening her hold when Peder squirmed in protest. "I trust all is well."

Merrick shifted, easing his foot into a slightly different position. "There's nothing Ranulf cannot deal with," the lord of Tregellas replied, and in such a tone, Beatrice surmised it would be useless to press him further. Perhaps later she could speak to Constance alone, and her cousin would be more forthcoming.

"I hope your leg isn't bothering you too much, my lord," she said.

He made a sour face and grunted as he shifted again. "No."

His wife frowned. "There's no need to be rude to Beatrice," she said. Her expression changed to one of sympathy. "You'll be up and about eventually, my love, but until then, you should perhaps consider this a just punishment for overindulgence in wine."

Her husband's only answer was another muted grunt as he set the letter on the table beside his chair.

"Your leg's healing very nicely, the apothecary says, so it would be a shame if you were to injure it again," his wife noted.

The baby started to whimper and Merrick held out his hands. "Let me hold my son while you two gossip."

In spite of the glower that accompanied his words, his tone was more conciliatory than annoyed.

Beatrice gave him the baby, which he took in his powerful hands as gently as if Peder were made of crystal. Meanwhile, Constance rose and gestured for Beatrice to follow her. "We two can *gossip* better over here by the window, where our talk won't disturb the menfolk."

She paused a moment and looked back at her husband. "May Beatrice read Ranulf's letter herself? Her reading's come along very well these past few months, but a little practice wouldn't hurt."

Merrick shrugged. "I see no reason to keep the contents secret."

Beatrice couldn't keep the joy from her features as she retrieved the scroll from the table, and she silently blessed Constance for teaching her to read and write. Her father had considered it a waste of time to teach noblewomen anything except the words and simple arithmetic necessary to keep tally on the household expenses.

"If there's a word you don't understand, please ask. I shall sit here by the window in the sun and enjoy doing nothing," Constance said as Beatrice sank down into another chair by the window, where the light fell upon the parchment and the writing that was like Ranulf himself—upright and firm.

"Greetings to my lord Merrick and his most gracious lady," she read, hearing his deep, smooth voice as clearly as if he were speaking in her ear. "I have nothing new to report since my first letter. I continue to attempt to make some progress with the villagers with the help of Hedyn, who justifies his position daily. Unfortunately, despite my obvious charm and friendly...

"What is this word?" she asked, pointing it out to Constance.

"Overtures."

"Ah," Beatrice sighed as she returned to reading.

"Despite my obvious charm and friendly overtures, the villagers appear reluctant to discuss much beyond the measure of the daily catch with their new castellan. Nevertheless, I shall continue to investigate the matter of Gawan's death until I am either satisfied it was an accident, or convinced it was not, and if it was not, bring the guilty to justice."

Puzzled, Beatrice looked up at Constance. "Who's

Gawan? How did he die? Why does Ranulf suspect he was murdered?"

"Gawan was a fisherman," Constance explained. "He was found dead on the shore the day Ranulf arrived, apparently drowned. The sheriff has some doubts about whether it was an accident, since nothing of the poor man's boat has been recovered."

"It may have been an accident, though, as the man had set sail alone two days before," Merrick interposed. "Ranulf will find out the truth."

"Yes, yes, he will," Beatrice said, returning to the letter, now held in hands no longer quite steady. Things were not nearly as peaceful at Penterwell as she'd believed although, she told herself, the castellan had the protection of his garrison, so he would surely not be in any danger.

"In the meantime, I must petition you for some funds and, if you can spare them, a mason or two. Due to some personal concerns, Frioc has let several portions of the castle defenses fall into disrepair. They should be fixed as soon as possible, or I fear the place may collapse about me. I suggest, my lord, that you journey here for a day or so to confer on what should be done, and what first.

"And perhaps, my most gracious and generous lord, as well as oldest friend—and thus I trust I have duly appealed to both your loyalty and such vanity as you possess—you could bring some provisions with you when you come, such as a few loaves of bread, some smoked meat, a wheel of cheese, and a cask or two of ale. I regret to say the food here is rather lacking, unless one likes fish, and until I can devote more time to hunting game, likely to remain so. Also, you might consider bringing your own bedding. What is here is adequate, but not as comfortable as Tregellas affords."

Beatrice had a sudden vision of Ranulf huddled in a crumbling castle, wrapped in a moth-eaten blanket and lying on a pallet of fetid straw after a meal of watery stew made of rotten fish heads.

She jumped to her feet, the parchment falling to her feet unheeded. "You can't let him live in squalor!"

Merrick raised a brow as little Peder, surprised and confused by her abrupt motion, burst into tears. "Squalor?" he repeated loudly enough to be heard above the baby's cries. "I hardly think—"

"The household must have gone to rack and ruin after Sir Frioc's leman left him," Beatrice said, wringing her hands in dismay. "Especially if Ranulf's busy trying to find out what happened to that Gawan."

"How do you know about Sir Frioc's leman?" Constance asked incredulously as she rose and went to take the baby from her husband.

"Demelza told me," Beatrice replied, following her. "Her sister's brother-in-law lives in Penterwell and she knows all about it. Apparently they quarreled because Sir Frioc wouldn't offer her marriage.

That must be why Ranulf comes home to terrible meals and filthy bedding—there's no chatelaine to organize things.

"Oh, Constance, you must let me go to Penterwell," she pleaded, equal parts appalled and determined to see that Ranulf didn't suffer a moment longer than necessary. "I can take Ranulf some decent food and linen and you know I can ensure the servants mend their ways and the cook does better. Oh, please say you'll let me go!"

Sitting beside Merrick, Constance lifted her baby from her husband's arms and loosened her bodice in preparation to nurse him. "Beatrice, as much as I'd like—"

"You've been telling me what a fine job I've been doing helping you," Beatrice persisted, going down on her knees beside Constance's chair and gripping the arm.

Her vivid imagination had already gone from picturing Ranulf cold and hungry to Ranulf lying on his deathbed if she didn't get to him, and soon. "I can make the servants listen to me—you know I can. And I can organize his household so that it can run smoothly for a time before anyone need return."

She clasped her hands together, quite prepared to beg, for Ranulf's sake, as her gaze flew from Constance to Merrick and back again. "*Please*, let me do this!"

A grim-faced Merrick shook his head. "No."

Constance had once said her husband found it difficult to refuse a woman's pleas, but he seemed to be finding it very easy at the moment. "That's a fine way to repay your friend, letting him suffer when there's someone at hand who can help him," Beatrice declared as she scrambled to her feet.

Despite both her petitions and defiance, the expression on the face of the lord of Tregellas remained unchanged. "You cannot go to Penterwell. You're neither married nor betrothed. It wouldn't be proper, and as your guardian—"

"No one would dare to say anything if *you* sent me."

"Not to *us*," Merrick replied. "But it might turn away some men who would consider marrying you."

"If any man thinks so little of me, I wouldn't want him anyway," she retorted. "Besides, everyone knows Ranulf is an honorable knight, or he wouldn't be your friend or castellan. Surely you don't think I need fear for my honor if I go to his aid? That he'll suddenly go mad and forget your friendship and the oath of loyalty he swore to you and attack me?"

"Beatrice," Constance said soothingly as her son suckled at her breast. "Merrick's only thinking of your reputation."

"My father has already destroyed my family's name," Beatrice returned. "As for Ranulf's reputation, anyone who knows him knows he would never abuse your trust, or me."

"This isn't a matter of trust, Beatrice," Constance said softly. "Of course we trust him, and you."

Calmer in the face of Constance's placating tone and gentle eyes, Beatrice spread her hands wide. "Then why not let me go?"

Constance looked at her husband. "I agree the situation must be dire, or Ranulf wouldn't say anything about it. And *I* certainly cannot go. Neither can you."

"Who else could you send to set the household to rights?" Beatrice pressed, beginning to hope Constance was coming around to her point of view. "Demelza? Another of the servants? How much authority would they wield over the servants of Penterwell?"

"We could always send Maloren with Beatrice, along with the masons, as he asks," Constance mused aloud. "Ranulf can tell the masons what needs to be done as well as you, my love, and God knows he's not extravagant.

"Beatrice is also right about the servants. It will likely take a lady to get them back in order.

"As for any possible scandal, Ranulf is an honorable knight and the trusted friend of the lord of Tregellas. Any person of intelligence would realize that Ranulf would risk your enmity by taking advantage of your ward, and Ranulf is certainly no fool." She regarded her husband gravely. "Besides, I don't see any alternative, do you?"

Merrick shifted again and didn't answer. Beatrice was about to state her case once more when he abruptly held up his hand to silence her. "Oh, very well. You may go with the masons—for three days, and no more. And Maloren must go with you."

"Oh, thank you, thank you!" Beatrice cried, flinging her arms around the lord of Tregellas's neck for a brief but fervent hug before she ran to the door. "I'll go and tell Maloren. She hates traveling and she's likely going to complain the whole time, but I don't care. We simply must save Ranulf!"

CHAPTER FOUR

"No unfamiliar ships have been spotted along here, either?" Ranulf asked Myghal as they rode along the crest of a hill a short distance from the coast two days after Beatrice had begged to be sent to Penterwell. They were near enough to see the water, but a safe distance from the edge of the cliffs. Venturing any closer would have made it impossible for him to hide his fear.

"No, sir, not a one, not for days," Myghal replied, his shoulders hunched against the wind blowing in from the sea. Above, scudding gray clouds foretold rain, and the gulls wheeling and screeching overhead seemed to be ordering them to take shelter.

"And still no one has said anything to you about Gawan's death?" Ranulf asked, repeating a question he posed to the undersheriff at least once a day, while Hedyn led other patrols on the opposite side of the coast from the castle.

Myghal shook his head.

Ranulf stifled a sigh. How was he to discover who had killed Gawan, and perhaps those other two, if nobody would speak to those in authority about what they knew? Surely somebody in Penterwell had to know *something*.

Gawan's widow, Wenna, had been willing to talk to him, but she'd been nearly incoherent with grief, the tears rolling down her cheeks as she told him that she was sure her husband had been murdered. "Been a fisherman since nearly the time he could walk, my lord," she'd sobbed through her tears. "It would take a storm to sink him, and there wasn't one."

Ranulf had gently suggested that perhaps her husband had set out to meet some evil men, assuring her that if that were so, and even if her husband was engaged in activities that broke the law, he was still determined to find the culprits who had killed her husband and bring them to justice.

"He went to meet a Frenchman, my lord," she'd admitted as she wiped her nose with the edge of her apron, her rounded belly pressing against her skirts. "He's traded with the man before. My Gawan didn't trust him, but the Frenchman paid more than most, and Gawan wanted as much as he could get because of the baby. My poor fatherless baby..."

She'd broken down completely then. He'd sent Myghal, who'd been with him, to fetch a neighbor's wife. He'd also taken several coins from his purse and left them on the table before he slipped away.

For years and years he had believed love to be a lie, a comforting tale told to keep women in their place, for no one had ever loved him. Then he'd fallen in love—passionately so—and found out that feeling could be real, and so was the pain it brought.

Wenna's grief was an uncomfortable but necessary reminder of that anguish. Otherwise, he might forget and allow himself to—

He heard something. Behind them. On the moor.

Pulling sharply on his reins, Ranulf held up his hand to halt the rest of the patrol, then wheeled Titan around.

"What is it?" Myghal asked nervously, twisting in his saddle to see what had drawn Ranulf's attention.

"There," Ranulf answered, pointing at a galloping horse heading toward them at breakneck speed, its rider bent low over its neck, the bright blue cloak of the rider streaming out behind him like a banner.

Ranulf rose in his stirrups, the better to see, and realized almost at once that it wasn't only a cloak flapping. There were skirts, too.

That horse looked familiar. Very familiar.

God's blood, it was Bea's mare, Holly, so that must be Bea, riding as if fiends from hell were chasing her.

Drawing his sword, Ranulf bellowed his war cry and kicked Titan into a gallop. God help any man who sought to hurt his little Lady Bea!

THE FIERCE CRY SOUNDED like a demon or some other supernatural creature, wounded and in pain. Startled, Beatrice pulled sharply on the reins to halt Holly. As her mare sat back on her haunches, Beatrice felt her grip slipping and the next thing she knew, she'd gone head over heels onto a patch of damp, grassy ground.

For one pulse-pounding moment, she lay too stunned to move as the thundering hooves came closer. Then she saw shoulder-length red-brown hair, a familiar forest-green surcoat, and the great dappled gray warhorse that belonged to Ranulf.

As she struggled to sit up, the castellan of Penterwell brought his horse to a snorting halt, threw his leg over the saddle and slipped off. He rushed toward her, his sword still clutched in his right hand as he fell on his knees beside her.

Still somewhat dizzy from her tumble, surprised by Ranulf's sudden arrival and taken aback by the obvious and sincere concern on his features, Beatrice blurted, "I hope you don't think I didn't care about Merrick making you castellan. I was delighted for you, although it's no more than you deserve. But nobody told me before the evening meal. I suppose all the servants thought I already knew, and Constance and Merrick probably expected you to tell me. You didn't, so I didn't know you were going until you were already gone."

Ranulf sat back on his ankles, looking as dazed as if he'd tumbled from his horse, too.

Her heart thudding with a combination of excitement and dread, Beatrice decided that, since she had started, she might as well try to find out where she stood with Ranulf. She wondered if she should begin with their kiss, but couldn't bring herself to mention it. "I was afraid you were upset with me when you didn't say goodbye."

"I expected to see you in the morning," he replied with no hint of embarrassment or shame as he rose. "Unfortunately, you were still asleep and I thought you needed your rest. I would have said a better farewell when you retired from the hall if I had known it was the last time I would see you before leaving Tregellas."

The last time…? It suddenly dawned on her that he might have been too drunk to remember their embrace or the words they'd said. If that was so, she should be both glad and relieved. But she wasn't. She was dismayed and disappointed.

His expression inscrutable, Ranulf surveyed her from head to toe. "Are you hurt?"

She was, although not in the way he meant. It pained her to realize that what had been such a momentous occasion for her was not even a memory to him. "I fear I'm going to have a terrible bruise, and this cloak may never be free of stains, but I'm otherwise unharmed," she replied, managing not to sound as upset as she felt.

He reached down to help her to her feet, his strong, gloved hand grasping hers. Even that touch was enough to warm her blood and make her remember the heated passion of his kiss.

She must deal with the present and ignore the painful past.

Looking toward the group of soldiers drawing near, she said, "I trust those are men from your castle."

He followed her gaze and nodded. "Yes, and the undersheriff."

"Surely it isn't safe for you to get so far away from them if men of Penterwell are being murdered."

Ranulf's ruddy brows contracted. "Your own safety is something *you* should have considered, my lady, when you decided to ride about this unfamiliar countryside all by yourself."

"I'm not all by myself," she protested. "Two soldiers rode ahead with me."

"Unless they've become invisible, my lady," he said, still frowning, "you are most certainly alone."

Taken aback, she looked over her shoulder, expecting to see her escorts from Tregellas riding toward them.

"I *wasn't* alone," she amended apologetically. "Holly must be faster than their horses. I didn't realize she was so swift."

As she spoke, Ranulf's men and the undersheriff arrived and drew their horses to a halt.

Suddenly aware of how disheveled she must look, and worried that they might think she often rode about like some heedless hoyden, Beatrice blushed and stared at the grassy ground. She had so much wanted to arrive the way Constance would, as a lady of dignity and worthy of respect, the better to impress Ranulf. Instead, she'd shocked and angered him. It was obvious he was annoyed by the way he pressed his full lips together, and by the appearance of that deep, vertical furrow between his brows.

"I was mistaken. The lady wasn't being chased," he announced to his men, and if she'd had any doubts that he was angry, the tone of his voice would have dispelled them.

He turned back to her. "Lady Beatrice, these are some of the men in the garrison of Penterwell. I believe you've met Myghal, the undersheriff of Penterwell."

Her pride demanded that she act as composed as Constance, or Ranulf himself, so she forced herself to smile at the slightly plump man she guessed was in his early twenties. "Yes, I have. Good day, Myghal."

The undersheriff nodded and mumbled a greeting.

"Myghal, Lady Beatrice is apparently going to be visiting Penterwell, along with Lord Merrick."

Beatrice shifted uneasily, wondering if she should tell Ranulf here and now that Merrick had not come with her party—except that would surely only upset him more.

She was spared mentioning Merrick when Ranulf went on before she could speak. "Continue the patrol. You should check that cove again."

Myghal nodded, but his eyes were not on his overlord. They were on Beatrice. All the other men in the patrol were watching her, too.

This was not the first time men had looked at her, and while she told herself it must be because of her unkempt appearance, in her heart Beatrice knew their attention had another cause, even though she wasn't as beautiful and graceful as Constance. That sort of masculine scrutiny always made her uncomfortable, and so she did what she always did in such circumstances. She started to talk.

"I was so sorry to hear about Sir Frioc. I never met him, but he sounds a most genial sort of fellow, and the fact that Lord Merrick approved of him says much about his character. And I'm very sorry if I caused Sir Ranulf, or you, Myghal, or you other men any alarm. I assure you, I didn't mean to. I rode away from my party because I simply couldn't bear my maidservant's complaints another moment. You'd think I was dragging her on a pilgrimage to the Holy Land. She ought to be quite comfortable in the cart on the veritable *mound* of cushions I prepared for her, and warm with all the blankets and shawls, as cozy as Cleopatra on her barge. But no, Maloren must moan and groan until I thought I'd go mad. So I said to Aeden, the sergeant-at-arms, that I was going to let Holly have a good gallop over the open moor. You haven't met Maloren or I dare say you'd understand. I love her dearly, but she can be most exasperating."

In spite of her heartfelt explanation, Ranulf looked more than a little exasperated himself. "My lady, I regret I must interrupt this charming justification for your astonishing behavior. However, these men have work to do."

Beatrice blushed and smiled again. "Of course they do. Please, don't let me detain you."

"It's a pleasure to see you again, my lady," Myghal murmured as he tugged his forelock before he turned his horse and led the patrol toward the shore.

Ranulf watched his men leave, and as he did, he tried not to grind his teeth or otherwise betray his annoyance. But what the devil was Merrick thinking, bringing Beatrice along with him and then letting her get so far from their cortege?

Likely that was as she said: she'd ridden ahead of the guards Merrick had assigned to her—although why wasn't Merrick himself watching her? Surely as her guardian, he should be taking more care…unless he was as tired of her cheerful chatter as she'd been of Maloren's complaints.

Even so, that wouldn't explain why Merrick had brought her to Penterwell in the first place, especially when there was the mystery of Gawan's murder to solve. She could be of no help there, and they certainly didn't need the distraction of Bea's bubbly, inquisitive presence when they were trying to find answers from the recalcitrant villagers.

Perhaps she was bothering Constance too much. The lady of Tregellas must still be weak from the effort of childbirth, and he could understand that she might find Bea wearying.

As for the reaction of Myghal and his men, he shouldn't be the least surprised by the attention Bea attracted. She was a beautiful young woman, even more beautiful and graceful and charming than her cousin, and certainly more vivacious. Myghal was a young, unmarried man—a young, unmarried commoner who should harbor no hopes of anything from Bea save a polite smile, no matter how friendly she was. She was friendly to everyone, rich and poor alike. A smile from her didn't necessarily mean anything significant—

"I really am sorry for causing any distress to you or your men," Bea said. "You know Maloren, though. I thought I'd go mad if I had to listen to her for the rest of the journey."

She smiled apologetically, looking up at Ranulf with the innocence of a novice while he, jaded reprobate as he was, tried not to notice that her buttercup-yellow woolen gown seemed molded to her body beneath her wode-blue cloak.

Or to feel like a heartless rogue for leaving Tregellas without bidding her farewell, even though he'd been the worse for overimbibing.

He'd also been afraid he might slip and say something that would reveal his foolish longing.

"You came riding to my rescue just like Lancelot," she said with another glowing smile.

God help him, why did she have to look at him like that? Why couldn't he stay angry with her? Then he might be able to ignore his wayward desire.

"I saw a woman riding as if her life was in danger,

so naturally I came to her aid," he replied, doing his best to control his tumultuous emotions as he marched to her mare and grabbed the dangling reins.

"Naturally," she said, following him like an eager puppy. "You are a most chivalrous knight."

"Whether these lands are safe or not, it wasn't wise to get so far ahead of your party. I'm surprised Merrick was so remiss."

"Oh, but he wasn't," Beatrice hastened to reply. "Merrick had nothing to do with it."

Ranulf made no secret of his confusion. "What do you mean? As leader of your party and your guardian—"

"He's not. Well, he's still my guardian," she amended, "but Merrick isn't with the cortege. He can't leave Tregellas. Indeed, he can't ride at all, or even walk because of what happened the night little Peder was born."

Ranulf stared at her as if she'd just spoken in tongues. "What are you talking about?" he demanded. "Merrick merely sprained his ankle."

"I know Merrick didn't think he'd done anything serious, but the apothecary discovered that he'd broken his leg, so it's a good thing Constance insisted on sending for someone more learned, isn't it? Fortunately, it's a clean break, so it shouldn't leave Merrick crippled, provided he stays off it for several more days, or so the apothecary says, and he seems a wise fellow, so I think we can take comfort in his opinion."

Ranulf felt the need to sit, but as there was no chair, bench or stool nearby, he didn't. "Who is in charge of your party, then?"

She beamed a smile. "Well, I suppose I am, although Aeden's in command of the soldiers, and I can hardly tell the masons what to do. That's for you to decide."

"I don't believe it," Ranulf muttered.

Bea's smile died. "I wouldn't lie about a thing like that. In fact, I don't generally lie about anything, unless it's how a gown looks or something equally unimportant." She crossed her arms beneath her perfect breasts. "I must say I'm offended you would accuse me of making up a story like that."

She certainly sounded offended, so what she'd said was almost certainly true. Merrick had broken his leg and wasn't coming. But *she* had, and without a proper chaperone or escort, just some soldiers and two masons, all of considerably lower rank.

Had Merrick lost his mind? What, in the name of the saints, was Bea supposed to do at Penterwell, except aggravate and distract him?

And tempt you, too, a lustful little voice prompted in the back of his mind.

"That doesn't explain why Merrick sent *you* here," Ranulf said brusquely, his anger now partly directed at himself.

"Well, naturally when Merrick received your

letter, he was concerned—and Constance, too—about the conditions at Penterwell. So was I, so I've come to oversee your household the way the masons will oversee the repairs to the walls. It sounds as if you could use some assistance with the servants, at the very least. And I've brought food and wine, too."

Ranulf drew his broadsword and took a moment to calm himself by swinging it from side to side, as if decapitating the grass.

"I know the news about Merrick must come as a shock," Bea went on, "but I thought you might be a little glad to see me."

God save him from apologetic young women with the eyes of an angel and a body to tempt even saints to sin!

"Coming here without Merrick or any other relative was not wise and I'm surprised Merrick and Constance allowed it," he said as he sheathed his sword.

Bea's bright blue eyes sparkled with what looked remarkably like defiance. "Surely you're not telling me I need to be protected from you?" she asked. "Are you implying you would forswear your oath of loyalty and friendship to my cousin's husband and ravish me?" She cocked her head to study him. "Or are you suggesting I'll throw myself into your arms because you're irresistible?"

He tried to ignore the wondrous vision of Bea rushing into his open arms, then pressing her soft, shapely body against his as she lifted her sweet face for his kiss. "No, of course not," he growled.

"Then why should I not come here when you need help, and the sort a woman can best provide?"

Had she *no* idea how that sounded? The notions it gave a man, especially a lonely one, and even if he didn't think her the most beautiful, tempting woman he'd ever met? "Because other people will talk and make assumptions that could call your honor into question."

She drew herself up to her full height, which was about even with his nose. "I appreciate your concern for my reputation, Sir Ranulf, but I point out, I have little honor to lose. My father was a traitor, and executed." Her eyes flashed with a stern determination that surprised him, for Bea was usually the most gentle and softhearted of women. "If other people wish to see a sin where none exists, they are not worthy of my acquaintance."

"How do you intend to get a husband if—?"

"If a man thinks me a loose woman, why would I care if he wants to marry me or not?" she demanded. "And surely if neither Constance or Merrick object to my coming here, you shouldn't. They are legally obligated to protect me, not you."

Exactly. "Which is why they never should have let you come here as you have."

Her eyes grew cold, like blue ice, and her tone just as frosty. "Very well, Sir Ranulf," she snapped, "as you see fit to question my guardians' decision and wish to decline my assistance, I shall gladly return to Tregellas at once."

He told himself he ought to be relieved.

And then a drop of rain fell upon his nose. Another fell on her cheek.

She glanced up at the cloudy sky before regarding him with grim triumph. "It seems, my lord, that the rain is not going to hold off. Given that we are closer to Penterwell than Tregellas, we shall be forced to spend this night at the castle you command. Otherwise, I might take a chill and die. Then Merrick and Constance will hate you and Maloren will no doubt attempt to assassinate you in revenge."

She was, unfortunately, right, at least about staying the night in Penterwell. "As you say, my lady, given the weather we have little choice," he agreed, determined to sound as stern and commanding as he could. "You may come with me to Penterwell, but in the cart with Maloren. Now that you're under my care, I won't risk another fall."

Bea frowned as she wrapped her cloak more tightly about herself, her brow wrinkling and her lips turning down at the corners. "Maloren won't like sharing."

"I point out, my lady, that this is not a request. I am your host and responsible for your welfare while you're at Penterwell."

As he spoke, it suddenly dawned on Ranulf that Bea would be his first noble guest. Just as suddenly, he recalled the state of his hall, and the kitchen, and got a sinking feeling in the pit of his stomach. He had no idea at all what sort of chamber might be available for a noble female guest and her maidservant, either. He'd spent most of his days out on patrol, or in the village with Hedyn, meeting the villagers and trying to find out what had happened to Gawan and those other two missing men. When he returned to the hall, he ate whatever the cook had prepared—which was always fish of some sort—and climbed into his messy bed too tired to care if the linen was clean as long as he didn't wake up flea bitten in the morning.

Had his first guest been Merrick, he wouldn't have worried about creature comforts. Like him, Merrick would be more concerned about possible enemies, not what was served at the evening meal or where he'd be sleeping. But this wasn't Merrick. This was Bea.

As if that realization were not bad enough, the cart bearing Maloren crested the rise in the distance. The old woman was already half standing, her hands on the driver's shoulders as if she were some sort of Amazon, urging him to hurry, while the beleaguered driver flicked his switch with a desperation Ranulf could well appreciate.

"Oh, my poor lamb!" Maloren cried when she spied Bea. "What's happened? I could kill those two soldiers who came back without you. Winded horses, indeed! What's that blackguard doing here? Why is your cloak muddy? Has that Satan's spawn laid a hand on you? I warned you not to ride off!"

God help him, Bea *and* Maloren. He'd rather have the plague.

Bea slid him a reproachful look, as if she'd somehow guessed what he was thinking. "At least *you* won't have to ride in the cart with her," she said under her breath. "She'll be chiding me all the way to Penterwell."

For a moment, Ranulf was tempted to rescind his order.

But only for a moment. Otherwise, Bea would be riding beside him all the way to the castle, and that was surely something best avoided.

AS MALOREN STOOD beside Beatrice in the entrance to the hall of Penterwell, she threw up her hands in disgust. "By the holy Mother and all the angels, I wouldn't keep pigs in this place!"

Beatrice silently agreed with her servant's assessment. This was much worse that she'd expected, and her expectations had not been high. Indeed, she'd never seen such an ill-kept hall, with torn and smoke-darkened tapestries and scarred, battered tables bearing evidence of past meals. If the tables had been wiped at all, she doubted the rag had been clean, or even wet. The lord's chair on the dais, a massive thing, had no cushion and looked more like an instrument of torture. The fire in the central hearth smoked and smoldered as if the wood used to make it had been left in the rain for a week.

She shuddered to imagine what the kitchen and bedchambers must be like. Mice in the pantry, no doubt, and bugs in the beds. No wonder Ranulf had written that letter to Merrick, and no wonder he'd muttered something about seeing to the horses and baggage instead of coming with them to the hall. Yet there was no need for him to be ashamed. He was the castellan, not the chatelaine, and a man couldn't be expected to run a household.

She'd also seen why he'd asked Merrick to send masons. The outer wall, and there was only one, was crumbling at one corner, and parts of the wall walk had already fallen away. Planks had been put in the gaps, but wood could catch fire if attackers used flaming arrows, and wet wood was as slick as ice in the rain.

The castle itself wasn't overly large, and the inner buildings consisted of the hall, where most of the soldiers and male servants must sleep, with family apartments and quarters for female servants above; the stables; the kitchen; a keep with a dungeon below, no doubt; and various storage buildings made of wood or stone. The yard itself was cobbled and relatively free of clutter or anything that might cause overcrowding or other danger.

"Gah! Just look at this rubbish," Maloren muttered, kicking at the rushes on the floor. "Been here for months, these have, or I was born yesterday.

No fleabane either, by the smell of it. We'll be scratching bites within a day. And there's *bones* in it. Rats, too, no doubt. We can't stay here. We should turn around and go back to Tregellas. It's only raining a little, nothing to speak of."

Beatrice silently sent up another prayer for patience. Maloren had complained only moments ago that she was going to be soaked to the skin walking from the cart to the hall. "It's raining too hard, and it's too late in the day to start back. You wouldn't want to be benighted on the moor or in a wood, would you?"

Maloren's immediate response was a sniff, and then to point at the water dripping through a hole in the slate roof. "We'll be drowned in our beds—if we're not too busy slapping at fleas and Lord knows what else."

Beatrice spied some women huddling in what appeared to be the corridor to the kitchen. Because of their simple homespun attire, she guessed they must be servants. They were less slovenly than the state of the hall would have led her to expect, so perhaps it was merely lack of leadership that explained the mess here, not an unwillingness to work. If she were staying here, she wouldn't accuse the servants of being lazy. She would simply assume they wanted to do their work and tell them...

She was here for at least this one night. Why not do what Constance and Merrick had sent her to do, even for that short time? She could surely make a bit of difference, and what did it matter if Ranulf wasn't cooperative? She had a duty to fulfill, and she could try to achieve as much as possible before she was sent away.

Determined to do just that, she started toward the wary women. It would be better if Ranulf introduced her to the household, but since he wasn't here, she would simply introduce herself.

And she would not feel grateful that not one of these women was pretty.

She smiled kindly and spoke gently, as if they were a group of nervous horses. "Good day. I am Lady Beatrice, the cousin of Lady Constance, the lady of Tregellas. I've come to visit Sir Ranulf and help set his household to rights since he has no wife or female relative to do it for him."

The women exchanged guarded looks. None of them ventured a word or smiled in return.

Beatrice gestured for the one who looked the youngest and least frightened to come forward. "What's your name?"

"Tecca, my lady," she murmured in reply.

"Thank you, Tecca. Who is the most senior of the maidservants here?"

"Eseld, my lady."

She looked over the women. "And which one of you is Eseld?"

"She isn't here, my lady," Tecca said quietly.

"Where is she?"

"Don't know, my lady."

Beatrice was quite certain Tecca did know, and so did the other servants who were likewise avoiding looking directly at her. However, this wasn't the time to press the point. What mattered now was what had brought her here in the first place. "Well, when you do see her, tell her to come to me. Lady Constance has charged me with ensuring that Sir Ranulf is as comfortably accommodated as a man of his rank deserves to be, and I intend to see that happens. First, though, I would like one of you to take my servant, Maloren, to the kitchen. She will be in charge of the evening meal today."

Behind her, Maloren muttered, "I don't know how I'm expected to have anything decent on the table. The food's probably full of maggots."

"Maggots?" a rough male voice cried from behind the serving women. "Who accuses me of having maggots in my food?"

A man nearly as wide as he was tall pushed his way through the serving women. He wore an apron liberally spattered with grease and his sleeves were rolled up to display fleshy arms. One eye squinted and he was missing a front tooth. His plump fingers were covered with tiny scars; he was also completely bald.

In spite of his unappealing appearance and rude manner, Beatrice gave him a smile, too. "Am I to assume that you're the cook?"

"Aye, and the best one in Cornwall," the man

boasted. "Sir Ranulf can have no cause to complain about the food."

Beatrice decided this was not the time to discuss that, so she gave him a rather empty smile. "When will the evening meal be served?"

"When it's ready."

No wonder this place was in such a condition, if this servant thought he could speak to her like that.

Beatrice drew herself up and straightened her shoulders, then regarded him with the contempt his insolence deserved. "You are the cook in Sir Ranulf's household. I am the cousin of his overlord's wife. When I ask you a question, you will give me a proper answer, or you will no longer be the cook here. Do you understand me?"

The man glanced about him uncertainly while all the other servants stared at their feet.

The cook seemed to appreciate that he'd made a serious error in thinking this young beauty lacked any authority, or the will to use it. He colored, cleared his throat and wiped his hands on his apron. "Sir Ranulf wants me to wait until all the patrols have come back."

Beatrice inclined her head in a gracious nod. "I see. Then so it shall be. What is your name?"

"Much, my lady."

"Thank you, Much. You can tell Maloren what you'll be serving and help her direct the unloading of the foodstuffs we brought from Penterwell."

"Aye, my lady."

She turned to Tecca. "While you will show me to my lord's bedchamber."

CHAPTER FIVE

BEATRICE WASN'T SURPRISED to find the castellan's bedchamber in no better condition than the hall below. The massive curtained bed was a mess of wrinkled linen and likely hadn't been made since the day Ranulf had arrived, if then. It looked as if Ranulf merely crawled into a sort of nest when he wished to sleep, on a rough-looking mattress with straw poking out of several small holes and through the poorly sewn seams. The curtains themselves would probably release a cloud of dust if one so much as touched them.

Ranulf's chain mail and helmet rested on a stand in one corner; clearly, Ranulf was not about to let that fall into neglect, although he had no squire. Perhaps he had one of the soldiers or servants tend to it. Or, more likely, he trusted that duty to no one else.

As for the rest of his clothing, it was surely in that battered wooden chest near the narrow arched window that didn't have even a linen shutter to keep out the chill breezes or night air. Inside the chest, his clothes, such as he possessed, were probably a feast for moths.

There was also a spindly sort of small table holding a large wooden bowl that must serve as a basin for washing, and a simple clay jug for an ewer. Some small pieces of other linen for drying, none too clean, lay folded beside the bowl.

Saying nothing to Tecca, who remained near the door, Beatrice ventured farther into the room, reflecting that at least the open window meant it didn't smell.

She hesitated when she saw something black and furry on the floor on the other side of the bed. It looked like the hind end of a large shaggy dog.

"It's a bear pelt," Ranulf announced from the doorway.

Beatrice wheeled around to find him leaning against the frame of the door, his arms crossed, his expression impassive.

"Is it meant to be on the floor, or has it fallen from the bed?" she asked, deciding she would act nonchalantly, too, or as much as possible, even though she was acutely aware that she was in Ranulf's bedchamber, and memories of the last time she'd been alone with him in such a room kept pushing their way into her thoughts.

Ranulf continued to regard her dispassionately. "It's meant to be on the bed. Last night, I grew too warm and kicked it off."

She tried not to envision Ranulf in that bed, warm or otherwise.

"I regret I didn't pick it up earlier," he said,

pushing off from the door frame and strolling closer, his gait easy, his shoulders relaxed.

Yet there was a tension in his body, too, and she was reminded of the times she'd seen his ease disappear, replaced with a warrior's readiness to defend his honor, or that of his friends.

She'd often wondered if he would react that way if someone offered an insult to her. Would he fight to uphold what remained of *her* honor?

"I would have picked it up," he continued, "had I known my bedchamber was going to be subject to a lady's inspection. I must point out, my lady, that it's highly improper for a maiden to be in a man's bedchamber unless it is her wedding night and he the groom. Since I have no intention of taking you for my bride, this chamber should be exempt from your efforts, and thus your presence."

He truly must not remember anything about what had happened the night before he left Tregellas. "I thought that since I was already here, I might as well do a little of what Constance charged me to do," she replied honestly, "such as ensuring that your living quarters are as comfortable as they can be. Besides, it's not as if we're alone. Tecca is…"

She fell silent when she glanced at the open door. The maidservant was no longer there.

Beatrice swallowed hard and told herself to stay calm. There would not be—could not be—a repetition of what had happened the last time they were alone.

"I take it you're referring to the wench who was standing in the corridor," Ranulf said evenly. "I dismissed her. I didn't think she needed to hear us arguing."

"Arguing?" Beatrice repeated warily. "What have we to argue about? I'm only going to make sure you have fresh linens and a clean hall and some decent food. Why would you want to quarrel about that?"

"Because it isn't your place to do such things for a man to whom you aren't married, or betrothed."

Bea went to the window and stood with her back to him. The last remaining light of day illuminated her as if she were an angel about to ascend.

"As for my comfort," he continued, forcing himself to consider more mortal matters, "I'm a knight, my lady, not a pampered prince. I am comfortable enough."

And she should *not* be in his bedchamber, most especially not alone. As it was, he didn't dare so much as glance at his bed because of the impure thoughts that Bea near his bed aroused.

She slowly turned to face him, regarding him not with anger or indignation, but with a sorrow that was heart-wrenching to see. "Constance has done so much for me, and since she couldn't come herself because of the baby and Merrick's leg, I was happy to take her place. Now you command me to go back and tell her I'm unable to do even this one simple thing for her husband's dearest friend."

He felt like the most callous brute in Christendom, but he was right, nonetheless. She simply couldn't stay. "Leave my chamber, Beatrice."

Before I do something I will regret.

Her expression questioning, she slowly walked toward him. "Is Maloren right to say you're an immoral scoundrel? Is that why you're so upset I've come? Am I not safe with you, Ranulf?"

He nearly groaned aloud. Could she truly have no idea how appealing she was, to him or any man? Was that why she saw no danger in her actions? She was safe with him because he willed it so, but his restraint was fraying fast.

Perhaps, that small voice prompted in his desperate mind, it was time she learned to take more care around men, even those she could trust. Maybe she should be made to realize that even those most determined to be honorable could be tempted beyond their strength. And many men wouldn't care that she was innocent and naive, more girl than woman. They would see only the beauty of her face and form, and have no care for the tender heart within. They would think her seduction a test of their manhood, a battle to be won, a prize to be gained, or a way to restore lost or wounded pride.

As he had with other women, once upon a time.

She should learn that hard lesson, and who better than he to teach it—he, who knew how selfish and heartless men could be?

"I may be an honorable knight, Beatrice," he crooned as he gave her a decidedly wolfish grin and began to approach her, "but I'm not a saint. And you are very beautiful."

She stared at him in wide-eyed disbelief as he backed her against the wall and trapped her there.

"Go, my lady," he whispered huskily, "out of this chamber and away from Penterwell, before you discover that even honorable men have their limits. I mean it, Beatrice. Go now, before I carry you to that bed and do what my lust demands."

Despite his harsh words, he saw not fear in her eyes but wonder, followed swiftly by delight.

"Other men have told me I'm pretty," she whispered, the corners of her delectable lips curving upward in a smile, "but you never have."

He wished all other men to the devil.

"I'm not afraid to be alone with you, Ranulf," she said, reaching out to caress his cheek. "I'm not afraid of anything you might do."

This was not going the way he'd intended.

And then she smiled. Gloriously. Joyously. As if she wanted nothing more than for him to carry her to his bed and make love with him.

He forgot this was supposed to be a lesson. He saw only the desire that mirrored his own in her trusting, lovely eyes, and he could no longer refrain from acting on it.

"Bea," he murmured, her name a sigh, a hope, a

plea, as his arm went around her waist and he tugged her to him, capturing her mouth in a fierce and passionate kiss.

"Ranulf," she whispered, and she returned his kiss as if she had been waiting years for just that moment. Her arms locked around his body, holding him so tightly he could feel her breasts pressing against him. She parted her lips and touched her tongue to his, eagerly deepening the kiss.

The desire he had long tried to contain with his iron-willed resolve broke free. Need, affection, passion and longing bloomed like seeds, long dormant in winter, that leapt into life with the warmth and light of spring.

Overpowered by emotion, Ranulf forgot honor and duty and chivalry. In his arms, she was all he knew or cared about—her beauty, her spirit, her friendly kindness bringing light where there was darkness, joy where there was desolation, affection where there had been only pain.

With burgeoning need, with increasing desire, he held her close, kissing and caressing her. He felt her respond to his lips and his touch, and the realization fueled his ardor.

"I'm glad you're not a saint," she murmured breathlessly just as he was about to sweep her up into his arms with the half-formed intention of carrying her to his bed, "although I wish you'd cut off your beard. It scratches."

Reality hit him like a blow. He had grown his beard to make her see that he was too old for her. She was more than ten years younger than he, and barely out of girlhood.

He was a landless knight, without wealth, or power or family. She was a young, beautiful lady, beloved of his friend and overlord, cousin to his best friend's wife, entrusted to his care because she was a visitor here.

He was tainted by his sinful past; she was sweet and pure.

He flushed with mortification for his lustful weakness. Kissing her was a mistake. Being alone with her was a mistake. Anything except dispassionate reason was a mistake when he was near Bea.

He had erred and he must correct his error. He must destroy whatever was developing between them while he still had the strength and the will, or her honor, and what remained of his, would be lost forever.

"You're the first woman to complain about it," he replied, struggling to sound coolly calm as he stepped away from her. "I would ascribe that to your lack of experience, except that kiss would seem to indicate I must be wrong to think you've never been kissed before. Might I inquire, as a friend of the family and thus one who cares about your fate, who has been so fortunate as to be the object of your affections? Young Kiernan perhaps?"

For the first time in his experience, Bea's lip curled

with scorn. "There is no need to bring Sir Jowan's son into this. He's a friend and nothing more."

Ranulf ignored the brief spasm of relief that answer brought him and focused on the fact that she had *not* said Kiernan had never kissed her. "It could be you're not as naive as I think. After that kiss, perhaps I should reconsider. Maybe you have more experience than I assumed."

"You're the first man who's ever kissed me like that, and the first man I ever wanted to," she retorted. "Nor is this the first time we've kissed."

As he stared at her in stunned surprise, she put her hands on her narrow hips and glared at him with suspicion. "Do you truly not remember what passed between us the night before you left Tregellas?"

Snippets of Ranulf's incredibly arousing, vivid dream came back to him, of kissing Bea and being kissed. Had that really happened? And if so, he thought with sudden shame and horror, was there more he had forgotten? Had he, in his inebriated state, totally lost all self-control and taken advantage of his best friend's ward?

"You needn't look so stricken, Ranulf. We kissed just as we did here, and nothing more. Then you sent me away—and made me feel like the worst, most sinful woman in Christendom because I had dared to kiss you. Nevertheless, I should think that would tell you who is the object of my affection, and it most certainly isn't Kiernan."

His eyes narrowed as he clutched at one reason not to be completely ashamed. "*You* kissed *me?*"

"That night I did. But here and now, and with all memory of our previous embrace apparently absent from your mind, *you* kissed *me.*"

Relieved that they had only shared a kiss, yet dismayed that he had done that much, he forced himself to laugh. "God save you, Lady Beatrice, you make far too much of a kiss, which tells me just how ignorant a maiden you are. Now go home to Tregellas and take your romantic fancies with you. Love is not a tale told by troubadours or minstrels."

Instead of fleeing the chamber as he'd hoped, her brows lowered and her eyes flashed. "Do you think I don't understand the difference between minstrels' songs and real life? Of course I do—because the love they sing about so often leads to disaster, for one thing, and that doesn't always happen in real life. Look at Constance and Merrick if you wish an example. Would you say their love is doomed to fail?"

"I will grant that, in some instances, love does last," he replied, "but that sort of true love is more rare than minstrels would have us believe. In any case, this over-heated affection you apparently have for me isn't love. It's nothing more than a maiden's moonstruck fancy."

Her sharp, bright eyes held his. "That only tells me how little you know of my heart, Ranulf," she said as she walked toward him. "And if you believe what I feel for you is ridiculous, why then did you kiss me?"

He began to back away. "I was attempting to show you what can happen when an innocent, ignorant young woman allows herself to be alone with a man."

She regarded him with blatant skepticism. "You chose an interesting method of instruction. Did it never cross your mind, sir knight, that your embrace might have the opposite effect, and rather serve to make me crave your kisses more?"

Oh, God, he was caught in a trap, and one of his own making.

"Fortunately," she said, coming to a halt at last, "I know full well you're not a fiendish rogue. You're an honorable knight, the trusted friend of my cousin's husband. No woman need ever be afraid of you."

God help him! She shouldn't be making him feel proud, trusted and valued. She was supposed to be shocked, horrified and appalled.

"That kiss we shared in Tregellas was not the first time I realized you felt more than mere friendly affection for me. What about Christmas, Ranulf, when we very nearly kissed? Will you tell me now you didn't want me then?"

He flushed, cursed his weakness and planted his feet, crossing his arms as he tried to act nonchalant. "I suppose I might have been momentarily addled by the mulled wine that night."

"You weren't drunk, Ranulf. You'd barely had any wine at all."

Oh, Lord.

He steeled himself to answer as he must, although the lies fairly curdled on his tongue. "I admit I contemplated a kiss that night to see how you'd react. However, any kisses we've shared since, as well as your willingness to put yourself at the mercy of a man's desire, have only shown me that I was right to think you're much too young and inexperienced to be trusted around men. As for any unfortunate fantasies my actions have caused you to entertain, let me assure you that my taste doesn't run toward moonstruck maidens. I will not kiss you again."

She tilted her head and searched his face, as if she would see into his very heart and expose the secrets he sought to hide. "What's the matter, Ranulf? Why are you saying such things? Why are you so afraid to admit that you want me? Is it because another woman once broke your heart?"

Shocked, he stiffened and had to fight not to betray his dismay. "I've never spoken of such a woman."

"That doesn't mean she doesn't exist," Bea returned. "That's why you're pushing me away, isn't it? You don't want to be hurt again. You'd rather reject what I offer without giving me—giving *us*—a chance."

She had no idea of the pain she was causing, the long-buried memories she was summoning to the surface of his mind—memories that only served to remind him more strongly why he must not take what Bea, in her youthful inexperience and purity, offered him.

He glared at her and answered harshly, determined to push her away, for her own good. "Have you been stricken deaf, or are you being wilfully stupid?" he demanded. "How many times and in how many ways must I tell you that I don't want to be the object of your silly, girlish fantasies?"

Still she didn't look away, but continued to regard him steadily. "Is it because I'm the daughter of a traitor then?"

He flinched, for his reaction had nothing at all to do with her father. "Your father's crime is his shame, not yours."

"I promise you, Ranulf, that although my father betrayed his king, I would never betray you."

He believed her, and that was another reason to drive her away. He didn't deserve such loyalty from a woman, not after what he'd done.

Determined to make her see that her cause was hopeless, for so it must be, he took hold of her shoulders and stared into her eyes, which were sparkling like blue diamonds. "Listen to me, Beatrice, and get this through your head. You're nothing but a foolish girl with a head full of romantic fancies. Granted, you're a pretty little thing, and your kiss was not without some merit, but pretty women who kiss as well as you are easy enough to find. If and when I take a wife, I want a woman of maturity and experience in my bed, not some green girl. I don't want *you* and I never will."

The truth, or such as he wanted her to believe,

finally hit home, and it was like watching an innocent, wild creature perish. He had seen death before. God forgive him, he had killed men himself. But that was different from watching Bea's heart break before his very eyes—to see the light and spirit in her shining eyes dim, and pain bloom where before there had been trust, affection, happiness and hope.

Had he looked like that when Celeste had told him she was marrying Lord Fontenbleu? Had Celeste felt the same shame and remorse? Did she silently curse herself and wish herself dead for what she'd done?

He steeled himself for Bea's tears, which did not come. She straightened, tall and slender, as poised as a princess, while regarding him with haughty dignity. It was as if a changeling had swooped in and taken his little Lady Bea, replacing her with a woman of power and majesty who took his breath away.

"I'm seeing to your comfort at the behest of Constance and your overlord," she said with calm composure. "It's my duty to do what they sent me to do, the same way you do your duty to Merrick and the king. Whether I'm welcome or not, and whether you want me to or not, I shall fulfill that duty for as long as I'm able until you force me to leave."

Then she swept out of the chamber and left him.

WHEN SHE WAS GONE and the door had closed behind her, Ranulf leaned back against the nearest wall and hung his head.

He felt like a murderer, a cruel and merciless villain.

He hadn't wanted to hurt her, yet this was the way it must be. Bea deserved a finer, better man than he could ever be. He knew it and, one day, so would she. Then, hopefully, she would realize the folly of her youthful affection and be grateful he had rejected her. She could be glad she hadn't thrown herself away on a poor and landless knight, and might even find it in her heart to forgive him the things he'd said and done today.

Meanwhile, he would live without her love, finding contentment where he could.

Ranulf drew in a deep, ragged breath as he pushed himself off the wall. Not for him the joys of marital bliss such as Merrick and Henry had found in the arms of their beloved wives. He would never know that deep happiness, or have his children gathered 'round him, with a wife he cherished and adored looking on beside him.

He would be alone, as he must and always would be.

As RANULF SLUMPED against the wall, Beatrice ran into the first empty chamber she could find. She shoved the door closed and fastened the latch, then splayed her hands upon the door and laid her forehead on the rough wood, breathing hard.

How could she have been so wrong? How could she have believed he was a good, kind man? He was a cad, a scoundrel, a lustful beast, just as Maloren had always said. He was an ungrateful wretch, too, making sport of her duty and her wish to help him. He'd acted as if she carried the plague and was trying to sicken him with it. It would serve him right if she let him wallow in filth and misery, eating moldy bread and rotten meat, sleeping in musty sheets in a room thick with dust, finally dying loveless and alone.

She must have been mad to think she loved him! She didn't. She couldn't. She wouldn't. His kisses were lies...

She took a deep breath, then shook her head. No, if there was one thing that had been truthful between them, it had been the kisses they had shared. He could claim he didn't want her and give her a score of excuses, but his kisses had told her the truth.

Whatever he said about not wanting her—that was the lie.

Why would he reject the love she offered?

Her age should be no barrier. People with far greater differences in ages married all the time. Indeed, her youth should be to her advantage, although he was right that she had no experience in loving a man. But that, too, would be considered a good thing by most men.

And he could teach her what she needed to know.

She warmed as her mind strayed to sharing Ranulf's bed, but she quickly returned to the obstacles he seemed determined to put between them.

Until she understood why he claimed not to want her, she couldn't hope to become his lover.

She recalled the look in his eyes when she spoke of another woman and there, she felt sure, was the answer. Some foolish, stupid woman had spurned him and made him feel unworthy, and the blow still stung.

How could she make him see that whatever had happened before, the woman had been at fault, not him? He was more than worthy of a woman's love. She had to make him understand that—and to do that, she must find a way to stay. She *couldn't* leave here tomorrow.

She turned into the room and looked at the open, unshuttered window and the rain still falling. If it were raining like that in the morning, they wouldn't be able to depart. Ranulf wouldn't dare make them set out for Tregellas in a deluge, lest they get stuck in the mud, or otherwise have difficulties. She was, as he had said, the cousin of his best friend's wife.

As she silently prayed for the rain to continue, she sneezed. Like every other chamber in Penterwell Castle, this one was dusty and dirty and full of cobwebs. It was also empty, save for an upright bed frame leaning against the wall.

She walked farther into the chamber. Yes, this would do for her and Maloren, with a little cleaning. They'd brought their own bedding and linen, and a small, portable table and two stools. She'd also brought her little box of medicines, including one the

apothecary had shown her how to make after he'd
tended to Merrick's leg and she'd wondered aloud
how Constance might ensure that her husband got
some sleep despite the pain.

An idea popped into her head like a gift from
heaven or the answer to a prayer. There was one way
to ensure that she wouldn't be leaving first thing in
the morning whether it was raining or not, and all it
would take was a potion made of poppy seeds slipped
into some wine.

Beatrice smiled as her usual good humor returned.
The proud and mighty Sir Ranulf was about to discover she wasn't simply going to surrender without
a fight.

CHAPTER SIX

HIS EYES STILL CLOSED, Ranulf groaned as he lay in his bed the next morning. God save him, his head felt as heavy as a lead weight, and his arms, too.

It was as if he were suffering the effects of too much wine, except that he hadn't had much wine at all last night when Bea had sat beside him at the evening meal, looking lovely and ethereal and hardly saying a word.

How many times had he told himself he wished she would be quiet? Yet it had been distinctly disconcerting having her sit silently beside him throughout an entire meal.

As disturbing as it was having Bea so obviously angry at him, she simply had to go back to Tregellas, taking her avowals of devotion, her bright eyes, her lovely lips and his heart with her. Her anger was easier to bear than the anguish he would feel if she learned the truth about his past.

As for her assumption that a woman had broken his heart, she was right. A woman had. But it was not Celeste's rejection that made him turn away from Bea now, or think himself unworthy of her innocent devotion. It was the terrible thing he'd done after, and the worse thing he'd done before, when he was still a boy.

No, it was better this way. Bea must not want him and they mustn't be near each other, lest he give in to temptation. She had to go back to Tregellas.

At least Maloren had looked pleased for once, he thought, trying to find something good about the situation as he threw off the bear pelt and other coverings and tried to get out of bed. It was as if he were trying to move through mud.

He lay still and took a deep breath, inhaling the light scent of lavender from the clean sheets. Last night when he'd retired, he'd found the bed made with fresh sheets, the mattress repaired and stuffed with new straw, and the floor swept. Tapestries depicting colorful scenes of a hunt and ladies playing instruments, cleaned and free of soot, covered the walls. Closed wooden shutters kept out the wind and the rain. A large beeswax candle burned on the table that had been moved beside the bed, and there'd been a goblet of spiced wine beside it, too. This chamber that had once been little better than a cold, barren storeroom was now a place of warmth, comfort and ease.

He'd drunk the wine as he stood staring at the newly made bed, knowing Bea must be responsible for the changes in spite of what had passed between them. He couldn't deny he'd been pleased when he'd crawled naked between the sheets, and he'd had the most restful sleep he'd had in weeks.

He smacked his lips, where the taste of wine and exotic spices lingered. It had been very good, that wine, but surely not enough to render him…

He pushed himself up and reached for the goblet. Leaning close, he sniffed the dregs in the bottom and cursed softly.

He'd been drugged. Someone had put something in that wine to make him sleep.

Wide-awake now, he threw off the covers and jumped out of the bed, hissing as his bare feet touched the cold stone floor. Someone had wanted him insensible—to do what? His soldiers could hold off an attack without him, at least for a little while, and there was nothing worthwhile to steal from his chamber, except his armor and sword, and they were still there.

Or perhaps that dose was intended to do more than make him sleep. Perhaps his death had been the goal, and only by chance and God's mercy had the dose not been lethal.

He grabbed his clothes from the top of the chest and started to dress. God save him, what o'clock was it? He went to the window, threw open the shutters and cursed again. Rain was pelting down from the sky like the biblical deluge.

The door to the chamber banged open. Maloren marched in carrying a bucket of water and with clean linen over her arm.

"So, you're awake at last," she grumbled as she ran a scornful gaze over him. "*Some* people think they can sleep the day away once they're in command. And close those shutters or there'll be water all over the floor."

"Do you know who put that goblet of wine by my bed last night?" Ranulf demanded, paying no heed to anything else she said.

As soon as he asked the question, it occurred to him that it might have been Maloren's doing, some scheme to keep her "lamb" safe from his supposedly nefarious designs.

"Who else but my good and gentle lady?" she replied, glaring at him as if he'd gone mad. "She even helps them as don't deserve it."

Bea had put the wine there?

Someone must have gotten to it before she had brought it to his chamber. "Where did she get it?"

Maloren made a sour face. "We brought it from Tregellas, of course. She prepared it for you with her own hands, too, and after that long journey."

Surely Bea hadn't…?

Maloren sniffed derisively as she continued to glare at him. "Although why she bothered, I don't know. You don't even have the grace to be grateful."

Between his heavy head and the realization that his wine had been drugged, he had no patience for Maloren's impertinence this morning.

"Since it's raining, you and your mistress will

have to remain under my roof for the next day at least," he said through clenched teeth. "Might I suggest, Maloren, that in that time, you curb your tongue. Otherwise, you may be forced to contemplate your insolence in the dungeon."

The maidservant's mouth fell open and a look of fear came to her eyes. "You wouldn't dare!"

"You think not?" he asked. In truth, he would never put a woman, especially an elderly one, in a cold, dank cell merely for being impertinent, but he wasn't above letting her think he would.

"M-my lady wouldn't let you!" Maloren stammered, backing away.

"Your lady has no power here, Maloren, so take care how you speak to me," he said as he followed her. "I neither know nor care why you hate me as you do, but hear this and believe it—I grow weary of your baseless accusations and rude remarks. I have no seductive designs on Lady Beatrice. She is my friend's relation, and therefore sacrosanct."

The old woman's hands fluttered to her chest. "You…you won't touch her?"

Would that he could promise that! "I give you my word as a knight of the realm and Lord Merrick's brother-in-arms that I have no wish to seduce her," he answered instead.

Maloren's whole body seemed to slump with relief. "Thank God."

"So now that you have my word, I expect you to

address me with the respect my position deserves, if not my person."

Maloren meekly bowed. "Yes, my lord."

"And now you can go."

"Not yet, my lord, sir," Maloren said. She bustled over to his clothes chest and threw open the lid with so much force it banged against the wall.

"What are you doing?"

"My lady's ordered that all your clothes are to be washed and mended."

He instinctively looked down at his rumpled breeches and the shirt still in his hand.

"Not what you're wearing," Maloren said. "Those'll be taken care of on the morrow."

With that, she headed for the door, carrying his one other shirt, his extra tunic, two pairs of breeches and some stockings in her thin, wiry arms. Ranulf thought of stopping her but decided against it. His clothes could stand to be cleaned, and he had something more important to do than argue with Maloren.

He had to talk to Bea.

He quickly washed and finished dressing and hurried to the hall.

Where he discovered pandemonium. It seemed like a hundred servants were busy there. Some were sweeping the old rushes into a pile near the door. Others were scattering new ones, followed by children sprinkling herbs and getting nearly as many on themselves as on the rushes. The hounds were tied in a corner, apparently too occupied by the bones they were chewing to mind their restraints. Another group of servants, with buckets and rags and what looked like pots of beeswax, were at work cleaning the furniture. More, on ladders, were sweeping away the cobwebs from the beams and corners. The tapestries were missing, and a large fire crackled in the central hearth. Torches burned in cobweb-free brackets on the wall, illuminating the chamber so that it was nearly as bright as on a sunny day.

This had to be Bea's doing, too.

"Oh, there you are, Sir Ranulf!" he heard her call out and then saw, to his shock and chagrin, that she was one of those standing on a ladder, where she'd been brushing away a spider's web with a small broom.

He immediately had visions of her plunging to her death, lying on the flagstones with her neck broken.

"What do you think you're doing?" he demanded as he strode toward her ladder. "Get down from there!"

Mercifully, she didn't hesitate to obey. She climbed down quite nimbly, which didn't excuse her taking such an outrageous risk.

Once on the ground, he saw that she was dressed no better than a peasant in a gown of simple doe-brown homespun, with a square of plain white linen on her hair. She had a smudge of dirt on her nose, too.

Yet she'd never looked more beautiful. Or kissable. Or desirable. And although she was dressed like a peasant, he was still very aware that she was nobly born, worthy to be a lord's wife, and the chatelaine of any castle in the land.

What he would not give to have her chatelaine of this castle—as long as he was castellan. To be with her every day and see her leading his servants like a pretty, merry general.

What he would not give to have Bea for his wife…except that he had nothing to give.

He mentally gave his head a shake, for such thoughts could avail him nothing—and she'd put herself in danger *again*. "You could have fallen and broken your neck, and then what would I tell Constance and Merrick?"

"That I had been behaving in a most unladylike manner and it was not your fault," she replied with a disarming, devilish little grin.

Why wasn't she still angry with him? She ought to be. He'd said terrible, hurtful things to her yesterday. "I'm serious, Beatrice. You shouldn't be doing that. And you shouldn't be working like a servant, either."

"But I like it," she answered cheerily. "And have I not heard you say more than once that a good commander doesn't shirk any tasks he asks his men to do?"

Her eyes sparkled as her tone grew gently wheedling. "Besides, isn't your hall more pleasant and comfortable when it's clean?"

He fought to hold on to his necessary anger. "The fact remains that you shouldn't have been climbing on a ladder. It's much too dangerous."

She raised a golden brow. "Whereas you never do dangerous things?"

"I'm a knight. It's my duty to take risks."

"And it's *my* duty to get this hall into a livable condition."

"You were supposed to be leaving."

"We can't go in the rain—or haven't you noticed the weather?"

"I have." He recalled the other reason he should be angry with her. "But if I hadn't, it might have been because somebody put something in my wine to make me sleep last night."

"And did you sleep?"

"Of course, and you know it, since you were the one responsible."

"Yes, I was," Bea brazenly admitted, and without a particle of contrition. "You looked so exhausted I used a potion the apothecary taught me to make after he'd tended to Merrick."

She grinned as if she'd just won first prize in a joust. "And you do look much more rested this morning, even if you're grumpy. Why don't you go to the kitchen and get something to eat? Maybe that will improve your mood. There's porridge that should still be simmering, and some smoked ham and bread and cheese from Tregellas." She surveyed him in a matronly sort of way. "You've been working too hard and not getting enough to eat. You look far too thin."

"My lady—" he began sternly, telling himself it didn't matter how he looked to her.

"My lord," she interrupted, her bright blue eyes shining. She clasped her hands together as if she was about to plead for mercy. "All I want to do is to act as your chatelaine for as long as it continues to rain, as Constance and Merrick asked me to. When it stops, I'll meekly and mildly go back to Tregellas just as you command." Her expression softened and turned sorrowful. "I haven't forgotten what you said to me last night, Ranulf. I doubt I ever will. But can we not be friends for now?"

As he hesitated, wanting to agree and yet wondering how he could he possibly be friends with Bea given the feelings she aroused within him, he realized that the hall had become as quiet as a cathedral on a midsummer's afternoon. Every single one of the servants—including Maloren—had stopped working, or doing whatever they were doing to watch them.

Bea darted a glance at them, and they immediately went back to work.

"Well, Ranulf?" she asked quietly, her voice so low, only he could hear. "Will you agree to my request, or will you order your servants to stop what they're doing and go back to doing nothing, even though you feed and shelter them?"

How could he refuse when she put it like that? He gritted his teeth a moment, prayed for strength, then raised his voice so that all in the hall could hear.

"While Lady Beatrice graces us with her presence," he announced, "you will obey her as you would me."

Her grateful smile seemed to reach right into his chest and grab hold of his heart. "Thank you, Ranulf."

He didn't know whether he wanted to shake her or embrace her. He wanted to think of some clever, cutting thing to say to her.

No, what he *really* wanted to do, he realized as he turned on his heel and strode to the kitchen, was take her in his arms and kiss her until they both were breathless.

"SACRE BLEU!" the Frenchman muttered as he climbed over the slippery rocks at the entrance to the cave near the village that same morning and despite the pouring rain. "A thousand sea battles I have survived, yet now I may fall to my death on some rocks!"

He glanced up at the young Cornishman holding a smoldering pitch torch on the relatively dry ledge above. "That would be too bad for you, eh?"

Myghal frowned as he watched Pierre climb the last few feet. The Frenchman had been smuggling tin between Cornwall and France for over twenty years, and he had the look of a man who'd spent his entire life at sea: weathered skin as brown as aged oak, hair liberally sprinkled with gray, and gnarled, callused hands that looked strong enough to bend metal. He wore a leather tunic and breeches, boots and a shirt of coarse linen. His sword belt was wide and its buckle silver, like the hilt of his broadsword. He also had two daggers stuck in his belt and, Myghal didn't doubt, at least one in his boot. He'd lost an eye from a loose rope whipped by a fierce wind and the empty socket puckered beneath a thick black eyebrow.

Pierre followed Myghal some twenty feet back into the cave to a dryer grotto. Another torch, stuck between the rocks, burned there. A hole leading upward from the grotto drew the smoke, which then dispersed through several small cracks until it appeared as no more than mist outside. That was why Myghal's family had used this cave as a secret cache for their goods for generations.

"You have the tin?" Pierre asked.

Myghal nodded and moved back into the dimmer recess of the grotto. He rearranged one of a pile of rocks and brought forth twenty pounds of tin he'd purchased from several tinners who mined the moor around the village.

Pierre examined the metal in the light of the torch. "Although naturally I don't suspect you of cheating, not after what I've done for you, I think there is more you owe me."

"This is the last," Myghal protested. "This is what we agreed."

"For killing Gawan, *oui*. But things have changed now that Sir Frioc is dead."

"Was that your doing?" Myghal asked warily, and with sickening trepidation.

"*Mon Dieu,* no!" Pierre cried as if appalled at the very idea. He settled himself on one of the large rocks. "I would never have killed such a valuable fellow—so content to let smugglers ply their trade, as long as they kept the peace. But this Sir Ranulf... well, if I get the chance, he may go to the devil sooner than he plans. And the devil it will be, if even half the stories I've heard of him are true."

Myghal slowly sat on another rock. "What sort of stories?"

Pierre grinned. "I fear Sir Ranulf is not so genial a fellow as Sir Frioc. He's a vicious branch from a vicious tree. They say he drowned his own brother."

Myghal's eyes widened with disbelief. "Who told you that?"

"It's common knowledge among the brothels of London. That is why his father cast him out with nothing. Somehow he convinced Sir Leonard de Brissy to train him, and thus he came to be friends with the mighty lord of Tregellas. They tell other stories about him in the brothels, too. He is quite the lover, Sir Ranulf."

Myghal frowned, finding it difficult to reconcile this notion of his overlord with the man he knew.

"You don't believe me, *mon ami?* You should. I make it my business to learn about the men who oversee this coast. And now Sir Ranulf wants to find out who killed Gawan. That must be very uncomfortable for you."

"I didn't do it," Myghal retorted. "You did. The night Gawan died, I spent the entire evening in the tavern and plenty of people saw me there."

"That is true, but if I am caught by the vicious Sir Ranulf, I may be forced to confess that you paid me to do it, so I should think you would want to make sure that I am never captured."

Myghal's stomach turned and he felt as if a trap were closing around him, a feeling that had been growing ever since the terrible day he'd made his devil's bargain with Pierre. "Then you shouldn't come back to Penterwell for a long time, and not just because of Sir Ranulf. The villagers have their suspicions, too, and some of them are planning to take you prisoner if you set foot ashore. They think you killed Rob and Sam, too."

Pierre's face was the epitome of innocence. "Who, I?"

"Yes, you, or your men."

"Well, well, I say we did not, but it seems your friends in the village have other ideas. Perhaps it would be wise to stay away." He grinned at the young man. "You see? You did have something with which to pay me."

And, Myghal realized with a horrible foreboding, he would likely continue to pay for Pierre's silence, either with tin or information, for the rest of his life.

"But let us speak no more of murder," Pierre said amicably as he pulled a small wineskin from beneath his tunic. "Let us talk of more pleasant subjects. How goes your wooing of the widow?"

He offered the wineskin to Myghal, who swiftly shook his head. "I don't want to talk about her."

The Frenchman chuckled. "Not well, I take it. You should ask this Sir Ranulf you seem to admire for assistance. He once made a wager he could seduce fourteen virgins in a fortnight—one for every night—and he won."

Pierre smirked. "You look shocked, my young friend. But he is a comely fellow, or so I've been told, and skilled in battle as well as the bedchamber. Such a combination is hard for women to resist. No doubt that explains the young beauty living with him now." Pierre kissed his fingertips to the air. "*Magnifique!* I could get a fortune for her at the slave market in Tangier."

Ignoring what Pierre said about that mind-boggling wager, Myghal stiffly said, "Lady Beatrice is a noblewoman and the cousin of the lady of Tregellas."

"Sir Ranulf aims high, but clearly, he succeeds."

"She's *not* his leman," Myghal said, disgusted by the man's carnal assumptions. "I told you, she's the cousin of his overlord."

Pierre laughed as he tucked the wineskin back into his tunic. "Such a romantic innocent you are! Just because you have not the courage to seduce the woman you want, you think all men have such delicate scruples, or that noblewomen have? Sir

Ranulf, at least, does not. Those women who suc-
cumbed to his efforts were all nobly born women of
the king's court."

"I'm *certain* Lady Beatrice isn't his leman,"
Myghal insisted. "He doesn't even seem to like her
very much—but you still shouldn't get any ideas about
trying to steal her away. If anything were to happen to
her, Sir Ranulf and the lord of Tregellas would never
rest until they found the men responsible, and it'd
surely mean a slow and painful death when they did."

Pierre put his hand to his breast as if offended.
"Have I said anything about abducting her? Although
now that you speak of it, a woman like that might be
worth the risk." His lips curved up into a sinister
smile. "Especially if she was properly trained."

Myghal felt sick to think of any woman in Pierre's
clutches, raped and beaten and bound for slavery.

"I would be willing to offer a portion of the profit
if you would help me catch her," Pierre proposed. "I
might even share the training with you."

Thoroughly revolted, Myghal shook his head.

Pierre sighed and shrugged. "Very well, but now
I have a desire to do a little slaving, for there is great
profit in that trade." His eyes gleamed in the torch-
light. "Your Wenna is a pretty woman. Big with child
now, of course, but in another month or two, she
might fetch a fair price."

"Wenna?" Myghal gasped, staring at him with
horror.

Pierre grinned, and there was scorn in his beady brown eyes. "Yes, your pretty little Wenna. So let us make another bargain, *mon ami*. Help me get the noble beauty, and your Wenna will be safe. More, you will never see me again. But if you do not help me, I will take the woman whose husband you paid me to kill, and the villagers will find out what happened to your rival."

CHAPTER SEVEN

THREE DAYS LATER, it was still raining and Ranulf was still frustrated and exasperated as he made his way to the sheriff's house on the outskirts of the village, on the side away from the sea. Water streamed from his cloak and his boots were soaking, but Ranulf didn't care. Although he and Bea had achieved a sort of truce, it was better to be drenched than around her, with her cleaning and her smiling and her busy chatter about what she was doing and what still needed to be done, or trying not to watch her and imagine what it would be like if she could stay. If she could be his wife.

He'd contemplated riding out with the patrol today, but he wasn't willing to expose the expensively purchased Titan to the risk of a broken leg from slippery mud, or a lung ailment from the damp.

Besides, the patrol had already gone without him. He'd overslept again. Bea refused to allow any of the servants to wake him, and he'd had another wretched night, not dropping off to sleep until nearly dawn. Then he'd dreamed of making love with Bea on the black bear pelt, her honey-blond hair spread out about her like a halo, her naked body undulating beneath him.

With that memory to torment him, he reached the sheriff's two-storied stone house and rapped sharply on the wooden door with his bare knuckles. Since Hedyn wasn't married, they could have a conversation about important matters without the distraction of wives, or women who acted like them.

A male servant, dark haired and middle-aged, opened the door. His mouth fell open when he saw Ranulf standing on the threshold, but he quickly recovered, bowed and opened the door wider to allow the castellan to enter.

"S'truth, my lord, I wasn't expecting to see you this morning. The weather's fit to drown a man!" Hedyn cried as he hurried from his comfortable seat near his hearth to welcome Ranulf.

He then ordered his servant to take Ranulf's cloak and invited the castellan to sit by the fire.

"Put your feet up on that stool," Hedyn suggested. "That should help them dry. I thought the rain might let up this morning, but it looks like it'll last awhile yet. One good thing, though—ships are more likely to stay close to shore or take refuge in a cove, so they'll be easier to spot."

When Ranulf was settled, with his feet raised near the crackling flames and a goblet of mulled wine in his hand, Hedyn regarded him questioningly. "Well, my lord, what brings you here? Have your men found something?"

Ranulf was not about to admit that he had come seeking refuge from overzealous young ladies with cleaning on their minds. "I was hoping you'd learned something more about those two missing men."

"Ah." Hedyn leaned back in his chair and shook his head. "Not a word. Which means, I think, that they're likely dead, or we'd be able to get news of them along the coast. Their vessel wasn't big enough to risk a longer voyage."

"So that would be three men dead, and probably murdered, in the past month, not to mention Sir Frioc's unexpected demise."

"Aye, my lord," Hedyn grimly confirmed.

Ranulf pushed away the memory of Gawan's body lying on the beach, gray and soaked and terrible. "And none of the villagers have given you any hint as to who might be responsible for any of these deaths or disappearances?"

Hedyn shook his head. "I think they're coming 'round, now that they've had time to get used to you, but they're not willing to say much. They're Cornish, when all's said and done, and they don't trust outsiders."

"They should trust *you*. You're Cornish."

That brought a wry grin to Hedyn's weathered face. "Aye, sir, I am, but from a village some miles away. That makes me from outside, too—just not so much."

Ranulf sighed and sank deeper into his chair. "I hope they don't wait too much longer before coming forward with information, if they have it. I don't want any more murders."

"No, my lord, and believe me, they want to know who's responsible and the louts punished. A few more days, and we might hear something."

A few more days, Ranulf thought dismally. He prayed to God nobody else ended up in a watery grave in a few more days. "What of Gwenbritha?"

"Still at her mother's, my lord. I'm sure she had naught to do with Sir Frioc's death. She was very upset when I told her about it. She wasn't sorry she'd left him, but she was sorry he was dead."

"Women can be deceiving."

"Aye, so they can. But I don't think she's guilty of anything with regards to his death. To be blunt, my lord, I don't think anybody is. We saw no signs of anyone else near his body—no footprints, no grass or ground disturbed. I'd be willing to wager Sir Frioc's death was an accident."

Ranulf hoped Hedyn was right.

"I hear you've got a visitor at the castle," Hedyn noted.

The arrival of a noble lady and her escort would hardly have passed unremarked in a small village. "Lady Beatrice is the cousin of the lord of Tregellas's wife."

"Pretty girl, so they tell me."

"Yes, she is."

Hedyn's eyes sparkled in the firelight. "Set down the cook right handily, so I've heard."

This was news to Ranulf, but he tried not to betray any surprise, although he found it hard to imagine Bea intimidating anyone, until he recalled her irate majesty. Still, it could be that Hedyn had it wrong, his grasp of events based on gossip and supposition. "She came to help me bring some order to my household." He gave Hedyn a man-to-man, I-don't-really-care smile. "That sort of thing is beyond my experience."

Hedyn chuckled and moved his feet closer to the fire. "Well, it'll do that fellow some good to have his nose out of joint. Neither Sir Frioc nor Gwenbritha could manage him."

Ranulf felt it necessary that Hedyn understand exactly how things were with Bea. "She'll be going back to Tregellas as soon as the weather clears."

"Oh, aye?" Hedyn replied. "I thought maybe she'd be staying."

"No, she will not."

"Seems a pity to me, my lord," Hedyn said evenly, "her being so pretty and a dab hand with the servants, too. I've heard nothing but good things about her, and that's saying something."

"Even from the servants she's making work so hard?" Ranulf asked, not hiding his skepticism. He was aware of the way soldiers grumbled when they were forced to do much more than polish their armor, and there were always those who'd complain about that.

Hedyn gave him a smile that seemed to indicate he found Ranulf's question rather naive. "There's a few—the lazy ones—would grumble if they had to get out of their beds, but most of 'em like having something to do and knowing when and where to do it. Idleness makes 'em cranky, and it seems her ladyship is a pleasant sort of mistress. Gave Tecca a new scarf for doing a good job getting her bedchamber ready. The lass was so excited, you'd think she'd been made Queen of the May."

"Didn't that upset the other serving women?" Ranulf asked, curious as to how female servants behaved. He'd spent his years among knights and soldiers; he could guess how they'd react. Female servants were more of a mystery.

"Well, if they envied her, it's made 'em that much more keen to impress Lady Beatrice with their efforts. I hear she promised them all a new gown if they got the whole castle clean and ordered to her satisfaction. And the children—Lord love you, they think she's the next thing to a fairy queen! She gives any that want them little jobs to do and sweetmeats when they finish."

Ranulf remembered the children sprinkling herbs on the rushes. They certainly seemed to be enjoying themselves. Nor would kindhearted Bea ever chastise them for getting nearly as many herbs on their clothes.

"I tell you, my lord, she's going to make some lucky man a fine wife."

Ranulf decided he needed to clarify still further. "I have no intention of marrying Lady Beatrice."

"No? You seem a goodly age to be married, my lord."

"Perhaps, but not to that lady." Since there was no reason to linger, Ranulf got to his feet. "As you've nothing new to report, I'll head back to the castle and wait for the morning patrols to return."

Hedyn rose and detained the castellan with a hand on his shoulder. "I loved a girl once, my lord, and she loved me," he said quietly. "But her father took a dislike to me and I was too stubborn and proud to go to him and ask for her hand. So I lost her. She took up with another, and there wasn't a day went by I didn't think of her and wish I'd crawled on my belly to her father, if that's what he wanted, and begged for her hand."

Ranulf's hazel eyes gazed steadily and impassively back at the Cornishman. "I'm sorry for your misfortune, Hedyn, but my situation is not the same. And in future, should I require your advice on matters of the heart, I shall ask."

SOME HOURS LATER, a dryer but no less disgruntled Ranulf stood on the dais of his hall that was now free of dust and cobwebs. Instead of smoke and cheap tallow, it smelled of fresh herbs, straw and beeswax. The tapestries had been beaten free of dust and the tears mended. The lord's chair sported a bright cushion from Tregellas, and so did the chair where Bea usually sat; it was, at present, conspicuously empty.

Tapping his foot, Ranulf gestured for Maloren to come closer. "Where's your lady? The meal's ready."

"She's gone to the village, my lord."

"Why?"

"To see Wenna, my lord."

Gawan's widow? "Why would she do that?"

Another serving maid, the young one, stepped forward. "Wenna's time's come, my lord," she explained with deference, and after glancing a little nervously at Maloren. "She sent a lad to fetch Eseld. The village has no midwife now and Eseld's attended more births than most of the women in the village, so Wenna wanted her to come."

"Lady Beatrice went with Eseld?"

Both women shook their heads, momentarily confusing Ranulf, until Maloren spoke with her usual peevishness. "That Eseld's a drunken *sot*. She's sleeping in the stables, where she's been since breaking the fast. When my sweet lamb found the woman half-gone from drink, she offered to go in her place."

"Lady Beatrice isn't a midwife," Ranulf noted with a frown. "What use would she be?"

"My lambkin's better than no one," Maloren declared. "She's learned a lot from Aeda and she talks to the apothecary every chance she gets, so Wenna could do worse—a lot worse. Despite what *some* people think, my lady's a clever girl who knows a lot about medicine."

Ranulf had often seen Bea chatting with the apothecary when he visited Tregellas, but he'd always assumed she was being more of a nuisance than anything else. It had never occurred to him that Bea was learning something from the man, or that her presence in Constance's chamber when she gave birth had any other motive than cousinly concern.

However, and despite Bea's urge to help, the weather wasn't favorable for dashing off to the village on a mission of mercy. "She went in this rain?"

Maloren frowned even more. "My blessed girl didn't want the boy to go back without help."

"How long has she been gone?"

"Howel came after the noon meal, my lord," Tecca said.

"How many soldiers went with her?"

Tecca flushed. "None, my lord," she finally ventured.

"She went *alone?*"

"Not alone," Maloren defensively replied. "I was going to go, too, but she told me to stay here and make sure that idiot of a cook prepared something other than fish for the evening meal. That Myghal said he'd take her."

Before Ranulf had time to be relieved, the door to the hall banged open, sounding like a clap of thunder in the silence.

"What weather!" Bea cried as she hurried into the hall, alone and clad in a wet cloak. "I feared Myghal and I might get swept out to sea before we got to Wenna's cottage."

She threw back her dripping hood. "Oh, Ranulf! You're back," she exclaimed, as if he'd been the one who'd departed the castle without leave or a proper escort. "Then it must be time to eat. Thank the saints, because I have to tell you, I'm starving. I rushed off before I could finish the noon meal and poor Wenna doesn't have much to spare, so I had only a taste of what she offered. She's really a very generous woman, Wenna. I quite like her."

Ranulf sent up a brief prayer of thanks as he walked swiftly toward Bea, while Maloren scuttled toward her darling and declared, "You've got to get out of those wet things, my lamb, before you catch your death."

"I'm not so very wet—just my cloak," Bea replied. She took off her soaking garment and handed it to Maloren.

Bea's round cheeks were flushed from her exertions, and slightly damp tendrils of hair had escaped from her braid to coil about her face. As always during the day, she wore a simple woolen gown—this one of soft green—as well as a plain leather girdle, with her hair drawn back in one long braid and tied at the end with a leather thong.

Yet no queen in all her finery could look more vibrant, more luminous or more naturally beautiful.

"I have to talk to you, Ranulf," she said, with un-expected determination. "Did you know there's no midwife in the village?"

"I have recently been informed of that fact," he replied, reminding himself that he was the castel-lan here, not a lover come a-wooing. "Now I sug-gest you do as Maloren proposes and get out of those wet clothes."

And he would *not* think about her clad only in a damp shift, which would hide nothing.

"I'm not that wet," Bea replied firmly, "and I won't get sick. I need to talk to you."

He wondered what she could possibly have to say to him that would warrant such resolve. "Village gossip is hardly a matter of urgency."

The look she gave him then!

Perhaps the meal could keep a little and surely he could risk being alone with her for a short while. "If what you have to say to me is that important, my lady, we can go to the solar."

The solar was a small, damp, musty room, but it had the virtue of privacy, and it wasn't a bedchamber.

It was obvious Maloren wasn't pleased with his proposal, but she could take her complaints to her mistress, Ranulf thought as he turned and headed for the stairs, with Bea following behind.

When they reached the solar, a quick survey revealed that this chamber had thus far been spared Bea's zealous ministrations.

Even so, when he turned to face her, he found her looking around as if contemplating what she could accomplish with a bucket of water and some rags.

"Well, my lady, what is this matter of great importance?" he asked.

"The midwife here has died and no one has come to take her place," Bea began, her bright blue eyes shining with eager interest. "The nearest one is in the next village, and that's five miles away. It would take half a day to send for her and get her back to Penterwell. That's why Wenna wanted Eseld—there's really no one else.

"Fortunately, I've learned quite a bit from Aeda, and the apothecary at Tregellas taught me some things about medicine—"

"I remember," Ranulf interjected.

She blushed, then continued staunchly. "So I went to see if I could be of help. There were other women in Wenna's cottage, but they knew even less than I did. All they seemed to want to do was talk about their own experiences rather than trying to assist Wenna. I must say, some of those experiences sounded quite horrendous. It would be enough to make most women determined never to bear children if they could possibly help it. I thought Wenna was going to faint listening to them, so I shooed them out as kindly as I could until it was only Wenna and me, and then I told her not to mind them. It's like men after a battle, I said. They all want to compare wounds and brag about their own. That got her to smile a bit and she calmed down, and in a little while, the pains ceased completely. It was a false labor, you see. That happens sometimes."

Bea grew even more intensely determined. "She's frightened, Ranulf, and I don't blame her. Something may go wrong and nobody here will know how to help her."

Ranulf remembered what it was like to be in pain and alone. "I'll write to Merrick after the evening meal. Perhaps Constance can find a midwife who'll come here."

"That's a fine idea," Bea replied with approval, yet her brows remained furrowed. "Unfortunately, that will take time, and since I didn't know you would make that kind offer, I…"

She took another deep breath, planted her feet and spoke as if about to announce that she was, in fact, a goddess. "I told Wenna that while I was no midwife, I would stay until the baby arrived and help her if I could. I gave her my word, Ranulf."

She hurried on as if he had ordered her to leave Penterwell that very moment. "I can't abandon her and it should only be for another week, a fortnight at the most. I know I should have asked you first, but she was so upset and it seems such a little thing. Please say you'll let me stay and keep my word."

Her staying here was no *little thing,* yet to refuse any help to the young, grieving widow…that he couldn't bring himself to do. And Bea was right. It might take Constance some time to find another midwife willing to live in Penterwell.

"All right," he reluctantly agreed. "You can stay here until Wenna has her baby. I'll inform Merrick of my decision when I write him tonight."

Bea's features lighted with relief and her eyes seemed to glow with joy. He feared she might embrace him, so he held up his hand and said, "You may stay only until Wenna has her baby. Then you *must* leave."

"Oh, thank you, Ranulf!" Bea cried as if she hadn't heard the last. "I knew you had a heart!"

Yes, he had a heart. A damaged one.

He began to back away. "You understand me, my lady? You may stay until Wenna has her child, and no longer."

"Of course," she said with another bright smile. "And in that time, I can help you in other ways, too."

He took refuge behind sarcasm. "Should I expect to find you discussing the repairs with Merrick's masons next? Or perhaps huddled with my garrison commander, planning the castle defenses?"

She didn't look the least upset by his remarks. Instead, she laughed. "Nothing so practical, I'm afraid, Ranulf. But I can act as a sort of go-between between you and the villagers.

"Well, the women, anyway," she clarified. "It isn't only Wenna who wants to find out who killed

Gawan. The other women want the guilty person caught, too, because they fear for their sons and husbands."

"Then they think Gawan was deliberately killed?"

"Oh, yes, they seem quite certain of it."

"If that's so, and they're worried, why don't they tell me who they suspect?" he asked, thinking of the frustrating wall of silence that seemed to surround the village.

"I think they'd like to, but you're *you*, while I'm me, if you follow me."

"Not precisely."

"Women find it easier to confide in other women," she said. "And not only are you a man, you represent their overlord and even the king. I don't. Not directly, anyway. I'm much less intimidating."

"Apparently not to cooks."

She flushed. "He was very insolent."

"Perhaps I should hire another cook," he suggested, quite willing to do so if she agreed.

"There's no need for that," she replied. "Much has learned his lesson. But I don't want to talk about the cook. Wenna told me something much more important. She said she told you about the Frenchman and how Gawan went to meet him, but she didn't tell you…"

Bea hesitated, went to the door, checked the corridor, then closed it.

No matter what she had to say, shutting them in here alone wasn't wise. Not wise at all.

If *he* were wise, he'd run.

Unfortunately, Bea stood between him and the door.

CHAPTER EIGHT

BEA DIDN'T SEEM to realize what she'd done as she launched into her revelation. "What Wenna didn't tell you was that the villagers are watching for the Frenchman's ship and the moment a landing party comes ashore, they plan to attack them, perhaps even kill them. Then they're going to scuttle the smugglers' ship."

Ranulf was no longer distracted by Bea's proximity and the fact they were alone. "By themselves?"

"They're very angry about Gawan," she said as if that explained it all, and perhaps it did. "There's a cove where the Frenchmen usually come ashore, and they're watching it day and night."

"Where is this cove?"

Bea shook her head. "I don't know. Once Wenna said they were going to scuttle the ship, some of the other women got a bit…well, I gather they thought I'd already heard enough and regretted that I'd even heard that much." Her eyes brightened with her usual enthusiasm. "Since I'm going to stay a little longer, maybe I can find out more."

Maybe she could at that, Ranulf thought, and despite his reservations. "Any information would be welcome."

She came closer. "Wenna will be even happier than I am to hear your decision about letting me stay, Ranulf. It's been so difficult for her."

He knew he ought to move away, but he felt as if he'd grown roots.

"It would have been more difficult if somebody hadn't left several coins on her table."

Ranulf blushed like a lad and wished he wasn't. "If that's all you have to say, Bea, we should go back to the hall."

"There's one thing more," she replied, coming mercifully to a halt a few feet away. "Do you trust Myghal?"

That was not what he expected to hear. "Is there a reason I shouldn't?"

"I hope not. It's just that when I was walking with him to Wenna's cottage, I felt…"

She shrugged her shoulders and looked at Ranulf as if expecting him to tell her what she felt.

He could certainly tell her what Myghal was likely feeling, and it wasn't something he was pleased to consider. The fellow seemed trustworthy enough, but he was young and young men could be fools. "Next time you go into the village, I want you to take some soldiers for an escort—at least two. I don't want anything to happen to you while you're in my care."

Her cheeks colored, yet her expression wasn't that

of a modest, obedient maiden. She looked offended. "Surely I'm perfectly safe in your village."

His village. Even without meaning to, she made him feel as if he'd accomplished something with his life. "I'd like to believe that, but your safety is not something with which I care to gamble. You're Merrick's ward, and I wouldn't want to face his wrath if something were to happen to you while you were under my protection. He nearly beat Henry to death when he only suspected Henry had put Constance in danger," he reminded her, not indicating by word, look or tone how devastated *he* would be if she were hurt or killed.

She lowered her eyes and nodded. "Of course. How foolish of me to want to do anything that might reflect poorly on your command of Penterwell."

"I'm relieved you appreciate my position, my lady," he said with every appearance of calm as he held out his arm, steeling himself for her touch. "Shall we?"

With a nod and not another word, she laid her fingertips on his forearm and let him lead her from the solar.

A FEW DAYS LATER, Beatrice did her best to ignore the two soldiers following her as she headed for the market in the village. Since Ranulf had agreed to let her stay until Wenna had her baby, she would abide by his decree that she take an escort when she left the castle, even though it made her feel foolish and conspicuous.

At least the weather had cleared, the rain giving way to the sun and warmth that heralded the start of a new growing season. Lambs frolicked on the slopes nearby, and everything smelled fresh and green and new. It was enough to put some spring in Beatrice's step, despite her dismay over the situation with Ranulf. Even Maloren seemed happier these days, and she didn't seem to mind having to spend so much time in the kitchen keeping a watchful eye on the cook.

"Good morning, my lady. Don't you look as fresh as a daisy today."

Her ruminations interrupted, Beatrice looked up to find Hedyn smiling at her. She liked the sheriff, with his fatherly voice and friendly mien, and she gave him a smile in return. "Good day to you, too. Isn't it lovely now that the rain has finally stopped?"

"Aye, my lady. Nearly as lovely as you."

Beatrice laughed as he fell into step beside her. "You'll be turning my head with such flattery, Hedyn."

He nodded at the basket she had slung over her arm. "Going to market, are you?"

"I want to get some new threads, and Tecca tells me one of the village women makes a lovely green dye. I thought I'd get some to take home to Tregellas."

"It'll be a sad day here when you leave us, my lady."

"I shall be sorry to go, too, but my home is in Tregellas."

"Pity, that is."

Beatrice wasn't sure what to say to that, and she

was a little relieved when Hedyn halted and said, "I must be off, my lady, to the shore. Something's washed up that might be from Gawan's boat."

"Are you any closer to finding out what happened to him?" she asked, for Ranulf had told her nothing more about Gawan's death.

Hedyn shook his head. "Sadly, no, though it's not for lack of trying. Sir Ranulf is dead keen to find out. He's made that plain enough."

"He takes his duties very seriously," she agreed, thinking of the way Ranulf sat brooding and staring into the fire after the evening meal every night.

"Aye, my lady, that he does, and it's to his credit. He's a fine gentleman. Impressed the fishermen and merchants, I can tell you, and that isn't easy to do. They were worried he'd be an arrogant…fellow," the sheriff said, catching himself and sliding her an apologetic glance for the derogatory term he'd been about to use. "No, my lady, we couldn't ask for a better castellan, and I hope you'll tell Lord Merrick so."

"I shall," she readily replied.

With a nod of his head and a bow, Hedyn strode off toward his horse tied outside the tavern, while Beatrice continued toward the stalls lining the main road.

Penterwell was a very snug sort of town, clustered on the rocky shore, the cottages built with their backs against the higher, windswept ground. There wasn't space for any kind of green; the main road served that function, with the stalls and shops of the merchants and tradesmen lining it. Smaller lanes led away from the main road, to the cottages or outbuildings.

The wives of the fishermen, however, set out their baskets near their husbands' boats and the drying nettle-hemp nets on the beach.

The merchants were all happy to see Beatrice. She laughed and joked with them, and was genuinely impressed with what they had to show her, making it difficult for her to confine her purchases to what she'd come to buy. That was especially hard when she spotted a lovely piece of silk hanging from the post of one of the stalls. It was an eye-catching, delicate shade of blue—almost the exact color of Constance's eyes. It would be a perfect present for her.

"I'd be willing to give you a special price, my lady," the brown-haired tradesman with a pug nose offered when he saw her interest. His eyes were likewise deep brown and very shrewd. "Here, let me get it down for you, and you can feel the quality. All the way from the East, that is."

She wondered how such a piece of fabric had managed to wind up in a stall in a little village in Cornwall, but decided it was better not to ask. "It *is* beautiful," she said with a sigh as she draped it over her hand. "Unfortunately, I brought very little money with me. I didn't think I would find such things in Penterwell."

"How much?" Ranulf asked from behind her, making Beatrice start.

She had no idea he was in the village. She thought he was still in the hall, listening to the reports from the soldiers who'd been on patrol that morning.

"Five marks, my lord," the merchant quickly answered, "and a bargain at twice that."

"If you say so," Ranulf replied evenly as he reached into his leather tunic, from which he produced a thin purse. "I'll purchase it for the lady."

"Oh, no, you mustn't," Beatrice said, flustered by his offer. He wasn't a wealthy man. "Thank you, Sir Ranulf, but—"

"It's to show my gratitude for all you've done at Penterwell," he said. His tone was so firm and so final that she realized it would be useless to argue.

"It'll suit you to perfection, my lady," the merchant said, beaming as he folded up the cloth and handed it to Beatrice.

"Oh, I wasn't thinking of it for myself," Beatrice quickly corrected.

To the merchant's obvious horror, Ranulf's fingers curled around the coins in his hand. "Who would it be for, then?" he asked, raising one questioning brow.

"I planned to give it to Constance. It's very early to be thinking of Twelfth Night, I know, but I've often discovered if I don't get a present when I see it, I never find one to compare later on," she explained, hoping he wasn't going to rescind his offer.

On the other hand, it really was expensive. "If you'd rather not—"

"I have another piece," the merchant swiftly interrupted, ducking down behind the table and reaching into a wooden chest. He drew out another piece of silk, in a slightly darker shade of blue. "I could give you both for seven marks."

"That's not the same blue," Ranulf noted.

"And that would really be too much," Beatrice said as firmly as Ranulf.

The knight looked at her, his expression impassive. "The second piece is more the color of Constance's eyes. The first matches yours. I'll take them both."

She flushed and found she couldn't quite meet his steady gaze. "I don't need any silk."

"You shall have it nonetheless, with my thanks, and the piece for Constance, too."

By now, several of the people shopping in the market had noticed them by the stall and ventured closer.

Unless she wanted to argue with Ranulf, Beatrice realized, she would do better to say nothing except thank you, so she did. "Thank you, Sir Ranulf. That's most generous of you."

"It is little enough for all you've done at Penterwell."

The merchant handed her the other folded piece of silk and swiftly pocketed the coins Ranulf gave him, as if he thought he had best get the money out of sight before Ranulf changed his mind.

"Are you finished with your purchases for today?" Ranulf solemnly inquired.

"No. I want to get some fish. The cook's been

complaining that fish is his specialty and he never gets to cook it anymore." When she saw Ranulf's expression, she said, "You don't have to eat it if you don't want to. There'll be plenty of other things."

"I'm sure," he said. He looked over his shoulder to address the two soldiers behind them. "You can return to the castle. I'll escort Lady Beatrice back when she's finished."

The soldiers nodded and departed.

"I don't think they were happy with that order," Ranulf noted as he walked beside her toward the fishwives with their baskets of gleaming pilchard and salmon, trout and the flat, spotted plaice.

He sounded almost like his old self, the way he had in Tregellas, making her remember the first time she'd ever seen him, when he'd ridden through the gate beside Merrick and Henry.

Merrick had been grave and stern, dressed in black. The merry, handsome Henry, dressed in brilliant scarlet, had been smiling as if delighted with everything. Attired in a more subdued forest-green, Ranulf had not smiled, but he certainly wasn't as grim as Merrick. After all three had dismounted, Ranulf had looked about him as if contemplating defensive strategies or perhaps the cost of the stone.

He had intrigued her far more than Henry with his smiles, or Merrick with his silence. Later, during that terrible time when Constance and Merrick had been at odds, it had been to Ranulf she'd appealed for help.

She thought he, rather than Henry, would be sympathetic. And so he had been, showing her that he wasn't nearly as cold and cynical as he pretended to be.

"No doubt it's more pleasant for the soldiers to come to the market than stand guard by the gates or on the wall, even if they have to trail after me," she said, giving him a bright and cheerful smile.

"Attending a pretty young woman as she goes about her errands is definitely much more interesting and entertaining than standing guard," he agreed.

He spoke as if he'd had that duty, once upon a time. "Did *you* have to trail after a lady as she shopped?"

"No."

She would try to ignore the feeling of relief his answer gave her.

"The merchants were certainly delighted to see you," he observed, "but that's not surprising. Everybody likes you."

"I try to be friendly and pleasant, that's all."

"And I do not." It was not a question.

What was she supposed to say to that? she wondered as they drew near the beach and the fishwives crying their wares.

A very odd expression came to his face. "What is it?" she asked, for it was obvious something was wrong.

"The smell," he replied. "Fish may be fine on a platter, but their odor is not one I appreciate."

His expression hadn't been one of revulsion. It had been something else entirely.

She dropped her voice to a whisper. "Do you sometimes get the feeling you're being watched, too?"

He regarded her as if she'd just said something incredible. "What?"

She suddenly felt ridiculous. This was Penterwell, after all, not a den of thieves. "It's nothing," she said, starting forward and wishing she'd kept quiet.

Instead of following her, he held her back. "You think somebody's watching you?"

"Once or twice I've wondered. I've had that feeling you get sometimes, when the hairs on the back of your neck stand up," she admitted. Certain he would dismiss her worries as another foolish product of her imagination, she gave a little laugh. "Well, perhaps you don't know what I mean, being a knight. Or maybe you have felt that sort of dread, before a battle or when you're about to ride into a melee—"

"Bea," he said firmly, cupping her shoulders. "Do you truly think somebody's been watching you?"

Conscious of how intimate this must look, she glanced at the people near them. "You're going to cause quite a bit of gossip if you don't let go of me."

He immediately did, as if her touch were like encountering an open flame.

"I'm sure it's nothing, my lord," she said.

Then, as if not the least concerned with anything, including the way he'd just been holding her, she strolled toward a woman with baskets of pilchard, the fishes' backs bluish black, their bellies silver.

He didn't say anything, nor did he come after her. Did he intend to leave her there and without a guard, despite his own order?

Even if he did, it was of no consequence. Nothing bad could happen to her while she was in the village. Nevertheless, she had to admit—at least to herself—that she did feel safer when Ranulf was nearby. Or perhaps she was simply happier then.

Trying to keep her attention on her task, she decided against the pilchard and went farther along the beach to choose something else. Much really was good with fish. It was too bad he was so terrible with everything else. Maloren complained day and night about his bread, his porridge, his stews, the way he burned the meat...

Ranulf hadn't gone away, but he wasn't coming any closer, either. He stood where she had left him, his arms crossed, his expression unreadable.

Well, why should he trot after her like a dog? Unless somebody decided to shove her into the water, she was perfectly safe. Still, it was disturbing having him standing there and watching her so grimly.

Perhaps the fish could wait until Friday.

Thinking that might be best, Beatrice made her way back to the castellan of Penterwell. "I think we'll not have fish until Friday."

"As you wish," he answered, turning back to the castle.

"After all," she said, and only a little pertly, "it's

difficult to make a choice when your escort is standing like a statue, staring at you as if the whole exercise is a waste of time. Honestly, one would think you were afraid of the fish, even though they're all dead."

"It's not the fish," he muttered.

She suddenly realized he'd led her back a different way to the castle, one that skirted the market and all the people there. They were in a back lane, and it was quite deserted.

Her heart started to beat rapidly, and not with dismay.

"It's the water."

"I—I beg your pardon?" she stammered, the warmth of her excitement doused by his grim statement.

"I don't like to get too close to open water. I nearly drowned when I was a child."

She was taken aback by his revelation, but also thrilled beyond measure that he would confide in her.

"When Merrick and Henry tipped the boat and you fell into the millpond?"

Henry had told her that Sir Leonard had insisted all his charges learn to swim. However, he'd said with a laugh, Ranulf seemed to spend most of his time in Sir Leonard's boat, rowing. One day, he and Merrick had decided to have a little revenge and before Sir Leonard embarked, tipped Ranulf into the pond.

"No, not then. The water was shallow where they did that, although I suppose I shouldn't be surprised if Henry exaggerated. I'm talking about something that happened long before that, before I was... Before I left my father's castle. Only Sir Leonard knew about it, until now."

"I'm shocked you'd tell me and not your closest friends," she admitted.

He flushed and made a wry, self-deprecating smile. "Is it so surprising I'd keep such a fear to myself?" he asked.

No, she realised, when she thought of the pride he, like most men, possessed.

"But it would be worse to have you think I'm afraid of dead fish."

She reached out to touch his arm, wanting, needing, to have some physical contact with him. "I shall guard your secret with my life."

Suddenly even more ashamed of his fear than usual, cursing himself for a weak-willed fool overpowered by the need to have her sympathy, Ranulf forced himself to laugh. "My dear Bea, there's no need for such dramatics. Indeed, I should probably just admit my fear to the garrison and be done instead of trying to think of excuses for why I won't go closer to the shore than I absolutely have to."

"If it wasn't when you fell into the millpond," she asked, ignoring his attempt to be flippant, "how did you nearly drown?"

That was something he definitely didn't want to talk about.

Fortunately, the sight of a boy running toward them spared him.

"Come quick, my lady, please!" the lad called out breathlessly. "It's Wenna! Her water's broke!"

MUCH LATER, Ranulf rose after a fitful night's sleep and climbed out of the clean, comfortable bed that was now made every day.

Bea must still be at Wenna's cottage. He'd ordered his guards to inform him when she returned, and he had made it very clear there would be a severe penalty if they didn't.

There was nothing to be worried about if she hadn't yet come back, he told himself as he went to the window. This was Wenna's first child and he remembered well what he'd told Merrick as they waited for his son to be born: first births could take a long time.

He threw open the shutter to see that a heavy fog had rolled in during the night. It was so thick, he couldn't even see the wall of the castle.

Surely Bea wouldn't try to return through that thick gray mist. She was no fool, after all, and there was no reason for her to rush back. Surely she'd be wise enough to wait until the fog lifted.

In spite of such optimistic reassurances, he wasted no time washing and dressing. Wearing a tunic, shirt, breeches and boots, he left his chamber and hurried to the hall, checking his steps when he drew abreast of the chamber Bea shared with Maloren.

He took a moment to breathe in the light, lingering scent of lavender. Through the open door, he noted the dressing table set up in one corner and the little jar of perfume, the ribbons and combs resting there. A stool sat in front of it, and he could easily imagine Bea at her toilette, chattering away as Maloren combed her hair.

How he wished he could do that simple thing for her. He'd stand behind her and listen to her musical voice as she talked about the domestic activities of the castle. She could make even the most mundane task entertaining, and many a time he'd smiled to hear her talk about the problems with the laundry or the kitchen.

As he went on his way it struck him that her chamber was much less comfortably furnished than his own. Bea had probably put items intended for her own use—cushions, pillows, linens and bedding—in his chamber. Bless her, but she shouldn't have done that, and he'd insist she take everything that belonged to her, or Tregellas, back with her. He could live with less. He had before.

Not for the first time, he wondered what might have happened had Sir Leonard refused to let him stay. If he'd been told he had to leave. If he'd been forced away.

As he was making Bea go away.

It was for her own good, he reminded himself, because he did care about her—far, far too much. He recalled all the reasons he didn't deserve her. His poverty. His lack of land. What he'd done to his brother, as well as that wager he'd won in London after Celeste had told him she was marrying another, richer man.

When he entered the hall, he found the soldiers who slept there stirring and some of the male servants setting up the tables in preparation for the morning meal.

"Lady Beatrice has not yet returned?" he inquired of Gareth, the garrison commander.

The short, stocky soldier, who wore his dark hair cropped close, shook his head. "Not yet, my lord."

"Where's Maloren?"

"Myghal came to fetch her," Gareth replied.

Although there was no reason to find that a cause for concern, Ranulf's blood chilled nonetheless. "When was this?"

"A little while ago, my lord. Myghal said she needed Maloren's help."

Although all could be just as Gareth said, and Bea and Maloren perfectly safe, Ranulf grabbed a torch from one of the sconces and started for the door.

"I'm going to Wenna's," he declared as he plunged into the fog-enshrouded courtyard.

CHAPTER NINE

THE MIST WAS SO THICK, Ranulf couldn't see the gate until he was nearly there. As he marched forward, droplets of moisture clung to his face, his hair, his beard. The torch spluttered but mercifully stayed alight as he passed the startled sentries and continued along the road toward the village.

As he neared the cottages and shops, the hairs on the back of his neck began to rise, just as Bea had described. His discomfort could be because of the fog, yet he couldn't shake the feeling that the thick mist was hiding something more sinister than buildings and the sea. His steps slowed and he drew his sword, every sense alert for anything that seemed unusual or out of place.

The sound of clucking penetrated the gloom and, through the fog, he spied a woman feeding her chickens scratching in the rocky soil. She stared at him as he approached, and no wonder. The castellan hurrying through the village carrying a drawn sword wouldn't be a reassuring sight.

He made no explanation as he strode swiftly

onward toward the widow's cottage. If there was trouble here, it would be better for that woman to wonder and worry, and go back inside.

He heard another sound and paused to listen. And then relief, as strong as his dread had been, washed over him. He knew that happy sound as well as he knew his own voice. Somewhere close by, Bea was laughing.

He started forward again and soon reached Wenna's small stone cottage. He doused the torch in a trough near the door and took a moment to catch his breath. He smoothed down his tunic and ran a hand through his damp hair.

God's blood, he hadn't even put on a cloak, he thought as he knocked on the wooden door before settling his expression into its usual mask of calm detachment.

Maloren opened the door, and the smile on her face died when she saw who was standing there. "Oh, it's you."

Obviously, and no matter how she'd been acting toward him lately, she still didn't like him.

"Ranulf!" he heard Bea cry with genuine delight, making him smile in spite of Maloren's unfriendly greeting.

"Wenna, may he come in and see the baby?" she asked.

It was like Bea to ask a peasant if the castellan could enter her cottage. By right, he didn't even have to knock.

Peering into the cottage that seemed full of women, he saw a bed in the corner, where Wenna must be, and a crude cradle beside it. A fire burned in the hearth and candles—too expensive for a peasant, so likely provided by Bea—lit the low-ceilinged building.

Then Ranulf saw Bea standing beside the cradle and forgot everything and everyone else.

She held Wenna's babe in her arms as if it were her own, and as he looked at her, a longing more powerful than anything he had ever felt before seized him. He yearned to see Bea with their child in her arms, a baby with golden hair and bright blue eyes.

Wenna murmured something and, smiling, Bea said, "You're welcome to come in, my lord."

He ducked under the lintel and the women made way for Bea to approach him. She was plainly dressed as usual, and her hair was in one long braid. Although her eyes sparkled with happiness, she looked as if she hadn't slept all night.

"Here he is, my lord. Isn't he lovely?" she said, raising the infant for him to see.

As far as Ranulf could tell, the child looked like most newborn babies, except that this one was completely bald. "Yes, he's a very fine baby," he agreed, once more imagining their child in her arms.

"He's going to be called Gawan, after his father," Bea said softly.

Ranulf wanted to vow then and there, in the

hearing of Bea and all these women, that Gawan's murder would be solved and avenged. But he wouldn't promise what he couldn't guarantee.

Instead, Ranulf went to Wenna, white and thin under the sheets, her belly still swollen from the pregnancy. After asking her leave to sit, he perched on the side of the bed. "Your son looks to be a very fine and healthy boy, Wenna. In time to come, I'll need a page. I would be pleased to offer your son that place."

And, it went unsaid, then he could become a squire and, quite possibly, a knight.

The dark-haired woman regarded him with wide, wondering eyes, although what he offered seemed little enough to him. The babe had lost his father, a fine fellow by all accounts, such as Ranulf's had never been. "I need good men, and from what I've heard of your husband, your son should serve me well and be a credit to his family."

Wenna burst into tears.

As Ranulf rather awkwardly got to his feet, the other women likewise started sobbing, and even Maloren surreptitiously dabbed at her eyes. Bea, however, looked at him as if he were an angel bringing glory, her eyes shining with happiness and a smile on her lips.

He was no angel, as he knew all too well.

"You must be tired, my lady," he said to her. "Let me take you home."

She nodded her agreement. "Maloren, come

take little Gawan," she said. "Please stay here and help Wenna."

Bea suddenly seemed uncertain as she glanced at Ranulf. "Unless you want us to leave Penterwell today?"

"Not today," he said firmly. *Not ever.* "You're much too tired."

"Thank you, my lord," she said, as if he were doing her a great favor.

If she only knew how much he wanted her to stay!

"I'll make sure she rests," he said to Maloren, and to prevent Maloren from insisting on going with them. "I'm sure there's no one better suited to look after a baby than you."

He gave the other women a courtly bow. "Although I'm also sure you'll not lack for willing and experienced helpers," he added.

As the other women blushed, exchanged pleased looks and whispered among themselves, he fetched Bea's cloak and wordlessly opened the door. Surprisingly, she said nothing. That told him she must be very tired indeed.

He saw at once that the fog was lifting, and they could easily make their way without a torch. They walked back toward the castle in silence. No doubt later, after she had rested, Bea would have much to say about the birthing.

Before she went back to Tregellas.

She tripped over a rock, stumbling forward.

Without thinking, he caught her and swept her up in his arms, holding her close.

"What…what are you doing?" she asked as she wrapped her arms around his neck.

"You're exhausted. I'm going to carry you back so you don't hurt yourself."

"I can walk," she protested, albeit halfheartedly.

"I don't think you got much sleep last night." *And I like having you in my arms.*

"No," she confessed. "It wasn't an easy birth, and more than once I feared we were going to lose the baby. I had to turn him." She clung to Ranulf more tightly. "Oh, Ranulf, I was so afraid I was doing it wrong, although I was fairly certain I was rightly remembering what Aeda said when I asked her about such things. But I've never even witnessed a breech birth."

Neither had he, and it sounded complicated and painful.

"Of course I couldn't let Wenna or the others know how frightened I was, so I simply had to pretend that I knew what I was doing and hope for the best. Fortunately, once he turned, everything went quite quickly—or at least it seemed to—and there weren't any more problems."

With a weary sigh, she laid her head against his broad shoulder.

"It was a good thing you were here to help," he said, thinking it would be a wonderful thing if she could always be there to help.

"Yes. Thank you for letting me stay." She raised her head. "I must be heavy. Perhaps I had better walk."

"It's all right, Bea. I don't mind."

She nestled wordlessly against him, close and soft and warm, and in another few moments, she was asleep.

As he looked down at her, he saw her for the beautiful, competent and—yes—talkative woman she was, and felt a warmth, a tenderness, a joy and fierce protectiveness wash over him.

His Bea. His little Lady Bea. How much he liked her "buzzing." He enjoyed hearing her describe things that other men might find mundane, or unimportant, but that spoke of simple domestic joys and security to him—things he had never really known. He loved the way her voice rose and fell with her enthusiasm, like a song. He liked to watch her mobile features, which could tell a story all their own, even when she didn't speak—although silence was rare with her. When Bea was quiet, he always feared she was ill and, usually, she was.

How worried he'd been on those few occasions! How thankful and relieved he'd been to learn her illness was nothing serious.

He didn't want her to leave Penterwell. He didn't want her to leave *him*. He wanted to be with her always, to have her for his wife, the mother of his children. He wanted to make Bea happy and keep her safe for the rest of his life, if she would give him that honor. If she would let him love her.

He'd tried to turn her away. He'd tried to make her hate him. Yet in spite of all his efforts, she still seemed to like him. Perhaps she really did love him.

It could be that God was truly merciful, allowing him to find happiness and contentment and love at last. It might be that God had forgiven him, despite what he'd done. Perhaps he *could* have lasting happiness with a wife he loved. With Bea.

If so, perhaps Bea would not despise him if she found out what he'd done. Maybe her respect, admiration and affection were strong enough to see beyond his past to his remorse and regret.

Maybe, he thought with a sudden flash of hope as well as self-recrimination, he was belittling her by thinking that she would see him for a monster, and not a man who had sinned and suffered and earned a chance for redemption.

One thing seemed certain as he held her in his arms: he could no longer continue this way, trapped between desire and dread. He had to find out, one way or the other, if Bea could forgive him his past. He must tell her everything and let her decide whether he was worthy of her, or not.

And if she reacted as he feared and turned away in horror? If she said she could never love him now?

He must, of course, accept her judgment. It would be no more than he deserved, because of what he'd done.

Having reached the gates of the castle, he ordered

one of the guards to go ahead and open the door to the hall for him. Carrying Bea inside, he assured the servants who rushed forward that she was merely tired and asleep.

He continued to carry her up the steps to her bed-chamber. Once there, he gently set her on the bed. She should probably be disrobed, but not by him. Not now. Not today. One day, perhaps, if he was blessed to call her wife.

Or never, if she came to hate him.

He did give in to one temptation. He leaned down and brushed his lips over hers in a gentle kiss. "Tomorrow, Bea," he vowed in a whisper. "Tomorrow I will tell you all about Ranulf of Beauvieux."

DAMN THE DRIFTING FOG, Myghal thought as his horse trotted down the rutted road leading away from Penterwell. And damn Pierre. Damn Wenna, too, for refusing him and making him do terrible things.

No, it wasn't Wenna's fault. She was innocent of any wrongdoing. He was the sinner. A cowardly sinner, fleeing the mess he'd made.

"Where are you going, Myghal?" a French-accented voice called out, as if a ghost were on his trail.

A ghost who sounded like Pierre.

Myghal punched his spurred heels into his horse's sides, sending his mount into a gallop.

He didn't realize men from the smuggler's crew had him trapped until he was surrounded. His horse shied and snorted, but there was no escape unless Myghal wanted to try to run them down.

Pierre, on foot, pushed his way through the wall of horses and men. "So, Myghal, you wish to flee?" he asked, his voice surprisingly gentle and his expression oddly mild.

Until he reached up and dragged Myghal to the ground.

When Myghal tried to get up, the fiercely scowling Pierre shoved him down with his foot and held him there.

"Fool," he snarled, his lip curling with scorn. "Do you take me for one, too? Do you think I don't know you are a coward? Who else but a coward hires someone else to do his killing? I knew I couldn't trust you, so my men have watched you night and day."

He bent down and, grabbing Myghal's tunic, hauled the terrified man to his feet. "What…what are you going to do?" Myghal stammered, his features as gray as the fog around them.

"Remind you of your bargain," Pierre said, pushing him back. "No wonder that woman didn't want you. You run instead of claiming her."

"I don't want any more people to be hurt because of me."

"Brave words, but you are still a coward. You could have had the woman you want and freedom forever when you brought Lady Beatrice to Wenna's cottage. It would have been the perfect chance to let us take her."

"I didn't think you'd be close by, because of the fog," Myghal lied. In truth, he'd thought of abducting Lady Beatrice then, but Wenna had needed her. And as the young noblewoman had walked beside him, talking happily, he had found turning her over to Pierre impossible.

"Where else would we be? Out at sea?" Pierre scoffed. "We are where we've been for days, waiting for you to fulfill your part of our bargain until my ship returns."

"You're right," Myghal agreed. "It would have been a good chance. I'm not likely to get another, so I think your plan is hopeless. You should give it up."

"Oh, you do, do you? You presume to tell me what to do?" Pierre drew his sword and pressed it against Myghal's heaving chest. "The only reason you're not dead right now is that you haven't betrayed us to Sir Ranulf, and you can still be useful. Otherwise…"

"What's to prevent you from killing me even if I do what you want?" Myghal demanded.

"Why, nothing, except that I am a man of my word," the smuggler replied. "I kept my word when I killed your friend. I could have taken your money and sailed away, leaving him alive. But *non,* I did what I said I'd do, the way I expect you to. Yet instead, what do I find? You are trying to betray me and run away."

"I can't do what you want!" Myghal cried. "I can't help you steal Lady Beatrice. It'd be death to me, same as it will be to you if you try it."

"And I said that was a risk I was willing to take," Pierre retorted. His sword blade flicked upward, nearly cutting into Myghal's stubbled chin. "I fear, *mon ami*, it is a risk you *must* take, or I will kill you where you stand, because you will be of no more use to me. So, my young friend, what is it to be?"

YAWNING AND STRETCHING, Beatrice opened her eyes. She was alone in her chamber at Penterwell and Ranulf had carried her home.

That's what he'd called it, too. He'd been speaking of Penterwell Castle and he'd called it home.

Of course, he might only have meant *his* home, so she'd been afraid to call his attention to the word he'd used in case he gave her one of his wry looks and replied with some droll mockery. But still, he'd said home.

Pushing herself up to a sitting position, Beatrice looked around the room. Maloren must still be with Wenna.

She closed her eyes and drew in a deep, relieved breath. It hadn't been easy turning the child and she'd been afraid things were going horribly wrong. Poor Wenna had been so brave, wanting to have her dead husband's child so badly.

And then—oh, blessed, thankful moment, after the pain and the tears, the cries and finally screams, the silent and not-so-silent fervent prayers to a merciful God—little Gawan had come into the world, well and whole, crying almost at once. Not as lustily as little Peder, perhaps, but certainly well enough, judging by the relieved looks on the other women's faces.

Little Gawan might have arrived safe and sound without her, Beatrice realized, but she was proud and pleased nonetheless, especially when she remembered the respect and approval in Ranulf's eyes.

There had been a tenderness in his hazel eyes, too, that had filled her with joy and made her heart beat quicker.

That look alone would have been enough, but then he'd carried her home in his strong arms and laid her on this very bed and kissed her. Softly. Gently. On the lips. He'd said he was going to tell her something.

If only she hadn't been so tired, she would have questioned him then and there, but by the time she'd roused enough to speak, he was already out the door and closing it behind him.

Surely, though, this was a hopeful sign that he'd changed his mind and she didn't have to go back to Tregellas. Perhaps he was even going to admit that he did care for her. Maybe she could have some hope that he loved her.

She clasped her hand over her mouth to stifle a delighted giggle, even though she was alone. Until she was certain just what was in Ranulf's mind, she shouldn't let herself get overly excited.

As her stomach growled with hunger, she got up

and washed her face, despite the frigid water in the ewer. She removed her woolen gown and shift stained with perspiration. Laying her discarded clothes on the bed, she put on her best shift, which was made of very thin and soft white linen. Ranulf wouldn't see it, but she always felt like a queen when she wore it, and she wanted to feel like a queen today. She pulled on a gown of blue wool with red cuffs that laced at the sides so she needed no help, and then a supple red leather girdle. She donned clean stockings and soft slippers, and combed her hair a hundred strokes before twisting it into a long coil and tying it at the bottom with a red ribbon.

Thus attired, excited, happy and rested, she hurried to the hall. Not only did she need something to eat, she wanted to see Ranulf and hear what he had to say.

Upon entering the large chamber, she immediately saw Ranulf standing on the dais with his back to her.

A woman was facing him, giving him the kiss of greeting.

A beautiful woman, tall and dark and slender as a reed, with almond-shaped brown eyes below arching brows. Her cheeks were round and had the merest hint of color, like the blush on an apple. She wore a cloak with an ermine collar and jewels sparkled at her shell-like ears, as well as at her neck.

She was looking at Ranulf as if she'd like to swallow him whole, while he stood with his back as straight as a mill's spindle, his shoulders tense, his feet planted.

Beatrice started to tremble, a sudden sick feeling of dread in her stomach. It wasn't just that the woman was beautiful. It was the way she looked at Ranulf and the way he stood, as if he'd been knocked off balance and only just recovered.

He knew this woman, knew her well. And she knew him.

Just as suddenly, Beatrice realized who she must be. This was the woman who'd broken Ranulf's heart.

CHAPTER TEN

THE STRANGER NOTICED Beatrice. Her brown eyes widened and glittered like wet mud in the tidal flats, although she continued to smile sweetly at Ranulf.

"I had heard you have a guest, Ranulf," she said loudly enough for Beatrice to hear. "This must be the ward of the lord of Tregellas."

Ranulf's expression was frustratingly bland as he turned to look at Beatrice. Unfortunately, she'd missed that first, important moment of reunion, when his reactions might have told her more about his feelings. "Lady Beatrice, may I present Lady Celeste de Fontenbleu, an acquaintance from my youth."

Acquaintance? That seemed a very casual word if they had once been in love, Beatrice thought, her happiness reviving as she approached and bowed her head in greeting.

An annoyed look flashed in Lady Celeste's eyes. "I thought we were much more than mere acquaintances," she said to Ranulf.

"Say friends, then," he replied.

Lady Celeste still didn't look pleased, but her

peeved expression disappeared as she spoke to Beatrice, replaced with a kindly smile. "What a pretty little creature you are," she remarked, her voice oozing condescension. "You certainly can't tell by looking at you that you're a traitor's daughter, my dear."

Beatrice struggled to hide her rising anger. As upset as she was, and even though what Lady Celeste said was true, she wouldn't show her real feelings to this woman. She wouldn't give Lady Celeste the satisfaction of knowing her words had any effect on her at all.

"Whatever her father's crime," Ranulf said before Beatrice felt calm enough to reply, "Lady Beatrice is the ward of my overlord, and a guest here."

Although his words were placidly uttered, Beatrice took some comfort in his implied criticism before he called to Tecca. "Bring wine for the ladies, and have a chamber prepared for Lady Celeste and her maidservant, and pallets found for the men of her escort."

This Lady Celeste was going to *stay?*

With a look of smug satisfaction, the woman moved her skirts aside with a graceful gesture before she sat. Beatrice, meanwhile, perched upon the edge of another chair and tried not to frown.

"One would think you have been in command of this castle for years," Lady Celeste said approvingly to Ranulf. "Your guards and servants are very well trained."

Beatrice glanced at Ranulf, wondering if he was going to acknowledge that if his servants, at least, were well trained, *she* had something to do with it.

He didn't. "I've learned many things about leading soldiers since we last met."

"And done rather well for yourself, too. I heard all about your recent triumph at Ecclesford."

"That was Sir Henry's doing more than mine. I merely assisted."

"I was told that after Sir Henry was wounded, it could have gone very badly for him and his men if you hadn't been there to take command."

"I did no more than any other would have in my place," Ranulf replied.

"You always were a modest fellow, Ranulf," the lady said with an admiring smile.

Never in all her life had Beatrice felt so invisible. It was as if she wasn't even there—or they wished she wasn't.

They were about to discover it wasn't easy to ignore Beatrice.

She fairly beamed at Ranulf. "Isn't he humble? I myself have often thought he doesn't brag enough," she said. She regarded Lady Celeste with wide-eyed, apparently genuine curiosity. "I'm surprised, though, my lady, that since you think so highly of him and take such an interest in his accomplishments, you haven't sought him out and visited him sooner. His whereabouts have not exactly been a secret. Tell me, how long *has* it been since you last saw Ranulf?"

Lady Celeste's lips thinned a little. "Too long."

"That would explain why he's never mentioned you. As for being castellan, he's more than earned this position of trust and responsibility. Lord Merrick doesn't simply hand out such rewards as if they were treats at Twelfth Night, you know. But I suppose some people cannot see merit even if it's right in front of their faces."

Lady Celeste ignored her. "Did you not occasionally wonder about me?" she asked Ranulf.

"Often," he replied. "I was sorry to hear of Lord Fontenbleu's demise. He was a good man. The court won't be the same without him."

Lady Celeste pulled a small square of linen out of her girdle and dabbed at her eyes. "It was a very unpleasant and lingering illness. I nearly fell ill myself taking care of him. And then I was so lonely in that big house in London all by myself, I thought I would visit you, now that I am free."

Free? What did she mean by that? Beatrice wondered. Free to travel? Free to seek out a man she'd once spurned and offer him her love?

And what of Ranulf? He was being polite, as she'd expect, but what was he thinking? More importantly, what he was feeling?

Whatever he was thinking or feeling, she had

better things to do than sit and listen to Lady Celeste fawn and flatter and flirt with Ranulf.

She got to her feet. "If you'll excuse me, I'll see to the lady's chamber," she announced.

And then she swept her skirts behind her with a swift flick and briskly walked away.

As Ranulf watched Bea go, he wanted to call her back and tell her that she had nothing to fear from Celeste, or any reason to be jealous. After the first shock of seeing Celeste again had passed, he had realized that whatever he'd felt for her before, it was dead and gone.

It had started to die, he realized, the day he'd first seen Bea standing on the steps of Tregellas, and it had been withering ever since. Whereas Celeste had been as beautiful and exotic as a flower from foreign climes, Bea was naturally lovely, as sweet and welcome as the first wildflower of spring. Celeste had been an unattainable goddess condescending to converse with a mere mortal. Bea was like a good friend and merry companion, someone to share his joys and his tribulations with when the day was over. He couldn't imagine shopping in the market with Celeste, or discussing the need for a midwife and the problems with his servants. Bea would not only discuss those things, she'd make him laugh about them and feel that everything would all work out, somehow.

Although he felt regret as he looked at Celeste's

still-beautiful face, it was because he was sorry he'd ever believed the excited, feverish desire he'd felt for her was love. He wanted nothing more than to tell her she couldn't stay; unfortunately, the courtesy of chivalry demanded otherwise.

"I was surprised to learn that young woman was here," Celeste noted, watching Bea's retreating form. "I confess I was rather shocked that anyone would allow their ward such liberties, but then I've never met the lord and lady of Tregellas."

"If you had, you wouldn't doubt that they love Lady Beatrice and would never put her in danger."

"Danger!" Celeste cried, smiling and touching his hand lightly before withdrawing her fingers. "Oh, no, that isn't what I meant at all. I'm sure you wouldn't dream of despoiling such a young and innocent girl, especially one who is so close to Lord Merrick, to whom you owe so much and despite her obvious attractions."

"No, I would not."

To think that for years he'd imagined what he would do, what he would say, if and when he ever saw Celeste again. Sometimes he'd planned a host of cutting things to say, hoping to hurt her as she'd hurt him. Other times he envisioned ignoring her completely, wondering if that would be painful for her. Sometimes, he imagined that she would throw herself into his arms and, sobbing, confess she'd made a terrible mistake.

God, he'd been so stupid.

"I meant no insult to you, Ranulf," Celeste said contritely and with some genuine distress.

Because he still had hope for a happy future with Bea, he decided to be polite. "Forgive me. I've spent too much time among soldiers, I fear." He gave Celeste a smile. "You don't look a day older than when I last saw you."

She returned his smile with a brilliant one of her own. "Flatterer! I don't know whether I should be pleased or disappointed."

"I hope I never cause you displeasure, my lady," he answered as if by rote. This was the sort of thing Henry could say and make sound sincere. *He* must sound like an idiot.

Celeste regarded him with a pout that highlighted the fullness of her lips. "You're beginning to sound like a courtier, Ranulf. I've had my fill of them and their insincerity."

"Forgive me. I'm still recovering from the surprise of seeing your cortege enter the courtyard."

"I was afraid you would tell me not to come if I sent word of my intentions," she admitted. "The way we parted, I wouldn't have been surprised if you never wanted to see me again."

"What happened between us was long ago," he said. "I told Beatrice you were a friend, and I see no reason it should not be so."

"Just friends?" Celeste asked with another coy smile.

Before he could answer, Myghal burst into the hall.

"My lord!" he cried breathlessly, his chest heaving, his face flushed. "It's Hedyn. He's dead, my lord! *Dead!*"

A SHORT WHILE LATER, Ranulf stood looking at the bloody, naked body of Hedyn and a woman, both lying dead in the sheriff's bed.

Daveth, the servant who'd answered the door when Ranulf had visited Hedyn that day, cowered in the corner. His hair half hid his narrow face, although Ranulf could see the track of tears down his sallow cheeks.

Below, in the main room of the cottage, three other servants, all women of various ages, huddled together and wept.

As far as Ranulf could tell, nothing in the bedchamber had been disturbed, except for the occupants, either before they'd been killed, or after. Hedyn had met his end from a single thrust of a thin dagger through his heart and lay as if still asleep, on his back. The woman had not died so quickly or easily. Her nude body lay half off the bed, her left arm dangling toward the floor. He guessed she'd given her attacker at least a moment's struggle. A trail of blood had dripped down that limp arm from the slash in her throat to puddle on the wooden boards.

Ranulf forced himself to sound—and to be—calm

and dispassionate as he addressed Myghal and the servant. "Who is the woman?"

"Gwenbritha," Myghal whispered.

God's blood. "Sir Frioc's leman?"

"Aye, sir."

"How long has she been Hedyn's lover?"

"I never knew she was till now." Myghal glanced at the servant, who shook his head. "Nobody did."

Ranulf certainly had not. He wondered if she was the woman Hedyn had spoken of that day, the one he had lost? If so, the sheriff might have wished Sir Frioc dead, as he had once wished Lord Fontenbleu to hell.

Yet he couldn't imagine Hedyn a murderer, although he knew that anger and rejection could make a man do things he wouldn't consider otherwise.

But who then had killed Hedyn and the woman, and why? "Even you were not aware your master had a lover?" he asked Daveth.

"I knew there was *someone*," the servant answered promptly, his voice quavering, yet determined, too. "But my master didn't tell me who, or anything except he'd be gone for the night when he went to see her. This was the first time she'd been to this house."

Ranulf saw nothing in Daveth's demeanor to suggest he was lying, although that didn't mean he wasn't. "I see. And what happened last night?"

"The master told me he wouldn't need me again, so I was in the kitchen, my lord, with the other servants, until it was time for me to go to bed."

They'd probably been talking about their master and Gwenbritha, no doubt at some length, if they'd been as surprised as he was by the identity of Hedyn's lover.

"The kitchen's attached by a corridor, my lord, separate from the house," Myghal clarified.

"That's right," Daveth agreed. "We was all in there, sir, having a bit of ale and a chat, until I went to bed."

Ranulf had already taken note of the general layout of the house, and the means by which someone could enter. "You don't sleep in the kitchen, do you?"

Daveth shook his head. "No, sir. I make my bed by the hearth in the main room below."

"And you heard nothing last night? No sound of an intruder or a struggle?"

The servant bit his lip and shifted his weight from one leg to the other. "I did hear some noises in the night, my lord, coming from this room. Woke me up, in fact, but I thought…well, I thought it was just my master and his woman."

If the servant had been somehow involved, directly or indirectly, it was unlikely he'd volunteer such information.

It could be that the attacker had entered and crept upstairs while the servants were in the kitchen. A fast and cunning thief or assassin could slip into a house and up the stairs in what seemed no more than a blink of the eye. "When did you realize something was amiss?"

Daveth glanced at the bodies, then quickly away. "Not till the noon, my lord. It wasn't like my master to spend the morning in bed unless he was ill—but it wasn't like him to bring a woman back here, neither. So I thought I'd best not disturb him, and waited for him to call me. Leastways, I waited till the noon, and then I wondered if they might be hungry, so I brung some bread and honey and wine. I never expected…"

He fell silent, having no need to explain what he hadn't expected to find.

Ranulf had seen the spilled wine and a broken carafe on the steps. A tray lay at the bottom of the stairs, a loaf of bread close to it, as if the fellow had been so shocked by his discovery, he'd dropped the tray.

"Go to the kitchen and wait," he ordered Daveth, "and have the other servants wait with you. I'll speak to them later. Close the door behind you."

As Daveth obeyed, Myghal suddenly bolted for the window, threw open the shutters, leaned over the sill and threw up.

Ranulf had wanted to react in much the same way to the sight of Gawan's corpse, so he couldn't fault the man's squeamishness. Once Myghal was out in the fresh air, he'd feel better, although the scene he'd encountered today would probably haunt his dreams for months and possibly years to come.

Making no comment, Ranulf went closer to the bed, and the bodies. He felt Hedyn's hand. It was cold and stiff, so he'd been dead for some time.

Myghal sat on the floor, his knees drawn up and his head in his hands. "Forgive me, my lord," he muttered miserably. "I'm not... I've never seen anything like this."

"Murder sickens me, too," Ranulf said. He went to help the younger man to his feet. "Have you any idea who could have done this?"

Myghal shook his head. "No, sir, no. Everybody liked Hedyn."

Whether the man was liked or not was not the issue, but Ranulf took pity on the distraught fellow. "It wasn't his friends I was thinking of," he said. "Was it possible somebody knew of his liaison with Gwenbritha?"

Myghal's eyes widened. "When his own servants didn't? Nor anybody else? Because if anybody in the village had known, you can be sure the man's servants would have heard about it."

It did seem highly unlikely that such a secret could be kept if anyone other than the lovers themselves knew. "He was also the sheriff, and as such, a representative of the king. Perhaps this crime has something to do with Gawan's death. Maybe Hedyn had discovered something about the other deaths, something that made someone think it was necessary to silence him," Ranulf proposed.

"Wouldn't he have told you, my lord?"

Ranulf scratched his beard. "If Hedyn had realized the import of what he'd learned. It might have been something that wasn't obvious, and Hedyn hadn't yet realized its significance. What did Hedyn do yesterday?"

"Nothing out of the usual, my lord," Myghal answered. "He talked to some of the fishermen in the morning after they got back with their catch, and a couple of the merchants. He ate his noon meal in the tavern, then sent me to the castle to see if your patrols had found anything. After that, well, I guess he went to fetch Gwenbritha."

"When was the last time you saw him?"

"When he sent me off to the castle. He was standin' in the main street, waving a farewell," Myghal finished with a tremor in his voice.

Ranulf sympathized with the man's sorrow, but he had one more question before he could let him go. "I want the names of the men he talked to."

Myghal listed eight men—five fishermen and three merchants, including the one from whom Ranulf had purchased the silk fabric for Bea.

Maybe if he'd been thinking less about Bea and more about catching the man or men responsible for Gawan's death, Hedyn would still be alive. Or maybe this murder had nothing to do with Gawan, and everything to do with Gwenbritha—except why then would she be dead?

Whatever the cause of these murders, there were things that needed to be done. "Why don't you go and fetch the priest?" Ranulf suggested to Myghal.

"You could ask some of the women to help prepare the bodies when I'm finished here."

"Aye, my lord," a relieved Myghal said before he immediately hurried from the chamber.

When he was alone, Ranulf concentrated on examining the room, trying to discover if there was a place where an assassin could hide, undetected, and perhaps for hours.

There was no arras, no tapestry or any large cupboard. There was a chest, but a quick look revealed that it was full of clothing and linen. Not even a child could fit inside with the lid closed. He supposed it was possible that someone could have removed the contents first, but where would he have put them in the meantime?

Ranulf went to the window, checking the frame for any evidence of a rope being attached, or a grappling hook thrown. There was nothing, and it was likely somebody in the village would have heard or seen that sort of activity. Surely they would have reported *that* to the watch. Otherwise he'd have to believe some of the villagers were culpable in these crimes.

He walked slowly toward the bed, looking closely at the floor. Unfortunately, Myghal's visit to the window and then his own had erased any signs of other boots that might have been there.

He should have been more careful.

Next Ranulf went to Hedyn's side of the bed and got down on his hands and knees to peer beneath.

It was remarkably free of dust, and there were a few marks that could be from a man sliding out from underneath, or a damp rag swished about to clean.

He couldn't imagine lying under a bed while a man and woman sported, waiting for them to fall asleep, and then killing them in cold blood—but then, he was no assassin.

He examined Hedyn's wound. The weapon that had killed him had been very thin and very sharp, and probably foreign. The fatal blow was nearly in the center of his chest, made by someone who knew exactly where to strike.

Ranulf walked to the other side of the bed. Slowly, carefully, he moved Gwenbritha so that she was lying on the bed, then brushed the hair away from her face.

Although she was pretty, she was no great beauty. She wasn't as young as Bea, but likely closer in age to Celeste. In the stillness of death, he could tell nothing of her personality, yet she must have had some qualities men found attractive.

Too many, perhaps, and it had led to her doom.

Her body was shapely, with trim hips and rounded breasts. He didn't think she'd ever had a child. He hoped not. He didn't want to imagine any little one crying for his mother, going to bed that night and for many others with damp cheeks and a heart full of sorrow because she was never coming back. She'd gone to heaven—a better, happier place, so the priest had said.

Ranulf shook away that memory and studied the wound on the woman's neck. It was high and on the left side. Judging from the position of the body in relation to Hedyn's, the killer had been facing her.

Had she awakened to find her murderer standing over her, ready to strike, Hedyn already dead beside her? If so, she'd been too shocked and terrified to scream, her mouth opening but no sound coming out.

And then the water choking...

He closed his eyes a brief moment. When he opened them again, he noted how high on her neck the wound was, starting just below her ear, as if her assailant had held her head by the hair in his left hand and slashed down with his right.

The poor woman. The poor, terrified woman. At least Hedyn hadn't seen his doom coming.

"I'll find them," he quietly vowed, as if they were still capable of hearing. "I'll find out who did this and he'll be punished. I give you my word."

Then, with respect and care, Ranulf drew the sheet up so that both bodies were covered, allowing them what dignity he could even in death.

WHEN RANULF RETURNED from Hedyn's house, he was more upset and agitated than Beatrice had ever seen him. Grabbing a goblet of wine from the table on the dais that she had poured in anticipation of his return, she rushed forward to meet him.

"Oh, Ranulf!" she cried, pity and sympathy for

him overwhelming her other tumultuous emotions. "I'm so sorry!"

"I don't want any wine," Ranulf snapped, brushing past her. He threw himself into a chair on the dais and stared at the floor at his feet.

She forgave his brusque manner, seeing it for what it was—his reaction to the death of a good man. She quietly ordered the servants gathered in the hall to leave him in peace. For a moment she thought of going, too, but she couldn't bear to leave him alone when he was in such a state. He might be angry on the surface, but she'd seen his eyes. There was pain there, too, so she would stay and offer him what comfort she could.

She set down the goblet on the table beside his chair.

"This is not your fault," she ventured softly.

Ranulf barked a harsh, mocking laugh. "Then whose, if not mine? I'm castellan here, charged with keeping the peace. I think the murder of the sheriff and his paramour could be accounted a failure to do that, don't you?"

She excused his rough sarcasm, too. "You didn't do the deed."

Ranulf jumped to his feet and strode to the end of the dais, then back again. "No, but I should have done more to prevent it."

She spread her hands. "What more could you have done?"

"I shouldn't have been so lenient, so damn patient," he snarled. "I should have put an end to the smuggling and questioned every man in the village about Gawan's death, and those other two, and Frioc's as well."

He began to pace. "But no, like a softhearted fool I waited for *them* to decide to trust me. Fool! Stupid, weak-willed fool!"

She couldn't stand to hear him berate himself so. "Yes, you could have done that," she agreed, her heart aching as she watched him. "You could have entered Penterwell like an avenging angel, and detained and questioned everyone. You could have thrown any man who smuggled into the dungeon, which would have been more than half the men of the village, and their women, too, if you went after anyone who profits by illegal trade. You could have put a cordon around the village, and forbidden any boat to put out. There are many things you *could* have done—but you would have made everyone in the village hate and fear you. They would never trust you, *ever,* and be far more likely to work against you. You might have made things a hundred times worse."

"How could it be worse?" he demanded. "A good man is dead because I let myself believe these selfish, stubborn villagers would see that I meant them no harm. I let them break the king's laws. From there, it must seem a small step to murder."

"And if they had still not given you the answers you sought, what then, Ranulf?" she asked. "Would it have been the rack or hot irons? Do you think that would have helped you get the answers you need? Or would it only have created more enmity, until every man, woman and child in Penterwell wanted *you* dead, too?"

His expression changed, from anger to bleak despair. "Why won't they help me?" he asked as he sat heavily and ran his hands through his hair. "Why won't they tell me what they know?"

"Perhaps now they will," she offered. "Maybe this will make them come to you. Let's hope so, Ranulf."

He continued to regard her with dismay. "And if not? What should I do then, Bea?"

She knelt beside his chair. "You may have to question everyone, as you suggested, and put an end to the smuggling until you find out who's done these terrible things, but you must tell them *why.* You must make them understand that you feel you have no choice, not if you're to discover who killed Hedyn and the others, and to keep them all safe."

Some of the tension left his body as he looked down at her and gave her a weary smile. "When did you grow so wise, little Lady Bea?" he asked, reaching out to caress her cheek.

"I don't claim to be wise, Ranulf," she replied, warmed by his gentle touch. "I've met the people of your town, and I think most of them want to believe they can trust you and put their faith in you, that you'll protect them. But they're afraid, too."

"They should be," he murmured, hanging his head

and sighing. "God's wounds, Bea, I've seen men killed before, but that poor woman…she saw her attacker, knew what was coming…"

Beatrice put her hand over his, offering him her silent comfort.

"It was done right in his house, in his bedchamber, with the servants sleeping below." His voice hardened. "Damn it, Bea, what kind of a man could do such a thing?"

Since he truly seemed to want an answer, she said, "An evil one an honorable man like you can't possibly understand. But you're clever, Ranulf. You'll catch him. I know you will."

"How can I, when no one in the village seems willing to tell me what I need to know? I confess, Bea, sometimes I feel as if the whole village is not only unwilling to provide information, they're conspiring against me."

She lifted his hand and pressed a kiss upon the back. "I don't think so. It could be they truly don't know anything more than you've already learned."

He gave her a sad and wistful smile. "Little Lady Bea, always ready to believe the best."

"I have faith in you, Ranulf. I know you'll find out who's done these terrible things."

His expression determined, he rose and pulled her to her feet. "You've got to leave here, Bea. Until I catch whoever's responsible, it's too dangerous for you to stay."

"I don't want to go," she said, unable to keep from voicing the wish of her heart. "I want to stay with you. I want to help you, even if it's only to bring you wine when you return."

He took her hands in his and looked down into her eyes. "I wish you could stay, too, but I won't put you at risk."

She gazed up at him with all the love and devotion she felt. "I would rather face danger with you than be safe without you."

"Would you really, Bea?"

"Yes, I really would."

With a sigh, he gathered her into his arms. She held him tightly, loving him. Needing him. Not wanting to leave here, where he might be in danger from unknown enemies. She wanted to protect him, and comfort him, and keep him safe and happy forever.

"Bea, Bea," he murmured. "Don't make it any harder for me to send you away than it is. If anything were to happen to you, I couldn't bear it."

He must love her! He must!

And then—oh, and then!—he bent his head and kissed her.

It was like the kiss he'd given her when she'd been half-asleep—soft, tender, wonderful—except that this time, she was very wide-awake. She could feel his affection, his warmth, how much he cherished her. His kiss told her better than words, more than anything he could say, that he must love her, this man who'd suffered. Who'd loved and lost. Who deserved to be admired for his strength and his courage, respected for his honor, cherished for the goodness that no one had been able to crush out of him, even though they tried.

With a low moan of encouragement, she relaxed against him, giving herself up to the desire flowing through her body. She let the love she felt for him come through her lips in a way different from words, but no less intense for all that.

Soon they were lost to everything but each other. Nothing else existed. All they knew was their passion as his hands shifted, moving with languorous exploration up her back. She slid her arms about him, holding him closer still, feeling his arousal and thrilled that she had caused it.

And then, as his kiss deepened and his tongue slid into the welcoming warmth of her mouth, his hand moved again, around her side to cup her breast.

Her breathing quickened and her hold tightened as her excitement reached a new height. Her breasts grew taut, her nipples pebbling beneath his still-light touch.

His beard began to tickle her and she smiled even as they kissed.

"I amuse you, my lady?" he asked huskily as his lips left hers to trail along her cheek.

"Your beard tickles," she breathlessly confessed.

"I shall have to do something about that."

"Please…"

Again they kissed, their passion fiercer now. She slipped her hands beneath his tunic, feeling the heat from his flesh through the shirt that remained between her hands and his skin. His lips took hers harder, with more urgency, and she responded in kind—until he drew back.

"You've got to go, Bea," he whispered as he rained light kisses on her cheeks. "Back to Tregellas, where you'll be safe. After this is over, once I've found the villains, I'll come to you there."

His lips found hers once more, and they kissed deeply, passionately.

Until somebody gasped.

They jumped apart as Bea remembered where they were. They were kissing like lovers in the hall of Penterwell, where anybody might see them.

It wasn't *anybody* staring at them. It was Lady Celeste, pale and horrified at the bottom of the stairs, one hand to her slender throat as if she were choking.

Nobody moved or spoke, until Celeste felt shakily for the handrail carved into the stone wall beside her.

"Ranulf," she stammered. Her eyes closed and her knees gave way.

Ranulf immediately rushed to her side, Beatrice right behind him. As he caught Celeste and lifted her in his powerful arms, Beatrice couldn't help wondering if this was a show on Celeste's part, a desperate attempt to regain Ranulf's attention.

"She feels very warm," Ranulf said, his brows knit with worry.

Beatrice put a hand to Celeste's brow. She *was* hot. A swoon might be bogus, but unless Celeste had somehow anticipated finding them kissing, she couldn't have planned to feign a fever. "Let's get her to her bedchamber, and I'll see if I can help her."

CHAPTER ELEVEN

"I DON'T KNOW why you have to tend that woman," Maloren muttered darkly as she watched Beatrice prepare some willow bark for Lady Celeste's medicine in the castle kitchen three days later.

Beatrice stood at a small worktable at one end of the large chamber, while Maloren sat on a stool with her back against the wall. In the main part of the room, the cook and the servants busily prepared the evening meal.

"She's rich," Maloren grumbled. "Let her pay for a physician, or go to the holy sisters and have them take care of her."

"She's Ranulf's guest, and fortunately not seriously ill. She should be well enough to travel in another day or two, and then she'll be leaving."

"Aye and good riddance to her! I see what she's up to, the hussy!"

Beatrice slid Maloren a questioning glance. "And what is that?"

"You're too sweet and innocent to see through her, my lamb," Maloren declared, waggling her finger at Beatrice as if Beatrice were five years old. "But *I* know *exactly* the sort of creature that woman is! Married for money and now that she's got it, she thinks she can buy another husband for pleasure."

"I don't think Sir Ranulf is for sale," Beatrice answered, looking down at the bark she was grinding with her mortar and pestle.

"Well, if Lady Celeste was as ugly as a boar, I'd say you might be right, but she's not. She's a beauty and knows it, and how to use it, too. I'll wager she's had men wrapped about her little finger since she was twelve years old."

"Perhaps once she had Sir Ranulf wrapped around her finger, but that was long ago."

Maloren sniffed derisively. "You think that means he can't be caught again? Of course he can, because she'll remind him of his youth and seem to promise him another."

Beatrice's teeth clenched as she continued to grind the bark and other ingredients to ease the pain in Lady Celeste's head. "I'm fairly certain Ranulf is too clever to fall into any traps Lady Celeste may set."

Especially since he had come to care for her, just as she'd always hoped.

Unfortunately, since Hedyn and Gwenbritha's murder, she'd seen very little of Ranulf. He was late for the evening meal every night and looked so tired and frustrated when he did arrive, she didn't want to pester him with questions. Not only was she anxious about the murders, she was still waiting to learn what he'd planned to tell her the day after Wenna had given birth, and to hear him say he loved her.

He would tell her eventually, she was sure, and in the meantime, she was confident enough of his affection to wait patiently. Well, perhaps not patiently, she inwardly confessed, but to wait nonetheless.

"You seem very concerned for Sir Ranulf's welfare," Beatrice noted, hoping Maloren's criticism of Celeste meant she was finally beginning to appreciate Ranulf.

"I hate to see any man the dupe of a rich widow. They've had their chance and ought to be content. But no, they must seek another husband, although there's women who can't even get one. But what's that to them, the selfish creatures?" Maloren sniffed with scorn. "Lady Celeste with her silks and brocades and perfumes, lying about pretending to be sick just so she can get her hooks into Sir Ranulf!"

Had she just learned a possible cause for Maloren's disgust with men? Beatrice wondered. "Did *you* ever want to marry, Maloren?"

"No," the maidservant snapped. "Let some oaf of a man order me about? Or try to sweet-talk me into doing whatever he wants?"

Beatrice refrained from pointing out that *she* had the right to order Maloren about, and she'd often resorted to sweet-talking her to get what she wanted. "Lady Celeste has no children," she suggested. "Perhaps if she marries—"

"If she marries, it won't be because she wants a baby," Maloren retorted. "It'll be because she wants a man at her beck and call, and beholden to her, too. She'll have her marriage contract ironclad so she keeps control of the purse strings—you just watch and see. She's a greedy, selfish bitch in heat, that's what she is."

Beatrice had to admit that in her own heart, her estimation of Lady Celeste was not far different from Maloren's.

"Is that potion going to be ready before the sun goes down?" Maloren demanded.

"Just as soon as I add it to the wine," Beatrice said, carefully doing so.

When the potion was ready, she said, "I don't suppose you want to come with me when I take this medicine to her?"

"Jesus, Mary and Joseph, no! The perfume that woman wears makes *my* head ache. I'll stay here and make sure Much doesn't burn the meat."

Beatrice felt a moment's pity for Much, but under Maloren's supervision, the food had definitely improved.

Covering the goblet holding the potion with a square of clean white linen, Beatrice made her way to the hall. She regarded the servants' work with a critical eye, but saw nothing amiss and much to praise with a quick word or smile. She had some words of compliment for the soldiers who were not on duty, too, all of whom were busy tending to their armor, either seeing to small repairs themselves, or polishing it until it shone. More than one of the soldiers blushed when the pretty young woman said something about their attention to their duty, or the zeal with which they polished.

When she reached Lady Celeste's chamber, Beatrice took a deep breath before she knocked on the door and waited until Lady Celeste's maidservant, Emma, opened it for her. Try though Beatrice might not to feel it, she was still a little intimidated by Celeste's exotic beauty and superior manner.

Lady Celeste lay in her bed, one made with linens she, too, had brought from home. They were finer and more expensive than those from Tregellas, and much better than those Beatrice had found in Penterwell. There was also a thick silk coverlet on the bed and fine white candles in a large brass candle stand beside it. Several small jars of unguents, perfumes and what Beatrice suspected were cosmetics, as well as a mirror, were on a collapsible table Lady Celeste must have brought from her home, along with the cushioned stool before it. She had brought a considerable number of garments with her, too, for several wooden chests and boxes also crowded the room.

Even sitting in a bed and unwell, Lady Celeste seemed to have the grandeur of a queen, making Beatrice feel, yet again, that she was very young and unsophisticated.

She never felt that way in Ranulf's presence, even

when he told her she was innocent and naive. She always felt very much a woman when she was with him.

"Ah, Lady Beatrice," Celeste said, raising herself slightly. "I don't know what I would have done if you had not been here."

"I dare say Ranulf would have sent for a physician," Beatrice replied, handing her the potion. "This should ease your aching head."

Celeste took a tiny sip and wrinkled her nose. "I hope so, for truly, the taste leaves something to be desired. It's too bad your medicine has to spoil Ranulf's fine wine."

It was too bad she'd fallen ill and been allowed to stay, Beatrice thought, but she didn't say it. Nor did she reveal that the wine had come from Tregellas.

Celeste glanced at her maidservant, standing expectantly in the corner. "Leave us, Emma. I want to talk to my benefactress alone."

Beatrice would rather talk to the poorest pauper in Penterwell than Lady Celeste. Indeed, she had, when she'd given the poor legless man some alms. He was certainly far more grateful for the loaf of bread she'd given him than this fine lady was for the medicine that eased her suffering.

As her maid departed, Lady Celeste patted the bed beside her. "Sit here, my dear, where we can chat like old friends. I think it's time I told you the history between Ranulf and me."

Beatrice didn't want to be her friend, but she couldn't resist the chance to learn what had transpired between Ranulf and this woman.

"I believe you may be somewhat aware of what happened," Celeste said as she continued to sip the wine.

"Enough to guess that a woman once broke Ranulf's heart," Beatrice answered honestly, "and that it was probably you."

"Guessed all that, did you? What a perceptive girl you are!"

Beatrice didn't appreciate being called a "girl" or patronized. "He never mentioned you by name until you came here."

That revelation did not sit well with the lady. Nevertheless, she grudgingly agreed. "The relationship between us didn't end well."

Celeste set the goblet on the table beside the bed. "My dear, I am going to be very frank with you, because I believe you care about Ranulf as much as I do."

Beatrice would have wagered a great deal that she cared more about Ranulf than this lady ever would, or could.

"When I was just a little older than you, I met Ranulf at court. Oh, you should have seen him then, my dear! So charming, so witty. And handsome! Half the girls at court were in love with him, I vow, which might explain…"

She hesitated, but Beatrice didn't think that was

from any sudden modest impulse. "Well, those were only rumors, after all, and I, for one, refuse to believe them, although I suppose it's not surprising that a young and disappointed man would seek solace in another woman's arms. Or more than one."

Celeste was watching her keenly, and although this revelation dismayed her, Beatrice wasn't going to give this woman the satisfaction of knowing she'd distressed her.

The lady seemed to realize no shocked queries would be forthcoming. "Anyway, before that, I fell in love with Ranulf, and he with me. We met in a rose garden, and oh, my dear, it was like something out of a minstrel's ballad! I had caught my sleeve on a thorn and he freed it and then he kissed my hand and looked into my eyes with such a look! I do believe we fell in love right then and there."

No wonder Ranulf had no use for minstrel's ballads of love and hated the romantic stories of Arthur and his court.

"I assure you, I loved him more every day and wanted very much to be his wife."

Celeste's expression grew mournful as she took hold of Beatrice's hands in hers, her grip strong and her fingers cold. "But when my family discovered our *tendre,* they were furiously angry. They had other plans for me, you see. They told me I was being both foolish and selfish. I had to make a marriage that would benefit the family, not just myself. Ranulf was a poor and landless knight, and worse, he'd killed his own brother—"

"What?" Beatrice gasped in stunned disbelief.

"Oh, didn't you know?" Celeste asked with a pitying look. "Yes, my dear, it's true. They lived in Lincolnshire, on an estate by the coast. Ranulf and his brother got into a fight, and somehow or other, they wound up in the sea. Ranulf held Edmond under the water until he drowned. Afterward, their father cast Ranulf out without a penny."

"It...it must have been an accident," Beatrice whispered. She couldn't believe Ranulf had killed his own brother, until she remembered what Ranulf had said about his family and their cruelty. "He must have been trying to defend himself."

"That's what I thought, too, but he would never talk about it, even though I asked him more than once."

Of course that would be a painful subject for him, and no wonder Ranulf dreaded the sea.

Nevertheless, the notion of Ranulf deliberately, viciously and cold-bloodedly murdering anybody was simply inconceivable. "Anyone who knows Ranulf can be certain he's innocent of willful murder. Sir Leonard de Brissy thought Ranulf was worthy of being trained as a knight. He wouldn't have done that if he believed Ranulf a murderer."

"That is what I told my parents, too," Celeste said. "He couldn't have done such a terrible, heartless thing. It had to be an accident. Yet they refused to listen and used his brother's death as another excuse to keep me from him. They forbade me to see him. They told me they would disown me if I disobeyed. I begged and pleaded and cried until I could cry no more, but they were adamant." Celeste wiped her eyes with the corner of her sleeve. "When Lord Fontenbleu asked for my hand, my family was at me night and day until I surrendered to their wishes."

Beatrice thought about her cousin and what Constance had been prepared to do if she hadn't fallen in love with Merrick. What Constance had counseled *her* to do if she found herself betrothed against her will. "You could have run away."

"But we would have had nothing—no money, no home."

"You would have had Ranulf." For Beatrice, that would have been more than enough. "Instead, you broke his heart."

"Don't you think I know that?" Celeste asked piteously. "Don't you think mine broke as well?"

Almost against her will, Beatrice's heart softened. Lady Celeste would not have been the first young woman to succumb to a family's pressure to yield. "I suppose it must have been difficult."

"Indeed, it was!" Celeste exclaimed. "I cried myself to sleep every night until the wedding, and that was three months later."

"At least you had the comfort of knowing you'd pleased your family, and you had a husband, too.

Ranulf had no one, for he told no one what happened. Even his closest friends don't know. I asked Henry once, you see, because I was sure someone had wounded Ranulf deeply."

"Oh, he had comfort, my dear," Celeste replied with a hint of a sneer. "And plenty of it. Many women were happy to rush into his arms once I had left them."

Beatrice had heard enough. "I think you should rest, my lady," she said, getting to her feet.

"You have no idea of the torment I endured," Celeste charged. "You have no right to stand in judgment of me—you who have the love of your cousin who allows you such liberties, in spite of what people will say. And her husband is so in her thrall, he won't gainsay a thing she does."

It was one thing for this woman to patronize and belittle Beatrice; it was quite another for her to insult Constance and Merrick. "You're right, my lady. I don't understand you. I don't understand how you could spurn the finest, best man in England. If I had Ranulf's love, I would run away and live with him in a ditch rather than marry another."

With that, Beatrice turned on her heel and started for the door.

"Would you really?" Celeste replied with undisguised scorn as she scrambled from the bed to follow her. "How brave and bold you are. Obviously you care little for your reputation. But then, what reputation have you to lose?"

Celeste grabbed Beatrice's arm to keep her there. "Your father was executed for treason, all his property and wealth forfeit to the crown. You have no land to bestow, and all the dowry you may hope for comes courtesy of your cousin's husband. You claim to know Ranulf—will he want to accept what is little more than his friend's charity? *I* can give him everything he deserves—money, land, and the power that goes with it. With me as his wife, he will be welcomed at court, even in the king's counsel. And he is a man of the world. Can you please him in bed? Do you know the tricks that can bring a man to such ecstasy, he'll never want to leave your arms? You're just a girl, a virgin—and he's had his fill of them. Fourteen in a fortnight, that was the wager he won. Do you think he'll ever be satisfied with you?"

Pale to the lips, Beatrice wrenched her arm free of the lady's grasp and again started for the door.

"What can you give him compared to what I have to offer?" Celeste demanded.

Beatrice whirled around and stalked toward Celeste like an enraged lioness. Blanching, Celeste stumbled backward until she hit the bed and could go no farther.

"I can give him a love that would risk anything rather than give him up," Beatrice declared. "I can give him my heart, and my body. I can give him my trust, my respect, my admiration. I can give him everything he deserves from a woman, everything I have and am. And in return, if he gives me his love and his respect, his heart and his body, I will be the happiest, luckiest woman in England.

"And know you this, my lady. I love Ranulf. I will continue to love him despite your pitiful efforts to blacken his name or to win him back with your lies.

"So I suggest, my lady," she concluded, "that as soon as you are able, you pack up your goods and go and find another man who can appreciate your beauty and your other considerable assets. Leave Ranulf to the peace he deserves and the happy life I hope to give him. And God go with you, my lady, because Ranulf won't!"

AS BEATRICE MARCHED out of Celeste's bedchamber, Ranulf watched the last of the fishermen leave Hedyn's house, taking the smell of the morning's catch with him.

"Is that all of them?" he asked Myghal, who had been with him during the questioning of the villagers.

"Aye, my lord."

Standing at the open window, Ranulf gazed up at the sky. It had been three days since Hedyn and Gwenbritha's murder—three days he'd spent questioning every adult in Penterwell, except for the time he'd spent at Hedyn's funeral mass, or sleeping, or grabbing a bite to eat in the hall. He'd barely seen Bea in all that time. Either he was asking questions trying to get answers, or she was nursing Celeste, who finally—thank God—seemed to be getting better. Even more thankfully, neither Bea nor anyone else had fallen ill.

He'd chosen to do his questioning here, in the house where Hedyn and his lover had died, because he hoped that would inspire those he queried to give him answers. He wanted them to think about the dead man and the poor woman who'd been his lover before they'd been so brutally murdered.

Unfortunately, not one of the people he'd questioned had told him anything useful. Nobody had any idea who could have killed Hedyn, Gwenbritha or Gawan, or who would want to. Nobody knew what had happened to the two others who'd gone missing earlier, or if there was anyone who had wanted Sir Frioc dead. To hear the villagers' responses, it was as if evil spirits had flown into Penterwell to do the dastardly deeds.

"Very well, Myghal," Ranulf said with a sigh, wondering what he'd do next to try to find the culprits. Perhaps he should lead the patrols of the coast himself, as he'd done before. Maybe his soldiers had missed something, or were protecting their relatives. He hated to think it, but it was possible.

"I beg your pardon, my lord," Myghal said quietly, as if wary of interrupting Ranulf's frustrated thoughts.

"Yes?"

Myghal shifted his feet. "The folks have been asking me when we're going to get a new sheriff and who it might be."

Ranulf had been thinking about that, too, and one candidate seemed obvious. "I see no reason why you should not be the sheriff."

Myghal stared at him as if he was thunderstruck. "M-me, my lord?"

"Why not?" Ranulf asked. "You were Hedyn's undersheriff for two years and he found you capable, as do I."

Myghal's cheeks turned scarlet. "I'm honored, my lord, but surely I'm not…there's got to be…"

"Would you really rather I named another?" Ranulf asked, sensing there was more than modesty to Myghal's protestations.

That wasn't surprising, given that his predecessor had been brutally murdered. "After what happened to Hedyn, I can understand if you're reluctant, although I'll be disappointed."

"It's not that," Myghal said. "But, um, you may have noticed, my lord, there's some that don't like me in Penterwell."

"I have noticed," Ranulf replied, recalling some of the looks he'd noticed Myghal receiving from the villagers. "But I have yet to meet anyone universally admired. It's also a sad truth that most men who represent the law are often regarded with suspicion. However, I need a man I can rely on, and one just as determined to find out who's responsible for these deaths as I am. Are you that man, Myghal?"

The younger man straightened his slightly beefy shoulders. "I am, my lord."

"Then you are now the sheriff of Penterwell, and I am going home."

CHAPTER TWELVE

CELESTE'S MAIDSERVANT hurried up to Ranulf as he dismounted in the courtyard and handed Titan's reins to one of the grooms waiting to take them. "My lord, if you please, my lord," the young woman said, looking as if she'd rather be anywhere else than talking to him.

"What is it?" he asked, frowning. "I hope your mistress's illness hasn't taken a turn for the worse."

"No, my lord, I don't think so," Emma said, speaking with great deference and not a little fear. "She wants to see you as soon as possible. She says it's important."

Ranulf's mind was instantly alert, as if an alarm had sounded on the walls. "Really? And what might this urgent matter be?"

Emma's thin face flushed to the roots of her mouse-brown hair. "I don't know, my lord. She didn't tell me. Just said I was to tell you it was important and that she needed to see you."

"In her bedchamber, I suppose?"

"She isn't well enough to get up yet."

Ranulf had not been born yesterday, and it had been ten years since he'd been that green youth of eighteen, anxious for love and blind to a clever woman's snares, so if Celeste thought to seduce him, she was most certainly going to be disappointed. On the other hand, perhaps it would be best if he made that perfectly clear.

"Please inform her that I shall be happy to speak with her as soon as I've given the night's watchword to the guard," he said, dismissing the maidservant.

He chose "wiser" for the word, then went to the chamber given over to Celeste's use while she was in Penterwell. He knocked briskly on the door, reflecting that it was a good thing that Celeste had brought her own servants. After he'd sent Eseld away—staggering dizzily and calling him a host of unflattering names—there was no one to spare to tend to a sick guest.

The door was immediately opened, although not by Emma. Celeste herself stood there, dressed—if one could call it that—in a bed robe of rich scarlet brocade loosely belted about her slender hips. Beneath the robe was a very sheer white shift, probably made of silk.

There had been a time he would have nearly died of desire to see her thus, and especially looking at him with that particular hunger in her eyes.

Unfortunately for Celeste, that time had passed.

"I had not anticipated finding you here alone and in

a state of dishabille, my lady," he said coolly. "Although I understand you have some matter of urgency to discuss with me, it will have to wait until—"

She didn't give him a chance to finish before she grabbed him by the arm and pulled him into the room with surprising force and shoved the door closed behind him.

"This is rather flagrant, isn't it?" he asked as he raised one inquisitive brow. "In the past you would have been more subtle."

"Don't play the righteous, pious prude with me, Ranulf," Celeste declared, her cheeks flushed and her eyes flashing with ire. "It doesn't suit you. I'm not trying to seduce you."

"I'm very glad to hear it," he calmly replied. "Since you must then only wish to converse, allow me to begin. You're obviously feeling better, so I think it's time you left Penterwell."

"What?" she gasped. "You would order a guest to go?"

Because she was a guest, and a woman, and despite her choice of garments and what she'd done in the past, he felt compelled to ease the order. "It's for your own good, Celeste. There has been some serious trouble here, including murder, and I don't want you to be in any danger."

Instead of looking worried, her eyes lit up with delight. "So you do care about me?"

"Yes, as a friend," he answered, and to make certain she understood there could never be anything more than that between them, he added, "Although there have been days I wished you dead."

She backed away. "You…what?"

"Is it really so surprising that I would want you to suffer after what you did to me?"

"And do you think I didn't suffer when I had to marry another? My family *forced* me to accept Lord Fontenbleu."

He thought of the morning she'd told him they must never see each other again. "I was too poor. You said so yourself."

She clasped her hands together, as Bea so often did. "That's what they kept saying to me—that you were poor and I would be poor, too, if I married you."

"I'm still poor, Celeste. I'm castellan here because of Merrick's friendship and generosity. I have no estate of my own, and few coins to my name. Everything I own can fit into a single wooden chest."

"But I am rich, and the man who marries me will be rich, too. I can give you everything you've ever wanted, Ranulf. Money, lands, power—and a wife who loves you!"

"All that, Celeste? You would give me all that?"

"Yes!" she cried, throwing her arms around him. "Whatever you want, Ranulf."

He gently pushed her away. "What I want is Bea. And I want *you* to leave Penterwell."

"Please don't hate me for what I was made to do!"

she pleaded. "Try to understand and forgive me. It's so difficult for a woman!"

"I know that, and I do pity you, Celeste," he replied, speaking not unkindly, but firmly, too. "As for forgiveness, if that is what you really seek, you have that, as well."

As he said it, he realized that was true. He did forgive her. "What's past is past, Celeste," he said gently. "Now let us speak no more of those days."

"But my husband is dead, and we're here—together," she said. "He never loved me, Ranulf, never. I was just a prize to him, something to decorate his hall and show off to his friends." She bit her lip and looked up at him, her eyes shining with unshed tears. "He never kissed me the way you did, never made me feel—"

"Please, Celeste," Ranulf said, turning away. "Don't say anything more. I'm sorry for you, truly I am, but I don't love you."

She stiffened as if a lightning bolt had struck her, and her expression grew as hard as that of a cheated merchant. "Do you no longer want me because I've grown old and ugly?" she demanded. "Is that why you'd rather dally here with that *child* and ruin your reputation—and hers, such as it is—beyond repair?"

To think there had been a time he would gladly have died for this woman. "Beatrice is not a child."

"And that makes what you're doing acceptable? You've taken that sweet innocent and made her your leman, despite your professed friendship with her guardian."

"Beatrice is *not* my mistress," he said through clenched teeth, trying to contain his growing anger.

"So you say, but that is most certainly not how it looks."

"If all you plan to do is insult me or Lady Beatrice," he said with cold deliberation, "I shall take my leave of you. Have your maid pack your things. You'll be departing Penterwell at first light tomorrow."

And he prayed God the weather would be fair.

"Wait!" she cried, running between him and the door, a truly desperate look on her beautiful face. "Ranulf, please! I'm sorry. I spoke harshly, and without good cause, I know. You would never seduce such a sweet girl, despite the stories I've heard."

A sliver of shame slid down Ranulf's back, cooling his anger with remorse. "Let me pass, Celeste. We have nothing more to say to one another except goodbye."

Rage flashed in her eyes and twisted the rest of her features. "You would have me believe you love that foolish, ignorant girl? What does she know of love or pleasing a man?"

Ranulf stepped aside, but again she moved to block him. "You would tie yourself to the daughter of a traitor? You would take charity from your friend, for that's what her dowry would be. What's happened to your pride, Ranulf? Your honor?"

"It will be the lady who honors me and makes me proud if she accepts my hand."

"So you haven't asked her yet. I wondered when she didn't know how your brother died."

A look of triumph came to Celeste's face when she saw Ranulf's expression. "Of course I had to tell her," she said with smug satisfaction. "And it's no wonder you didn't. You were afraid she'd never have you if she knew you killed Edmond. What do you think she'll make of that other tale I told her, of the wager you won after I accepted another?"

Ranulf grabbed Celeste by the shoulders and glared into her mocking face. "What did you tell Bea?"

Celeste smiled with triumphant glee. "Why, merely what was told to me about a certain wager— fourteen virgins in fourteen days, and that you won."

"Oh, God," he groaned, stumbling backward as if she'd hit him. Hard.

"What's the matter, Ranulf? Ashamed, are you? You should be!"

As Celeste stood before him, mocking him as his father and his brothers had so often done, Ranulf's pride arose, resolute and strong—the same fierce, determined pride that had taken him all the way to Sir Leonard de Brissy's fortress on foot.

"I was in the back of the church the morning you married, Celeste," he said. "I saw your satisfaction— nay, your *delight*—when you took Lord Fontenbleu's hand and kissed him. You weren't forced to have him. You—you grabbed the chance to be his wife. You threw me off with no more concern that you would a dress you tired of. God's blood, I was naive! But I'm not anymore, and I've found a finer, better woman to love than you could ever be."

"Love?" she scoffed. "What do you know about love? You mooned after me like a little boy! You wrote those horrid poems, those maudlin songs. It hurt my ears to hear you! To be sure, your adoration was flattering, and you do kiss rather well, but marry a penniless, landless fool whose own family cast him out for murder? I would have been mad!"

"As I must have been mad to think I loved you. Fortunately, I've come to my senses."

"You can't have if you're going to wed that tainted creature."

"If there is a tainted creature in Penterwell, you are it. Now I give you good day, Celeste."

The woman he had once desired beyond all reason fell to her knees and threw her arms around him. "Ranulf, I'm sorry!" she cried with seeming sincerity. "I lost my temper. I regret what I did all those years ago. I rue the day I let you go. I'll not speak against Lady Beatrice again, but please don't make me leave."

"I am castellan here and you are no longer welcome," he said as he reached down to raise her to her feet.

"Please, Ranulf, let me stay. I have nowhere else to go!"

"You have your lands, your estates, your castles. Go to one of them."

She shook her head, her hair flying about as if tossed by the wind. "They belong to my husband's nephew because we had no sons. Everything I possess is in this chamber."

He thought of her fine gowns, and the jewels she'd sported. "You're still rich. You can buy yourself a house in London, where you will surely find plenty of suitors anxious to share your wealth."

"No, no," she sobbed, real tears falling down her cheeks and genuine anguish in her no-longer-dulcet voice. "I have no family, no friends there. My parents are dead. They died less than a year after I was married. I have no one—no one cares for me—and London is a cold, cruel place for a woman no longer young."

Ranulf hesitated, torn between leaving this woman who'd once hurt him so deeply and offering her his sympathy, for he remembered well how it felt to be alone and friendless. "You're hardly an old hag, Celeste. You're still one of the most beautiful women I've ever seen, and you're far from ancient."

"Spoken like a man who loves another, younger woman," she said between sobs.

"What would you have me say?" he replied. "I do love another and yes, she is younger. That is not going to change. But you are hardly without resources."

Her hair disheveled, her bed robe gaping to reveal her thin white shift and the breasts beneath, Celeste wiped her eyes with the back of her hand. "May I at least stay here until I can make arrangements to go elsewhere?"

He had not the heart to refuse her. "Very well."

She gave him a sorrowful look that once would have made him do anything she wanted. "Thank you, Ranulf," she said, putting her hands upon his shoulders.

He started to pull back. "Celeste," he warned. "Don't."

"I'm not going to bite you, Ranulf," she murmured, holding him firmly as her bed robe came undone and fell open. "I only want to thank you. A kiss of gratitude and nothing more."

"I knew it!" Maloren screeched from the doorway. "Scoundrels and liars, the pair of you!"

AFTER LEAVING Celeste, Beatrice was determined to go straight to Ranulf until it occurred to her that might be precisely what Celeste wanted: that she go to Ranulf when she was angry and upset and accuse him until he got angry, too.

Even if Ranulf had returned from the village—and she wasn't sure he had—she wasn't going to fall into Celeste's trap.

Nevertheless, she yearned to talk to someone. If Constance had been in Penterwell, she would have run to her. Her cousin always knew what to say to make her feel better, or offer her sound advice. Unfortunately, Constance was far away in Tregellas.

Maloren was out of the question. Indeed, Beatrice fervently hoped Maloren never heard anything about Ranulf making a wager that required him to deflower virgins. That he would do so was ridiculous, of course, but Maloren would surely believe it and waste no time telling everyone she met.

So Beatrice went to visit Wenna, and soon sat holding little Gawan on her lap, tickling his chubby chin. "Oh, isn't he a handsome fellow?" she cooed.

Seated on a low stool nearby, working with her drop spindle, the young woman, who was only a year older than Beatrice, smiled. "I think he's a pretty boy, but then, I'm his mother."

"Oh, trust me, he's a very handsome baby," Beatrice assured her. "How are *you*, Wenna?"

Wenna sighed and stared at the spindle. "Well enough, my lady."

As her son reached up to tug at Beatrice's necklace of simple glass beads, Wenna suddenly regarded Beatrice intently. "Did he mean it, do you think, my lady? Will Sir Ranulf really make my boy a page?"

"I think that if Sir Ranulf said it, you most certainly can believe it," Beatrice replied. "Nor could your son have a better master. Why, Ranulf has made the garrison of Tregellas the most admired in the whole of England for their skill and discipline. One day, they'll say the same thing about the garrison and knights of Penterwell, you'll see. And," she added with significance, "once people start to hear that and know it for a fact, there'll be few places safer to live."

"I hope you're right, my lady."

"And then perhaps the merchants will come with wares that are rare so far from London. You should see some of the garments Lady Celeste has brought with her."

"Tecca says she's very lovely. You're not…?"

Although Wenna's voice trailed off, Beatrice could easily guess what she was wondering about. Probably plenty of other people in Penterwell were wondering, too.

"Lady Celeste knew Sir Ranulf when they were younger," she explained, taking little Gawan's hand and blowing onto his plump palm. "There's no reason she shouldn't visit him, although," she confessed with a wry smile, "I have had a few moments when I wished she wasn't quite so beautiful."

"Sir Ranulf surely couldn't prefer her to you," Wenna said with a conviction that Beatrice found pleasantly flattering.

"Well, for a long time, he didn't pay much attention to me at all," she replied, "and when he did, it was more with a sort of patient forbearance."

"But lately?" Wenna prompted as she reached out to take her child.

"Oh, Wenna, what would you have me say?" Beatrice replied, laughing as she blushed. "Would you have me tell you all my secrets?"

Her expression thoughtful, Wenna opened her bodice and put her baby to suck. "I want you to be happy, my lady, after all you did for me. I don't know if I'd have made it through that night if you hadn't been here."

"I didn't do so very much," Beatrice said, rising to put more wood on the fire.

"I think you did, and all the other women here do, too."

"You did the lion's share of the work," Beatrice noted with a smile.

"So you trust Sir Ranulf?" Wenna asked.

"Absolutely. There is no one I trust more, and the people of Penterwell should trust him, too."

"I'd like to, but I've heard some things, my lady," Wenna said slowly, and quietly, as if she didn't want even her baby to hear. "Things about Sir Ranulf."

Beatrice immediately thought of Celeste's unwelcome revelations. "What have you heard?"

"Myghal told me something about Sir Ranulf and a wager. It was about seducing women, my lady. Fourteen virgins in fourteen days."

Just because someone else had heard that lie didn't make it true, Beatrice told herself. "I'm quite sure Sir Ranulf would never do anything so sordid," she said with firm conviction. "Where did Myghal hear this astonishing tale?"

"From some fishermen down the coast. You also know about Sir Ranulf and his brother, then?"

"I'm equally certain his brother's death was an accident," Beatrice replied. She wondered who else had heard these stories. "Is that why the villagers won't talk to him about what's been happening? Do they really think he's some sort of lascivious rogue who murdered his own brother?"

"Myghal's told nobody but me what he heard, and he only told me because he knows I admire and respect you, and want only the best for you after all you've done for me. He wanted me to warn you, in case you didn't know. He fears you've been deceived by Sir Ranulf."

"I certainly have not," Beatrice declared, rising. "Sir Ranulf is the best of men and it pains me to hear these lies."

Wenna held out her hand. "Please, my lady, don't be angry. That's what I told Myghal—that they had to be lies. I said that if nothing else, your regard for Sir Ranulf meant he was a good and worthy knight. And Myghal, of all people, ought to know how it feels to be mistrusted and looked down on when there's no cause."

"Really?" Beatrice said, sinking back down onto the stool, her curiosity overwhelming her dismay. "Is it because he was the undersheriff?"

"Not just that, my lady," Wenna replied as she moved little Gawan to her other breast. "His family hasn't been trusted here since long before he was born."

"Is there some kind of feud?"

"You could call it that, I suppose," Wenna replied. "Folks say Myghal's family's too sneaky and shifty by far."

"If they're smugglers, I'm not surprised they're devious," Beatrice replied. "But lots of other people here are smugglers. I don't understand why they'd consider those traits a failing."

"Because Myghal's family acts as if everybody else is out to rob them or turn them in. Suspicion breeds suspicion, as well as hard feelings, my lady. But no matter what anybody says, I won't believe Myghal is a bad man, or that he had a hand in Gawan's death."

"They've accused Myghal of that, too?" Beatrice asked, dumbfounded.

Wenna flushed. "He wanted me for his wife, you see, but I chose Gawan."

"What do *you* think?" Beatrice asked, remembering the discomfort she sometimes felt in Myghal's company and wondering if he was not the good-hearted, trustworthy fellow he seemed.

"He couldn't have killed Gawan. Myghal was hurt and upset when I married Gawan, that's for certain, and he said some nasty things, but plenty of men say things they don't mean when they're upset and in their cups."

"Did he ever threaten you or Gawan?"

"Oh, no, my lady, nothing like that! He, um, he called me a bad name. That did me no harm, though, as everybody knew I'd never lain with a man before

I married. Believe me, my lady, in a village the size of Penterwell, they would have known if I had."

Beatrice did believe it. "Then you're quite certain Myghal had nothing to do with your husband's death?"

"I'd swear to it on a Bible, my lady," Wenna confirmed. "He's a good man, is Myghal."

"Obviously Sir Ranulf believes he's trustworthy, or he never would have made him sheriff," Beatrice agreed.

Wenna smiled. "That's what I think, too, although some of them—the ones who should spend less time drinking and more time working—say Myghal's made some sort of devil's bargain with Sir Ranulf to be sheriff."

"I can assure you, he has not. Ranulf wouldn't bargain with anybody when it comes to such things."

As Wenna's expression grew both satisfied and triumphant, Beatrice sincerely hoped, for Wenna's sake, that Myghal was indeed a trustworthy fellow. Nevertheless, she couldn't forget that there had been times she felt less than safe with Myghal, even if she wasn't able to say exactly why.

Perhaps Ranulf should hear of the villagers' opinion of Myghal's family. It was possible Ranulf didn't realize the level of mistrust the villagers had for their new sheriff.

"I'd best be getting back," she said, rising. "Maloren will start worrying, and she doesn't worry in silence."

Wenna bade Beatrice a fond farewell, and as Beatrice left the cottage, the two guards she'd asked to accompany her and who'd been sitting with their backs against the west-facing wall of Wenna's cottage, scrambled to their feet to follow her.

When Beatrice went down the main street, the villagers and merchants greeted her as she passed, either with a smile, a nod or a few words. Then she spotted Myghal hurrying toward her through the small crowd, a smile on his round face. Since he was clearly intent on speaking to her, she waited for him to approach. As he did, she considered him as a possible suitor, as Wenna must have.

Myghal had much to recommend him. As under-sheriff, he had been trusted by Hedyn and Sir Frioc, as well as Ranulf.

In terms of his personal appearance, Myghal was not unattractive, especially when he smiled. His body couldn't compare to Ranulf's, but Ranulf was a trained warrior in his prime. To many women, Myghal would seem appealing enough.

Not to her, though. There was no mystery to Myghal, no sense of hidden depths, no hint of a struggle to overcome loss and pain that made a man more than mere flesh and blood.

What he did have was an air of watchful wariness, as if he was always looking over his shoulder and more than half prepared to flee. Perhaps that accounted for the uneasiness she felt in his presence.

She really shouldn't consider that a lack on his part, given all that had happened here, most recently to Hedyn and Gwenbritha. It couldn't be easy or particularly agreeable to be sheriff of Penterwell now.

Yet Ranulf had faced his share of troubles, and instead of unease, he exuded calm confidence and a willingness to confront whatever difficulties assailed him.

"Good day, my lady," Myghal said in greeting. "What brings you to the village today?"

"I came to visit Wenna," she replied.

"Are you returning to the castle, then?"

"Yes, I am." She saw an opportunity to talk to him about those tales of Ranulf, and took it. "Would you mind walking with me?"

"It'd be my pleasure, my lady."

Perhaps not, she reflected, when he found out what she had to say.

She glanced back at the soldiers a few paces behind. "Myghal will escort me back to the castle," she said to them, "so there's no need for you to follow us. Please go on ahead."

With a nod of acquiescence, the guards started back to the castle, leaving Beatrice and Myghal to make their way at a more leisurely pace.

Beatrice took a few moments to best decide how to begin, then finally chose to be direct. "I understand from Wenna that you've heard certain stories about Sir Ranulf."

Myghal flushed and looked around at the stalls and those studying the wares available there, or talking among themselves. "Yes, I have, but if you please, my lady," he answered quietly, "I'd rather not talk about this in so crowded a place. We can take the back lanes to the castle."

Although by rights she shouldn't be alone anywhere with any man to whom she was not at least betrothed, Beatrice didn't refuse. She wanted to speak to Myghal more than she feared censure.

"Wenna told me some things you've heard about Sir Ranulf," Beatrice said as Myghal led her past the chandler's and down an alley.

He colored, but his expression was resolute for all that. "I've been wanting to talk to you about them, too, my lady."

"Suppose you tell me exactly what you've heard, and where, and when?"

"I was in Terwallen the other day," Myghal began, "asking about those two men who went missing, and I met a boatman there who generally plies his trade on the Thames. He was down visiting his sister, and I happened upon him in a tavern. When he heard me speak of Sir Ranulf, he whistled and called him.. well, my lady, it's not fit for your ears. But it made me so angry, I wanted to hit him. I called him—the boatman—a liar and a rogue and a few other names I won't repeat.

"Then another fellow come up. He wasn't a

friend of the boatman, but he said the Londoner was right, for he'd heard the same thing—that this Sir Ranulf, now castellan of Penterwell, had drowned his own brother when they was both boys, so his father cast him out. Sir Ranulf trained with Sir Leonard, and then come to London, to court, a few years back. It took Sir Ranulf a while to discover Southwark, but when he did, he went…well, wild, I guess you could say. Drinking and carousing, and he made this wager with one of the tavern keepers. He bet the man fifty marks that he could bed fourteen virgins in a fortnight and bring the man their bloody shifts as proof."

Beatrice hadn't heard that last part, and while it sickened her, it was also more proof that this had to be a lie. She couldn't even begin to imagine Ranulf in a dirty, stinking tavern offering up women's soiled shifts as proof of such a disgusting wager.

"And according to the boatman and this other fellow, that's exactly what he did. I didn't want to believe it, neither, my lady," Myghal finished, giving her a sorrowful look, "but I thought you ought to know."

"I know Sir Ranulf, and that's enough to make me certain that wager could *not* have happened," she said staunchly. "And I certainly hope you aren't going to tell anyone else these terrible lies."

"This way, my lady," Myghal said, turning down another lane.

Beatrice halted in confusion. "Why this way? This doesn't lead to the castle. This leads to the road that goes to the shore."

"Aye, the main road. At a fork we turn left to the castle, instead of right to the shore."

"Why don't we go left now and make directly for the castle?"

"Because there's a stream that way we'd have to cross, and it's a bit far for you to leap, I think."

Because she'd seen the stream on her visits to the village, Beatrice couldn't dispute its existence; even so, she was reluctant to follow him.

She told herself she was being ridiculous. Ranulf trusted Myghal; so had Hedyn and Sir Frioc. Nevertheless, she couldn't ignore her qualms.

"We could turn back," she suggested, "and go another way."

"Trust me, my lady, this way is faster."

"I think you underestimate me, Myghal," Beatrice said as she headed in the direction of the castle. "I'm sure I can jump the stream and I'm too hungry to take the longer way."

Myghal jogged after her and, as he neared, she quickened her pace, even as she silently chastised herself for letting her imagination worry her when surely there was no need.

"My lady, please," he called out. "What's wrong?

She tripped and fell, landing hard on her ungloved hands, her knees somewhat cushioned by her skirt and shift. Biting back a curse, she scrambled to her feet as Myghal arrived beside her.

"There's no need to run, my lady," he said. "No rush to get where you're going."

His voice and his words made her blood run cold.

CHAPTER THIRTEEN

BEFORE BEATRICE COULD answer Myghal, a soldier carrying a banner, with more men behind him, came around a bend in the road.

Beatrice let out a sigh of relief. That familiar banner belonged to Sir Jowan, whose estate bordered Tregellas.

Her relief diminished somewhat when she realized it wasn't the jovial Sir Jowan leading the armed party. It was his fair-haired son, Kiernan, the man she was sure had wanted to marry Constance before Merrick had returned to Tregellas after his fifteen-year absence. Constance, however, had once told Beatrice that whatever Kiernan wanted, she didn't want *him*.

Beatrice had been glad. Kiernan was a nice enough fellow, but he was no Merrick or Ranulf.

For one thing, he was vain. At present he was wearing a heavily embroidered surcoat of rich deep blue and silver. His mail gleamed in the sunlight, as did his spurs and helmet. His horse, a fine black beast, was likewise attired in blue and silver, from its bridle to its britchens.

Kiernan had some right to his vanity, she supposed, for he was a good-looking fellow. However, he wasn't as handsome as Henry, or as darkly attractive as Merrick, and he certainly didn't make her heart race like Ranulf.

Having reached them, Kiernan ordered his men to halt. He sprang down from his prancing gelding, its trappings jingling, and hurried toward her. "Lady Beatrice, what's happened?" he asked as he surveyed her muddy garments. He darted a suspicious glance at Myghal. "What are you doing on the road with this fellow?"

"This is Myghal, the sheriff of Penterwell," she answered, quite calm now that her imagination was once again under her control and determined to ensure Kiernan didn't get the wrong idea. "He's escorting me back to the castle."

"You have no other soldiers with you?"

"I need no more," she said, not at all pleased by Kiernan's arrogant tone. "I'm quite safe with Myghal."

Kiernan's expression as he looked again at Myghal told her he didn't agree. "Sir Ranulf should take better care of his guests."

"I did have more guards with me, until Myghal offered to go with me."

Kiernan reached out to take her scraped right hand, bringing it to his lips. "Even so, Sir Ranulf should take better care of you. I would."

Sweet Mother of God! She'd always been pleasant

to Kiernan, but she'd never encouraged him to think there was anything more between them, and she never would.

"What a kind *friend* you are," she replied, trying to extricate her hand from his grasp without grimacing with pain.

He saw her reaction and examined her palm. "You *are* hurt. We must get you to the castle at once!"

He made it sound as if she was bleeding profusely.

"It's not that serious," she protested.

"I *insist*," he declared.

He had no right to insist she do anything. "I shall have to walk. As you can see, I couldn't possibly hold a horse's reins, even if one of your men was so kind as to lend me his."

"I'll escort the lady," Myghal said stiffly, and it was obvious he felt slighted by Kiernan—with good cause, too.

"I'm quite content to return with the sheriff," Beatrice agreed. "Just tell the guards at the gate who you are."

"I'm not about to let you walk to the castle in such a state and with this fellow," Kiernan declared, retrieving his horse.

"I'm quite capable of walking," she said firmly. "It's my hands that are hurt, not my feet."

"The sooner your wounds are tended to, the better," Kiernan replied.

And then, without so much as a by-your-leave,

he picked her up and hoisted her, protesting, onto his saddle. In the next moment, he'd mounted behind her.

Myghal drew his sword. "Sir, you'd best let the lady down."

Kiernan's men pulled their swords from their scabbards.

"It's all right," Beatrice quickly said before Kiernan's men hurt Myghal. "Sir Kiernan's going to let me down. Aren't you, Kiernan?"

It wasn't so much a request as a demand. She didn't appreciate being hauled up as if she were a piece of baggage, nor did she appreciate the way he held her tight against him, his arm like a vise around her stomach.

Kiernan's pursed lips told her that her request was falling on deaf ears and instead of answering her or letting her down, he addressed Myghal. "I assure you, I'm not going to harm her." His tone grew even more haughty. "Whoever you are, it is not your place to order *me*."

With that, Kiernan kicked his horse into a bone-jarring trot. Beatrice twisted to look back over her shoulder at an obviously enraged Myghal, who had to jump out of the way of the clumps of mud and stones tossed up by the hooves of Kiernan's horse.

Truly angry now, she said, "That was the sheriff, not some a beggar on the road."

"And you are a lady, not a peasant."

"Yet you can pick me up like a load of wood? You should have treated Myghal with more respect, as both the man and his office deserve."

"He should have found a horse for you to ride."

"What are you doing here anyway?" she demanded, quite certain Ranulf hadn't invited him. Not only did Ranulf have no time for guests, considering what else he was dealing with, but she was fairly sure, judging by the way Ranulf looked at Kiernan sometimes, that he thought Sir Jowan's son a rather pampered and spoiled young man—as, indeed, he was.

Kiernan looked down at her, his expression both grim and pompous. "I've come to take you back to Tregellas."

She squirmed in Kiernan's arms, trying to get a better look at his face. "Did Lord Merrick and Lady Constance ask you to fetch me?"

He flushed and stared into the space between his horse's ears. "Not precisely."

So they hadn't. "Who do you think you are? You have no right to come here and—"

He spurred his horse to a faster pace, making her gasp and clutch the saddle lest she fall.

"What's come over you?" she asked when she caught her breath. "What do you think you're doing?"

"I couldn't sit idly by while your reputation is destroyed. Your visit to Penterwell is the talk of every hall and tavern in Cornwall."

"So what if it is?" she retorted, her sore hands forgotten as her grip tightened on the saddle. "I have every right to visit Sir Ranulf, as Constance and Merrick obviously believe, too."

"Your guardians let you come because they love you and feel sorry for you and so they indulge you," Kiernan answered, managing to sound aggravatingly condescending even on a cantering horse.

She had had all she could stand of Kiernan, whose generous father indulged his every whim. "Halt this horse and let me down!"

He didn't. Instead, his arm clasped her closer, as if he feared she might jump, which she was tempted to do. She'd almost rather risk a broken limb than listen to anything more Kiernan had to say. Unfortunately, she knew from her conversations with the apothecary that any break could become very serious indeed, so she had no choice but to stay where she was.

"Stop this horse and let me down," she said instead, "or I'll scream."

"There's no need for hysterics."

Hysterics? He thought *this* was hysterics? The man had no idea. "Unless you want me to demonstrate just how *hysterical* I can be, you'll let me down at once!"

"I won't let you walk unguarded back to the castle," Kiernan replied. "Forgive me if I've upset you, but you have no choice in this matter."

"You force me to be blunt. My reputation is not yours to guard, and it never will be. Now let me down or I'll jump."

Instead of answering, he urged his horse into a gallop, making it impossible for her to risk a leap from the saddle.

If she could have gotten her hands around Kiernan's neck, she would have strangled him unconscious to get away. Unfortunately, she couldn't do that, so she had to endure the humiliation of arriving at Penterwell in this embarrassing, unnecessary fashion, which would surely be talked about in the barracks and tavern and cottages for at least a fortnight.

The guards at the gate stared in wide-eyed wonder as Kiernan finally reined in his horse. "My lady?" one of them asked, sounding as if he wasn't at all certain he could believe his eyes.

"Yes. And this is *Sir* Kiernan of Penderston," she replied, imbuing Kiernan's title with as much scorn as she could muster, for Kiernan was obviously *not* a chivalrous knight. "Please let us pass. The rest of Sir Kiernan's escort will be arriving later."

The guards dutifully made way for them, exchanging both quizzical and rather wary looks as they passed.

"Sir Ranulf isn't going to like this," the one who'd spoken to Lady Beatrice noted.

"Not at all," his comrade answered, sagely shaking his head.

BEATRICE, MEANWHILE, stifled a groan when she saw
Ranulf leaning against the stable wall, his arms crossed,
his expression inscrutable. What must he be thinking?
Damn Kiernan and his arrogant presumption!

"Let me go," she said through clenched teeth as
Kiernan brought his prancing horse to a halt, but her
captor only held her tighter.

She was never going to forgive him for this—*never!*

"Well, well, well, what have we here?" Ranulf
remarked as he sauntered toward them. "Young Sir
Kiernan of Penderston with Lady Beatrice on his
horse like a prize of war."

Beatrice tried to wiggle free of Kiernan's grasp.
"Kiernan met me when I was coming back with
Myghal and he *insisted* I ride back with him. Indeed,
he gave me no choice at all. He lifted me up onto his
saddle and left Myghal behind on the road."

When Kiernan replied, he didn't sound at all irked
by her answer. "She was walking on the road like a
peasant and without an escort. She'd also fallen and
cut her hands."

Ranulf's gaze flashed to Beatrice's hands and
worry darkened his brow.

"It's nothing. I tripped, that's all. And then Kiernan arrived and—"

"Was kind enough to bring you back," Ranulf
interrupted. "For which I'm grateful, although I ap-
plaud your indignation for Myghal's sake. However,

I'm sure he'll recover. In the meantime, you should thank Sir Kiernan for his kindness."

Beatrice kept her mouth shut, not particularly pleased with either of them at the moment.

"I have come to take Lady Beatrice home to Tregellas," Kiernan announced.

Ranulf raised a brow. "Have you, indeed? Am I to assume you mean to carry her back immediately and in such an interesting manner?"

Kiernan flushed with embarrassment, as well he should. "No."

"I'm glad to hear it, as she has her own charming little mare to take her back to Tregellas when the time comes."

Ranulf strolled closer to Kiernan's horse. "Since it is not yet that time, allow me to help you dismount, my lady."

Given the smile she saw lurking in his hazel eyes, and especially since he held up his arms to help her, it no longer seemed a totally terrible thing to have been brought home on Kiernan's horse.

Beatrice duly placed her hands on Ranulf's broad shoulders as he put his around her waist. Jumping down, she delighted in the feel of her body so close to his, although she had to wince as her palms rubbed against his tunic.

Ranulf immediately took her hands in his and turned them over. "Next time you ought to wear gloves," he said as he studied them.

"She shouldn't have been walking about the village without her maid *and* a guard, either," Kiernan said as he slipped from his horse to stand beside her.

Still holding Beatrice's hands in his callused ones, Ranulf turned his cool-eyed gaze onto Kiernan. "My lady's maidservant was otherwise engaged.

"Maloren's in the kitchen and likely to be engaged there for some time," he said to Beatrice. "Tecca will help you dress for the evening meal."

Although she was glad she wouldn't have to hear Maloren grumble as she changed, Beatrice couldn't help feeling that she'd been dismissed, until Ranulf tucked her arm in his.

He ordered the groomsmen who'd come out of the stable to take charge of the mounts and summoned the garrison commander to look after Kiernan's escort. Then he called for another servant to take care of their guest's baggage.

"I didn't bring any," Kiernan frostily replied, "since I won't be staying."

"Oh? What a pity," Ranulf replied with a complete absence of sincerity. "However, I'm sure you don't intend to ride back tonight. You would be benighted on the moor. So you're welcome to my hall and allow me to offer you some wine while I tend to Lady Beatrice's wounds."

"*You'll* tend to them?" Kiernan replied with both surprise and obvious disapproval.

Beatrice's heart, however, began to beat with

delighted excitement. She didn't enjoy being hurt, but if it meant some time alone with Ranulf, she couldn't be sorry.

"Of course," Ranulf replied in answer to Kiernan's query. "In my many years of tourneying and battle, I've often had occasion to tend to minor injuries. Shall we, my lady?"

Preventing any further objections from Kiernan, they turned and started toward the hall, leaving the young knight to follow.

Those terrible stories about Ranulf had to be lies, Beatrice told herself as she walked beside him. He couldn't possibly have callously murdered his brother, or seduced those women.

They entered the hall, to discover Lady Celeste enthroned on the dais, garbed like an empress. She wore a lovely gown of rich scarlet velvet trimmed with golden threads. She rose like an empress, too, when she saw them approach, making Beatrice feel woefully underdressed and muddy and disheveled.

"Lady Celeste," Ranulf said as they reached her, "may I present Sir Kiernan of Penderston, a noble neighbor of the lord and lady of Tregellas."

Celeste gracefully bowed her head. "Greetings, Sir Kiernan."

"I'm delighted to meet you, my lady," Kiernan replied with an even deeper bow as he stepped forward. Staring up at her face like one in a daze, he took her hand and kissed the back of it.

Perhaps, Beatrice thought, she had no more need to worry about Kiernan making her an unwelcome offer of marriage.

"I believe I can leave you safely in Lady Celeste's care while I tend to Lady Beatrice's wounds, Sir Kiernan," Ranulf said with the merest hint of a smirk. "She fell and cut her hands. I have some ointment that should help their healing and take away the pain. Come along, Lady Beatrice."

Although she was delighted by the opportunity to be alone with him, Beatrice couldn't resist teasing him a little. "Come along, indeed!" she whispered as they crossed the hall toward the stairs. "You make me sound like an errant child."

Ranulf gave her a look that made her heart race. "I assure you, Bea, I've never thought of you as a child."

Her heartbeat quickened and hot desire seemed to bubble in her veins. "My lord, didn't you once say to me I should never be alone in a room with a man, and especially with you?" she asked with merry insolence, the memory of that other time she'd been alone with him as fresh in her mind as if it had happened yesterday.

"I did, and I was quite right to do so," he replied. "This time, however, I'm acting as your physician. I assure you, I shall conduct myself with proper propriety."

"How disappointing."

"Expect nothing else, Bea," he cautioned.

She blushed with embarrassment, wondering if she'd been too forward. Well, she knew she had, but she'd hoped...wanted...

Once in his chamber, Ranulf went to his wooden chest and drew out a small clay vessel covered with a waxed cloth. "Sit on this stool," he said as he uncovered the jar.

A light, minty scent filled the air while she obeyed.

"Hold out your hands."

She did that, too. "Is that sicklewort ointment?"

He nodded. "Yes. Constance gave it to me. It's what she put on Merrick's arm when she sewed his wound from the boar spear."

Beatrice shuddered at that memory as Ranulf began to spread the slick ointment thinly over her open palms. "Does that hurt?" he asked, raising his eyes.

"No. I was just remembering Merrick's wound. I was supposed to help Constance then, but Merrick was so angry, I ran away."

Ranulf laughed softly. "When Merrick's angry, everybody runs away, except Constance. She's a very brave woman, and so are you," he said, smiling in a way that made Beatrice want to kiss him even more. "I doubt I could keep my head during a birthing."

He finished and wiped his hands on a square of linen. "There now. Better?"

She felt much better, and not just because of the ointment. "Yes."

"Then I suppose we should go below and join our guests."

Beatrice knew he was right, and yet she wasn't willing to let this opportunity to speak with him alone go by. "Not just yet, Ranulf, please," she said, rising.

Despite her outward bravado, she was suddenly afraid. What if those things she'd heard about him were true and he was not the man she thought he was?

She had to find out, one way or another. "Ranulf, did you kill your brother?"

As his face reddened, she rushed on before he could answer, driven by her dread. "That's what Celeste told me, and apparently other people here have heard it, too. Of course *I* don't believe it. Well, or if I do, it's only because you told me your brothers were cruel. I can believe that one of them attacked you and you had to defend yourself. Drown or be drowned, and so you did. That's why you're afraid to be too near the water. And oh, how terrible it must have been!"

He didn't speak.

"I'm sorry, but I had to ask, although I should have been more diplomatic. But I don't suppose there's a tactful way to ask such a thing, is there?"

His eyes were as cold as marble in winter, his expression hard as iron. "I did kill my brother, and I meant to do it."

She sat heavily on the stool and stared at him with horrified dismay.

Ranulf looked down at her lovely, trusting face.

The time had come to tell her everything. These were not the circumstances he would have chosen to make his confession, but he had lost the chance to choose.

"I killed Edmond, my brother, the eldest son and favorite of my father, heir to his estate. We were fighting and fell into the ocean, and I held him under the water until he drowned."

"But...but surely he attacked you first," she protested. "You were protecting yourself."

He shook his head. "I wanted to kill him. I wanted him dead."

"Because he'd hurt you?"

"He hadn't laid a hand on me that day. It was because he'd drowned my dog."

"Oh, Ranulf," she murmured, sorrow and pity in her beautiful blue eyes.

"I found Felix lying on the shore, whimpering, with a rock tied around his neck. Edmond was furious. 'Your mangy cur mated with my best bitch,' he said, and before I could stop him, he picked up Felix and the rock and threw them as far out into the water as he could. Edmond was very strong."

Ranulf closed his eyes and grimaced. "I can still hear poor Felix yelping. And then the splash."

He opened his eyes again and regarded her steadily, although his whole body began to shake. "I tried to go into the water to save him, but Edmond held me back. I struggled and kicked and hit him."

That same terrible feeling of helplessness washed over Ranulf. He was twelve years old again and unable to save the one creature he loved. "Edmond let go and told me it was too late. Felix must be dead. That's when I completely lost my head. I didn't think, didn't care about anything except that Edmond had killed Felix. I threw myself at him and we both went into the water. Later I realized I must have caught him off guard. That's the only way I could have managed to hold him down the way I did, although I nearly drowned, too. Our father came and hauled me out. By then, it was too late for Edmond. He was dead."

Ranulf ran his hands through his hair and drew in a ragged breath. "I didn't care. I didn't care about what I'd done. Nor did I care that my father cast me out. I was glad that day, Bea.

"Glad," he finished, the word almost a croak in his tight, dry throat.

Bea rose and went to him. Without saying a word, she put her arms around him and gently pulled him close.

In her warm embrace, in the softness of her encircling arms, he felt her forgiveness and understanding. Silently she gave him the comfort he hadn't known since his mother's death.

Sorrow for his lost dog, for the mother whose life had ended when he was so young, as well as for the boy he had been, welled up within him.

He closed his eyes, trying to hold back the tears,

because they were a weakness. "What kind of man kills his own brother and doesn't care?" he asked hoarsely, his throat constricted with the effort to be strong.

"A man who's never had a reason to care. Who's never had the love he deserved. Except that you weren't a man then. You were just a boy."

He drew in another halting breath and, as a tear slid unheeded down his cheek, he said, "I didn't feel guilt or remorse. I felt *free,* free to do what I wanted, and I wanted to learn how to fight, so that nobody could ever hurt me again. My mother had talked of Sir Leonard de Brissy, and I knew where his castle was, so I made my way there. Praise God, he took me in. The rest you know."

"Did you tell Sir Leonard what had happened?"

"Yes. That's why he didn't make me learn to swim like the others."

"Merrick and Henry don't know, do they? About your brother, or your fear of the water?"

"No, I've been too ashamed to tell them. And my family didn't seek me out to charge me with the crime. My father didn't want the family name besmirched, you see. Better my brother's death be deemed an unfortunate accident and I a useless, unmanageable runaway than have the truth revealed."

"If Merrick and Henry knew, they wouldn't condemn you, and they never would have dumped you from that boat."

Determined to confess all now that he had started

on this path, he said, "Celeste told you something else. About a wager."

Bea nodded. "She told me you wagered you could seduce fourteen virgins in a fortnight. She said you won, and you brought their shifts as proof."

Her eyes pleaded with him to tell her that was a lie.

He could not. He would not. If she was ever to really love him, she had to know everything. "I did make such a wager, Bea, and I won."

CHAPTER FOURTEEN

"BUT IT WASN'T fourteen virgins. It was four," Ranulf confessed as Bea stared at him with shock. "And as if that shame were not enough, I took the evidence of my success to the man with whom I'd made the wager."

His guilt and remorse increased even more as her expression changed to one of revulsion.

He rushed on, desperately trying—hoping—to regain what little might remain of her affection. "The moment Ollie put the winnings in my hands, I knew how Judas felt. I made him swear never to tell anyone. There were some who'd been in the tavern who'd witnessed the wager and—worse—the winning of it. I searched them out and threatened them with death if they breathed a word. I gave the money to the church, thinking the taint might be washed away if it was used for good. When I returned to Sir Leonard's castle, I told no one what I'd done. I still pray every day for God's forgiveness." He hung his head. "Now, Bea, I humbly ask for yours."

Her face a pale mask of disappointment and dismay, Bea answered like one in a daze. "But I've been championing you, proclaiming your innocence. Saying that story had to be a lie, that you were too good, too honorable to do anything so lewd and disgusting."

He held out his hands in supplication. "Bea, I'm sorry for what I did. I've *been* sorry ever since. I've cursed myself a hundred—nay, a thousand times, and felt sick with remorse. And never have I felt worse than when I met you. Never have I felt more soiled, more stained, than when you smiled at me in your youthful innocence and looked at me with love."

She raised her hands as if to hold him off and began to back away from him, her silence more upsetting than curses or a harsh denunciation would be.

He followed her and desperately tried to explain, to win back her good opinion, or at least a tiny portion of it. "When I made that wager, I was drunk, and half-mad with rage and jealousy."

She stared at him as if she'd never seen him before. Perhaps, in her determination to see him for a man worthy of her love, she never really had.

"Oh, Ranulf," she whispered, "what of those poor women you seduced? Whether it was four or fourteen or forty, you weren't drunk when you did that. You gave no thought to them at all, did you? You were cruel and selfish, more so than I would ever have believed you could be."

If he thought he'd seen her heart break before, it was nothing compared to the recrimination in her eyes as she regarded him now. "Bea, I—"

"No, Ranulf, say no more!" she cried, turning away as if she couldn't even bear to look at him. "Your brother's death, done in the heat of anger and sorrow when you were so young—your rage, the need for vengeance—that I could understand and excuse. But the way you used those women… You cold-bloodedly sought them out and seduced them only to win a wager to assuage your wounded pride." She shook her head. "You are not the man I thought you were."

Celeste's rejection had been painful, but it was nothing compared to this. The terrible despair. The awful sorrow. The horrible finality. The knowledge that in Bea's lovely eyes, he was despicable, not worthy of her regard, or her respect.

In spite of that bitter realization, he was still a man of pride, for his pride was strong—strong enough to sustain a boy as he walked toward his goal and enable him to stand tall when he reached it. What was left of Ranulf's shattered self-respect rose and came to his aid now.

"No, I'm not the man you thought I was," he said with cold deliberation. "I tried to warn you, but you would not listen."

She looked at him then, with sorrow and grief etched on her sweet face. Her eyes shone with unshed tears, the sight ripping into his wretched heart and making a mockery of that manly pride.

"Perhaps I *am* ignorant and naive," she said quietly. "I thought Celeste was trying to poison my mind against you. I thought everyone else was repeating the same baseless rumors. I wouldn't let myself believe you were anything but good and noble."

He had hoped and asked too much of her. He had killed his brother. He had callously seduced women. He had dishonored them, and himself. No woman of virtue and honor would—or should—welcome his love.

It had been a mistake to believe otherwise.

Never again. He would be alone, as he must and always would be.

"I was wrong to hope," he said at last. "I've been living in a dream, wishing that some of your goodness, your purity, would help to cleanse me. But I was wrong. I'm not fit to be near you, let alone to love you, and God knows I shouldn't ask to marry you."

Bea nearly groaned aloud. She had waited weeks to hear him say that he loved her and had lived in hope he would ask for her hand in marriage. Now her optimistic dreams seemed a cruel jest. Ranulf was not the man she'd fallen in love with. He was…something else.

He was not the noble knight, the chivalrous friend, the handsome, desired lover. He was a man capable of cold-blooded seduction, of heartless cruelty to women who'd done him no harm.

"There is one thing more I must tell you," he said, his face like a statue, his expression resolute.

"I don't want to hear any more," she protested, half commanding, half pleading, as she ran to the door.

He crossed the room and stood in front of it, blocking her way. "No, Bea, I want you to know everything, so you'll hear this, too, from my own lips."

Those lips that had kissed her with such passion and tenderness. Those lips that had uttered lies to woo women into his bed.

"Today I was in Celeste's chamber," he continued inexorably. "I was summoned there by her maid. Celeste embraced me and Maloren saw us together."

Beatrice closed her eyes, fighting her despair, summoning her strength. She should not care about this, not after the other things he'd confessed. But she did. God help her, she did, and it was like a dagger through her heart.

His voice softened, more like the loving Ranulf she'd wanted him to be. "No matter what else you believe of me, Bea, no matter what Maloren or anyone says to you, I'm innocent of any wrongdoing with Celeste."

Opening her eyes, Beatrice looked up at him, this man she'd thought she'd love until the day she died. The first man to arouse her passionate desires.

This stranger.

"Let me pass, Ranulf," she said as she forced her feet to move toward the door. "I can't bear to be near you now."

He stood aside and when she fumbled for the door

latch, he opened it for her. She wrapped her arms around her body as if touching him would kill her, then slipped past him and away.

WHEN SHE WAS GONE, Ranulf went to the window and stared out at the sky, then the castle he commanded.

He'd thought he had come a long way since he'd left Beauvieux. He had dared to hope that he might yet find happiness and contentment.

Obviously Bea had not been the only one to harbor impossible dreams that were doomed to fail.

He had been a fool and, unlike Bea, he didn't have the excuse of youthful innocence.

There was only one thing left to do: his duty as castellan of Penterwell. He must and would find out who had murdered Hedyn, Gwenbritha, Gawan and the others, and bring them to justice.

WITHOUT CONSCIOUS THOUGHT, knowing only that she wanted—needed—to be alone, Bea stumbled toward her bedchamber. She closed the door behind her and staggered to the bed. She sat heavily and stared at the wall opposite as she tried to comprehend the full import of Ranulf's confession.

Such terrible things, and especially the heartless seduction of those innocent young women. How could he? She had thought him the most noble and chivalrous of men.

She'd been wrong. So very wrong. She couldn't

love him now. Over and over, this rang through her mind. His reasons simply did not excuse his actions.

How could she have been so wrong? How could Constance and Merrick? And Henry?

As those tumultuous thoughts and questions whirled around her distraught mind, the door to the chamber burst open and Maloren appeared on the threshold.

"There you are, my lamb!" she cried as she hurried inside. She paused and regarded her mistress with both triumph and concern on her familiar features. "You've heard already, then?"

Beatrice raised her eyes, yet before she could speak, Maloren heaved a sigh full of motherly dismay and hurried to sit beside her. She put her arm around Beatrice and gently pressed her charge's head against her shoulder in a comforting embrace.

"There, there, my lambkin," she crooned. "He's not worth it. There'll be other men—better men. Don't cry now."

"I'm not crying," Beatrice said dully.

"No? Well, that's good. He's not worth a single tear. Didn't I warn you about that devil's spawn, my lambkin, and her, too, with her silks and velvets? I knew no good could come from that redheaded demon, and now he's hurt you, just as I feared. And then to see him with my own eyes with that woman! I just about fell into a fit when I saw them together. He knew he'd been caught, too, sending me off to the kitchen with barely a word except I was to stay there until sent for. Wanted to try to smooth it over with you, I don't doubt, and tell some pretty lies. But I can see you're too clever to believe them, whatever he said."

"What exactly did you see, Maloren?" she asked, wondering if Ranulf had lied to her about Celeste and determined to learn the truth, no matter how much it hurt.

"I don't think you need to hear—"

"Please, Maloren. I want to know."

Maloren didn't dare refuse, not when her darling used that tone, and even if she might upset her more. "They were together, close together, just about to kiss."

"But not yet kissing?"

"They either had or were going to. What difference does it make?" Maloren demanded as she got to her feet and went to the small chest nearest the table. She threw it open and began to pack the things lying on the table. "What a despicable, dishonorable lout! Thank the saints that nice young Kiernan's come to take us home."

Home? Maloren meant Tregellas. She thought they should go back to Tregellas.

She ought to want to leave here and never see Ranulf again. She should be anxious to get away from him, after everything he'd done. She was, wasn't she?

She rubbed her aching head. She couldn't think,

couldn't plan, with Maloren bustling about the chamber. "Maloren, please, that can wait until later. I'd like to lie down and rest. My head aches."

Maloren instantly ceased her packing and regarded Beatrice with worry. "I'll fetch you some wine, and something to eat."

Beatrice shook her head. "No, no, I'm not hungry." She couldn't even think of food. "All I need is rest and quiet, Maloren, please."

"You rest then, my lamb. I'll bring you something to eat later, something that Much hasn't managed to ruin. You lie down and leave everything to your Maloren, lambkin."

With that, Maloren mercifully crept out of the chamber as if Beatrice were already asleep.

But there was no rest for Beatrice then, or for the rest of the day. Her mind raced frantically, returning over and over again to the things Ranulf had said, the horrible truths he had revealed, as she tried to decide what to think. And what to do.

SHE STILL HAD NO ANSWER when Maloren returned with a tray containing fresh bread and a mutton stew that smelled delicious. Regardless of the savory aroma, however, Beatrice couldn't eat. Indeed, she felt as if she would never be hungry again. Nevertheless, for Maloren's sake, she managed to drink some wine and nibble on some bread.

That seemed to satisfy Maloren, who insisted on

doing some more packing before she finally stopped
fussing and prepared for bed. When Maloren fell
asleep on her pallet by the door, Beatrice rose from
her bed. She quietly drew on her bed robe and soft,
doeskin slippers. She walked slowly to the door and
eased it open without disturbing Maloren. Then she
went to Ranulf's bedchamber. The door was closed,
but a dim light shone beneath.

He wasn't asleep, either.

She had to see him, to speak to him. She couldn't
go another hour, another moment, with this weight
pressing on her heart.

She opened the door and stepped into his room.

Wearing only his breeches, Ranulf stood by the
window, his hands splayed on either side of the
window as he looked out at the night sky, seemingly
oblivious to the chilly air. Equally motionless, she
studied the broad, naked expanse of the powerful
warrior's back and shoulders, his narrow waist and
slim hips, the strong, muscular legs and arms that
bespoke hours in the saddle and wielding weapons.
She noted the myriad small scars from several minor
wounds that crisscrossed his flesh glowing bronze in
the candlelight.

At the same time, she saw another Ranulf. The
lonely, loveless boy who would fiercely avenge the
death of the only creature he'd loved, even if he died
to do it. The young man who'd offered his heart to a
woman who had not seen his merit and rejected him.

The spurned and angry man who'd sought some way to prove that he was worthy of desire.

Was it any wonder he'd sought revenge in a woman's bed? That in the first flush of his rejection, he would make that wager, and do his best to win it?

Too many people who should have loved Ranulf had not. His family had abandoned him and all but cast him off even before he'd killed his brother, as if he were garbage to be ground beneath their heels. The woman who had first won his love had chosen another.

How could she, who claimed to love him, abandon him, too? And if she could, what then did that say about her love? That it was as shallow as Celeste's, as selfish as that of his violent family?

It was not. She loved him as she always had. No, she loved him more. Before, he had been like a hero from a legendary tale, a figure of romance, of mystery and allure, forbidden and yet, oh, so seductive—but he had not been a man.

It was a man she loved now, one of flesh and blood, of sins and flaws, as well as honor and chivalry. A man who needed her love, as she needed his. A man she would never abandon, believing as she did that he loved her, too. "Ranulf?"

He whirled around. "Bea! What are you doing here? Go back to bed."

"No," she said as she walked toward him. "Not until you hear what I have to say."

He crossed the room to grab his shirt from the top

of the chest. "If all you want to do is berate me, consider me berated," he said as he pulled it on and started toward the door, presumably to open it for her.

"I don't want to berate you, Ranulf."

He came to a dead halt. "You don't?"

"No. I came to tell you that I still love you."

"How can you after all the things I've done?" he asked warily. "You shouldn't. You should find another, better man, Bea, one who can give you the pure and honest love you deserve."

"There is no finer, better man, Ranulf. Your father and brothers tried to kill what was good and honorable in you, but they didn't succeed. You have suffered and been made the stronger, better for it.

"How can I not love a man who's earned the admiration and respect of everyone in Tregellas, who's turned the garrison there into the envy of every lord in England, and who helped Henry fight off an army of mercenaries even though his forces were outnumbered—and who's done all this while claiming he's merely doing his duty or helping a friend. You take no vain pride in anything you do, Ranulf, even when you could."

She gently took hold of his upper arms. "You make light of everything, thinking nobody sees the pain you try to hide. But I see it, Ranulf, although you struggle to keep your pain to yourself, to bear that burden alone.

"I was upset by what you'd done. What woman

wouldn't be, to think the man she'd adored for months could be so callous? But you were hurt when you made that wager and didn't care if you hurt somebody else, so long as your own pain was eased."

He drew in a ragged breath. "Even so—"

"You shouldn't have done it and the remorse has tormented you ever since. That alone tells me that you're a good man, if one who has flaws, as I do. As everyone does. But Ranulf, how many noblemen despoil virgins for sport without a second thought? How many noblemen would have treated me, a virgin ripe and eager for the taking, as you have, if they had the chance?

"Don't you see, Ranulf? Your treatment of me has shown me better than a thousand words that you are not a lascivious lout who thinks only of his own desire. That the youth who acted as he did after being spurned by Celeste is not the man who stands here today. If that were so, I would have been in your bed months ago."

"Bea," he warned, her name almost a plea as she stood before him, close enough to touch.

"Are you going to tell me to go away? That I should leave before you have your way with me?" She smiled then, with all the love she felt. "I know that if I asked you to keep your distance, you would. That if I told you to leave this room, you would without hesitation. That my honor is as safe as it could ever be, even here, even now."

She clasped her hands together with all the fervor she felt. "But oh, my darling, I love you with all my heart, with every fiber of my being, as much as I *can* love. I'm yours, and I always will be. Please don't send me away tonight, Ranulf. Let me be with you, now and always, so that you're never alone again, for as long as we both live."

As he looked at her, loving her, cherishing her, honoring her, Ranulf knew what he should do. What he ought to do. What honor demanded. What his conscience counseled. He should make her leave. She shouldn't stay.

But he couldn't. He couldn't cast off the love she offered. He couldn't turn away the great gift she held out to him. He couldn't refuse her love, and the comfort and solace that came with it. He couldn't let her go.

He took her hands in his and gazed into her sweet face. "Do you mean it, Bea?" he asked softly, scarcely daring to hope, despite the words she'd said. "You would give your love to such an unworthy fellow?"

She shook her head. "Oh, no. I would give my love to the most worthy man in England."

Still holding her hands, he did what he'd wanted to do since the day he'd realized that what he felt for Bea was more than mere desire, and even though he'd believed he would never love a woman well enough to wed.

He went down on bended knee and softly, fervently said, "My lovely, wise and good lady, my kind and gentle savior, my heart, my home, will you save me from a life of loneliness? Will you be my wife?"

"Oh, yes!" she cried, smiling even more gloriously than the day she'd announced little Peder's birth. "Oh, Ranulf! Of course! Of course I'll marry you!"

She pulled him to his feet and threw her arms around him, almost knocking the breath from his lungs in her happy excitement. "I was so afraid you were never going to ask me and I would have no choice but to retire to a convent and try to be a nun, which would surely have been a dismal failure, because my darling, my dearest, I would have pined away and—"

He kissed her. He simply couldn't wait another moment. He kissed her with all the love, all the longing, all the desire and hope and happiness she inspired within him. He kissed her as he'd wanted to do for weeks, even before Christmas when it had taken every ounce of his self-control to offer her wine instead. He held her close, reveling in the joy flowing over them, feeling that here, now, at last, in her arms and in her love, he had found a home. A haven. A place where he belonged, safe and secure, no matter what troubles beset him or who wished to do him harm.

She kissed him just as fervently, her passion no longer held in check by doubt. He wanted her. He loved her. He was hers, and she was his. They would be married, husband and wife. There was no need to hold back or wait anymore.

She ran her hands up under his shirt, finally touching his naked flesh. How warm it was, how firm, how taut the muscles beneath. The ointment he had given her had soothed the cuts and scrapes on her palms, so there was no pain when she caressed him, simply a longing to feel more of his skin. He angled himself slightly and his knee ventured between her parted legs, while his hand moved slowly down her arched back.

Oh, this was a kiss! A kiss and an embrace of a sort she'd only ever dreamed of. No, this was better than anything her maiden mind had ever imagined.

He moved to undo the tie of her bed robe and she moved back a little to let him do it. She knew no modesty, no shame, just pleasure and anticipation as he slipped his hands beneath the robe and around her waist, with only the slender barrier of her linen shift between his palms and her warm and willing flesh.

With a low moan, she relaxed against him, and let the robe glide from her shoulders to fall upon the floor. His arousal pressed against her, sending a host of new sensations through her already eager body.

"Make love with me, Ranulf," she pleaded in a whisper. "We are as good as married now, for you'll never break your pledge and neither will I."

"My wife. My lovely, loving wife," he whispered in return as he swept her up in his arms and carried her to the bed. "I will never forsake you."

She watched with avid desire, frantic need, as he

threw off his shirt and peeled away his breeches. He was magnificent, from the top of his ruddy-haired head to the soles of his feet. He was wonderful and good and hers to desire.

And never had she desired him more.

CHAPTER FIFTEEN

SHE HELD OUT her arms to him in silent invitation, not wanting to speak. Not needing to, as he quickly joined her on the bed, covering her with his beautiful body. As they kissed again, he worked his hand beneath the hem of her shift and slowly, slowly, pushed it upward along her naked thigh.

She gasped when his hand slid between her thighs, to caress her there, too.

"Are you frightened, Bea?" he asked gently. "Would you like me to stop?"

"No," she answered honestly. "I...I think I like it." He stroked again. She closed her eyes and answered in what was almost a purr. "Indeed, I like it very much."

He smiled to hear her answer, delighted that she felt no hesitation, that she so obviously enjoyed her lover's touch. For love her he would, tonight and every night, if that was what she wanted. He was hers to love and hers to desire.

This time, he would take his time. This would be no quick coupling of the sort he'd had when the urges of nature grew too strong, or the sordid seduction he'd practiced on those other young women all those years ago.

He was going to make love with Bea, loving her as he'd never loved a woman.

And as he kissed and caressed her, he truly understood that this was true. What he'd felt for Celeste had been merely a combination of admiration and desire. He had never imagined a life with Celeste. Never dreamed of her holding their child in her arms. Never wanted to sit by the warm flames of a hearth with her, listening to her talk about the cook or the laundry or the hundred other little things that made a life complete.

"My dearest, sweetest angel," he murmured, brushing a kiss upon her forehead and then the tip of her nose. "I love you. I've loved you for weeks— months. I think I started to love you the moment I saw you standing on the steps in courtyard of Tregellas. But I thought…feared…"

"It doesn't matter now," she assured him. "I love you."

"You make me so happy, Bea!"

"I'm very happy, too." A sultry look came into her blue eyes, a look that made her seem far older than her years. "But unless I've misunderstood something, we'll be happier yet if you don't stop. Please don't stop, Ranulf."

His pleasure slipped into sensual desire. "I shall happily obey, my queen, my empress. My love."

He kissed her lightly, his lips barely touching hers, and with that same teasing touch, he moved down her neck to her collarbone.

"What have we here?" he whispered as his fingertip traced the neckline of her shift. "A barrier. I shall have to storm it."

"How do you intend to do that, sir knight? There's no room in this bed for a trebuchet or other siege machine."

"I believe…with my teeth," he murmured, biting the end of the drawstring that tied the neck of her garment and pulling until the knot came undone. "Success."

"And now?" she whispered breathlessly.

"Now I claim the prize that lies within."

She closed her eyes and sighed as he insinuated his hand beneath her shift to cup her breast.

"Very nice and worth the storming," he murmured as he nuzzled her shift lower. "Worth the waiting, too."

Arching, she ran her hands over his broad shoulders. "I didn't like the waiting," she confessed. "But now you and your magnificent body are mine."

His tongue found her nipple and swirled about the taut tip, sending a fresh wave of need over her. "I'm delighted I meet with your approval, my lady."

"Oh, you do," she sighed as she bent her knees, the better to bring her body close to his.

"Not yet," he cautioned. "I intend to have my way with you, and it's a very slow way."

"But—"

"But me no buts, my lady. I want you to be so sated and satisfied, you'll never look at a younger man."

"As if I'd want a younger man!" she returned, wiggling against him in a way that nearly sent him over the edge right then and there. "I want a mature man, not a boy."

"If you keep doing that," he warned, "I might prove to be as impetuous as the greenest lad in Christendom."

"Impetuous? You?" she teased. "That I would like to see."

"I can be impetuous," he vowed, shifting slightly until she could feel his shaft against her body. "I believe I'm impetuously about to make love with my betrothed."

His betrothed! She had only a moment to savor the words as he began to lave her breasts with his tongue and stroke between her thighs. His actions awakened an urgent, primitive need in her, one that must be satisfied, and quickly. She didn't want to wait another moment, as she'd waited all these months, and she reached down to guide him.

He gasped as her hand encircled him. "I was supposed to be the impetuous one," he said.

"Then *be* impetuous," she ordered, "for I swear, Ranulf, this anticipation might be the death of me."

"I can't have that, my lady," he said, the words ending in a sound between a sigh and a groan as he pushed inside her.

Bea felt the membrane tear and his hard shaft filling her. There was pain, and likely blood, but she didn't care. The rest was too wonderful and now they were as good as married, husband and wife. Joined in love and passion.

"Did I hurt you?"

"A little," she confessed, trying not to think about it, to instead enjoy the feel of his skin beneath her hands, the muscles tight and powerful, to explore her beloved's body.

"I'm sorry," he said huskily, and she knew he was trying to hold back on her account.

"I love you, Ranulf. This pain is nothing." She pushed her hips up to meet him, instinctively grinding them against him and being rewarded with a sensation like a different sort of kiss. "Not when I can feel this, too."

A brief smile crossed his face and then that, too, was gone, submerged beneath the passion and the need when he began to thrust.

She threw back her head, squirming with desire and pleasure as his mouth, his hands, played upon her body, urging her to new heights of anxious expectation. Overwhelmed by the sensations, too new to this great bliss, she let herself be swept along, guided by his knowledge, his touch, his whispered endearments, the gasps when she touched him, too.

She could make him feel the same fierce need? The

same excited longing? Her uncertain caresses, her hungry kisses, could arouse him as he aroused her?

Empowered, delighted by the unexpected revelation that she could be his equal in their bed, she met him thrust for thrust, his partner in this play, his match in passionate craving. She was free to be herself, unrestricted by conventions, by the role she so often had to play. Here she felt no need to explain or talk to hide her insecurity. Here she could be the woman she had always longed to be.

Yet she was a new Bea, too—one who was completely a woman, beloved of the man she loved.

With a cry, her body tightened, taut as a rope holding a ship anchored in a stormy sea. And then it was as if all the desire, all the longing, all the need met in a thunderclap. She was set loose upon that sea, tossed and tumbling in the currents of her passionate release.

As she gripped him tightly, his thrusts grew more frenzied, more powerful, as if his body was no longer under his control—and perhaps it wasn't, as hers hadn't been. With a groan, he stiffened, then bucked as if only the release commanded his flesh, until he collapsed, sated, his head upon her breasts.

For a long moment, neither said a word. They simply lay entwined, panting, satisfied and happy.

SURREPTITIOUSLY WATCHING those of his crew who'd come ashore with him, Pierre added another board from what remained of Gawan's boat to the fire before him in the grotto. As the flames shot up, one of his men left the other fire and staggered toward him.

Barrabas's shadow loomed to grotesque proportions on the cavern wall as the big man with the shoulders of a bull and arms like a bear splayed one hand on the side of the cavern to steady himself. In his other hand, he held a nearly empty wineskin.

"We've been talking," Barrabas announced in his sailor's patois, an amalgam of French, German and Italian that Pierre readily understood. "We all think you ought to forget this plan to take that woman and sell her in Tangier. It's a long way to Tangier and women at sea are bad luck."

Pierre moved his hand slowly and cautiously toward the dagger in his belt. He'd sailed with Barrabas for over ten years, but he'd no more trust him that he would his whore of a mother. "Surely the mighty Barrabas isn't afraid of a mere woman."

"It's bad luck. And it's too risky to stay here with that knight in the castle. He's not like the other one, the fat one who fell off his horse."

"I tell you this woman will make our fortunes," Pierre replied. "Besides, even supposing I agreed with you—which I do not—how do you suggest we leave? Our ship isn't due to fetch us until tomorrow. What is one more day?"

Barrabas sat heavily on a large rock on the opposite side of the fire. "If we hadn't wrecked that boat, we wouldn't have had to wait. We could have gone to Dieppe and met them."

"You would have sailed across the channel in that fisherman's boat?"

Barrabas took a swig of wine and wiped his mouth with the back of his hand. "We could have done it."

"Or we might have drowned."

"At least we wouldn't have had to be holed up in this miserable cave, wasting time and waiting for that dolt to bring us bad luck."

"We would not have to hide among these rocks if you had killed Gawan properly. Nobody would know if he was alive or dead, like those other two."

"I did do it right," Barrabas retorted before he took another pull at the wineskin. "He shouldn't have come up again with all the chains I put around his boots before I threw him over." He shook his ugly, shaggy head. "You should have let me use my sword. Instead I had to listen to him crying like a frightened child before I smothered the life out of him." He imitated Gawan's frantic pleading. "My wife! Our baby!" He scowled. "I wish I'd slit his mewling throat."

"It's a good thing you did not," Pierre said, "or they would have been certain he was murdered when they found his body. Now all they know is that he fell off his boat, although that is more than enough."

Barrabas scowled. "*You* used a blade, on that sheriff and his woman."

"There was no way to make that look like an

accident, not if I was to do it swiftly and get out without anyone hearing."

He'd nearly been caught as it was. He'd heard the servant stirring and it was only because that woman had been too terrified to scream that he hadn't been discovered.

He hadn't expected the woman to be there at all. He had believed the sheriff would be alone, and vulnerable in his bed. It had seemed hours that he'd had to wait beneath it, listening to the sheriff and his lover.

"If you hadn't decided to linger here, we would have been well away and out of danger."

Pierre couldn't refute that, but he wasn't about to let Barrabas win this argument. "Without the greatest prize I've ever seen? I tell you, that blond beauty will be worth her weight in gold, so she's worth the risk. Hedyn was too clever, and therefore dangerous. Now Myghal is the sheriff, and he'll never betray us to his overlord. He has too much to lose."

The still-scowling Barrabas took another swig of wine. "And I tell you it's bad luck to bring women on the ship," he repeated, shaking the wineskin at Pierre for emphasis. "And it's too damned far to Tangier."

Watching the man across the fire, his grip tightening on the hilt of his dagger, Pierre slowly got to his feet.

"Are you challenging me, Barrabas?" he asked,

not taking his steadfast, cold-blooded gaze from his crewman.

He could hear the rest of men muttering among themselves. They knew what had happened to the last man who'd tried to question Pierre's authority, as did Barrabas. Guido's death had been a gruesome lesson in the danger of inciting mutiny.

Barrabas seemed to be recalling that particular incident. He stepped back, his arms dangling at his sides and fear in his black eyes as he stared at Pierre's hand resting on the hilt of his weapon.

Because Barrabas was worth ten men in a fight, Pierre gave him a second chance—although it would be his last. "Women can bring good luck as well as bad, and I feel in my bones that blond beauty will make us rich. I appreciate we have small comforts here, but what will that matter when we are rich and fat in our old age, eh? We leave tomorrow at the night's high tide and we will take the woman and be gone, never to return as long as that knight is in command."

Barrabas had seen Pierre kill men and laugh while he did it. He'd seen him rape and heard him brag about it afterward. He had been there when Guido had met his slow, tormented end. Even so, he believed he was right, and if they took that woman on their ship, they would die. "What if Myghal betrays us and doesn't bring the woman? Will we go and get her?"

Pierre smiled coldly. Cruelly. As he had when he'd tortured Guido. "Myghal will bring her. I will make sure of it. Now, have you anything more to say to me, Barrabas? Or must we draw our knives?"

Barrabas didn't want the woman on their ship, but he saw death here and now in Pierre's stance and the murderous gleam in his eye.

"No," he muttered, picking up the wineskin and heading back to the fire.

While Pierre sat and thought about what he'd do when he had Lady Beatrice on his ship.

It was indeed a long way to Tangier.

As PIERRE WAS DEALING with the mutinous Barrabas, Bea stroked her beloved's ruddy hair in the spluttering flicker of the candle they had not even stopped to snuff. "Now I know why Constance smiles all the time."

Still lying with his head upon her breasts, Ranulf laughed softly. "Bea, you are the most remarkable woman."

"Am I?"

He raised his head and smiled at her, his eyes shining with love. "You most certainly are."

"You didn't seem to think so until I came to Penterwell. You used to ignore me until I wanted to cry."

He levered himself up upon his elbow and regarded her gravely. "I was afraid of what I might do if I let myself be near you."

"Like that time at Christmas when you almost kissed me?"

"Like that," he agreed. He lifted a strand of her hair and brought it to his lips. "I love your hair."

She mussed his with her fingers. "And I love yours." She frowned and rubbed his beard. "But I really don't like this."

He laughed again as he moved away to lie beside her, where he could see her whole luscious body. "I don't particularly like it myself. I only grew it to look older, to make you see that I was too ancient for a merry lass like you."

"Ancient?" she said skeptically, running her hand down his chest in a way that started to reawaken his desire. "With this body?"

He took hold of her hand and pressed a kiss upon her palm. "In some ways, much too old for you. I haven't lived an exemplary life, Bea."

"I know." She caressed his cheek. "I love you, anyway. I love you just as you are. I may even come to love your beard."

"I'll shave it off."

"When?"

"Would now suit you, my lady?"

She smiled. "What will you tell people in the morning?"

"That my betrothed doesn't like it and told me so after making love with me most passionately."

"You wouldn't!"

He sighed with melancholy melodrama. "Alas, you're right. I can't. I can't say we're betrothed until we have Merrick's permission to wed."

"I'm sure he won't withhold it."

Ranulf grinned. "Fortunately, I don't think he will, either, although he's liable to make me sweat before he agrees." His brows lowered and he spoke in gruff imitation of the lord of Tregellas's deep voice. "Well, Ranulf, what makes you think you deserve her?" He frowned more deeply still and some of the merriment left his eyes. "And what can I say to that, except that I don't?"

She answered him with unexpected solemnity. "All you have to say is that I love you and I won't marry anybody else, so he might as well give his consent because if he doesn't, I'll just run away and live with you anyway."

"Bea!" he cried, astonished. "You wouldn't."

"I most certainly would. I love you and I meant what I said—I'll never leave you." Her smile seemed to light the room. "So he will have no choice but to consent."

"I fear I have seriously underestimated you, my little Lady Bea."

"Lots of people have," she replied frankly. "But when I want a thing, sir knight," she murmured, lying back down and pulling him with her, "I don't give up until I get it."

"There is one thing *I* want," he said as he bent his

head to kiss her. "To see your hair spread about you on the bear pelt."

"Is that all?" she said, shifting until she was lying atop the thick fur, her hair loose about her just as he had dreamed.

His lips curved up in a devastating, devilish smile. "Come to think of it, no."

LATER, RANULF OPENED his eyes and slowly became aware that the candle must have gone out. They had been in bed together quite a while. For too long, perhaps, he suddenly thought, waking more completely.

"Bea? Beloved, I fear it's time for you to go back to your chamber," he said, giving her bare, beautiful shoulder a little shake.

She sighed and opened her eyes. "What?" she asked drowsily.

"You should go back to your chamber," he said as he got out of bed. "I don't want anyone to accuse me of seducing you."

She grinned, a hint of mischief in her beautiful blue eyes. "You could simply admit *I* seduced *you*. I came to your bedchamber, after all." She twisted a strand of her hair around her finger as she watched him dress. "*I* fear I'm a total wanton where you are concerned. And I thought we were going to denude your chin of that beard."

"I regret that there's no time, at least for you to

help me, and as much as I might enjoy that—" he hopped on one foot and tugged on a boot "—perhaps I should leave it until we're married, and we can do that on our wedding night."

She shook her head. "I'm going to want to do other things that night, my lord."

His brow furrowed and he frowned with mock disapproval as he straightened. "You are indeed a very wanton wench." His eyes shone with a smile. "Much to my delight."

He glanced at the window and sobered. "But you really must go, Bea. Maloren will have a fit if she discovers you're not in your bed."

Bea grimaced. "You're right," she agreed as she, too, got out of the bed and smoothed down her disheveled shift.

"God's wounds, you can't go back looking like that!" he exclaimed as he tucked his shirt into his breeches.

"Like what?" she asked, starting to run her fingers through her tangled hair. "Has my nose grown hooked? My face haggard?"

He pointed at her shift, and in the first dim light of dawn, she saw what he was looking at—the small streaks of blood that proved she'd been a virgin.

She quickly stripped off her garment and hurried to the basin. There was cold water in the ewer beside it and she poured some into the basin and proceeded to wash out the stains as best she could.

Ranulf came up behind her and wrapped his arms around her naked body, warming her in more ways than one. "I'm sorry."

"It was to be expected. I think I've got most of the blood out."

"Are you going to wear it wet to your chamber?"

"I'll carry it and put it in the laundry later, before Maloren sees it." She slid him a questioning glance. "Should we go to Tregellas with Kiernan? Maloren expects us to, after what happened with Celeste. You could come with us and ask Merrick for permission to marry me."

"You should go back to Tregellas," he agreed, "where you'll be safe, but although I want to marry you with all my heart, I can't go with you. The people here still don't trust me, and it might seem to them that I'm putting my own happiness above my duty and the safety of the people of Penterwell if I go to Tregellas before I've caught the men responsible for the murders."

He finished with such a sorrowful sigh, Bea readily, if reluctantly, accepted his decision to remain here until justice was done. "Very well," she said, turning in his arms to face him.

Then she smiled brightly, and with determination, too. "But in that case, I'm staying, as well. Your larder needs more food. You need some new clothes or—oh!" she cried, her eyes widening. "I promised all your maidservants a new gown for doing a good job. I simply can't leave here until I've kept my promise to them, can I? Even Maloren won't argue with me about that, as she's to get a new gown, too."

He laughed softly. "Bea, Bea, you continually amaze me. Is there nothing you can't manage with that clever imagination of yours? But you would be safer in Tregellas."

She wrapped her arms about him and looked up longingly into his hazel eyes. "I don't think so. I think I'm perfectly safe right here."

"Bea," he warned, trying to resist her persuasive efforts and ignore the fact that she was naked. "You're distracting, too."

"Am I?"

"Very."

"But I can help you if I stay. Don't the women trust me? Didn't I already provide good information?"

"That's true," he conceded. And there was a full garrison here, and those who had been killed had been in more vulnerable places—at sea or in a secluded house, not a well-manned castle.

"You don't really want me to go, do you, Ranulf?" she wheedled, pressing her shapely body against him. "Please let me stay and help you, Ranulf. Please?"

He tried to look as if he was giving in under duress. "Oh, very well, my lady. I yield. I do require your able assistance in my investigation, and you absolutely cannot leave Penterwell until you've provided all my maidservants with a new gown as you promised—although I'll pay for them, of course," he added.

"You will?"

"It seems only right." He cocked his head and regarded her quizzically. "How did you intend to pay for them?"

She blushed and slid him a coy, incredibly alluring smile. "I hoped I could convince you of the wisdom of rewarding your servants for doing a good job."

He laughed and held her close. "God preserve you, Bea, you are too clever for me!"

"Since I'm staying, may I come to you tonight?" she asked, her voice low and seductive.

"I probably shouldn't let you, but I fear I, too, have grown wanton after such a night of bliss with my Lady Beatrice. I want more. If you think you can come here undetected, you'll find me waiting."

"I'll do my best," she promised. "Now I'd better go before Maloren wakes."

She left Ranulf's warm embrace and picked up her discarded bed robe. She drew it on, and then bundled up her damp shift while he went to the door and cautiously opened it. After checking the corridor, he moved out of the way for her to pass.

"Until tonight, I hope, beloved Bea," he said, giving her a kiss and caress.

"Until tonight, my love," she whispered before

she hurried down the corridor and slipped inside her chamber.

Where Maloren waited, wide-awake, with her arms akimbo and murder in her eye.

CHAPTER SIXTEEN

"WELL, MY LAMB?" she demanded as Bea quickly closed the door behind her lest Maloren rouse the entire castle in her rage. "Just where have you been?"

"Washing my shift," Bea replied, which wasn't precisely a lie.

"In the middle of the night?"

Bea was seriously tempted to tell an outright falsehood, to make up a story about falling from the bed and reopening a wound in her hand so that it bled on her shift. But Maloren would want to see the cut, to wash and tend to it anew.

"I was with Ranulf," Bea admitted as she set the damp shift on her dressing table.

She cringed as Maloren threw up her hands in horror and cried, "Oh, my poor lamb! You didn't! Not after— how could you? That scoundrel! That blackguard!"

"Maloren, listen to me," she said quietly, regarding her surrogate mother with steadfast resolve. "He's not evil incarnate, nor did he seduce me. I went to him willingly and without an invitation. He tried to send me away, but I wouldn't go. I love him. I'll always love him. He's a man who sinned and feels terrible remorse for what he did, but he's good and kind and honorable, and I'm going to be his wife."

"Wife!" Maloren gasped. She felt for the dressing table, then sat heavily on the stool, staring at Bea as if she'd just announced she was a ghost.

"Wife," Bea confirmed as she went to her former nursemaid and took Maloren's hands in hers, regarding her with the love of a daughter who hates to disappoint her mother but knows that, this once at least, she must. "I love him, and he loves me, and we're going to be married."

"Married!"

"Yes, married," Bea repeated, still determined, although she was sad that Maloren didn't share her joy. "I know he's done bad things. Believe me, Maloren, so does he—none better. He doesn't claim to be innocent. He's confessed everything to me, and with such heartfelt remorse, you would call him noble and more than worthy of my love if you had heard him, too."

"Was he kissing that woman?" Maloren demanded.

"Of that he's innocent," Bea answered. "Because I love you like a mother, Maloren, I'm going to tell you what Ranulf has told me about his past. You aren't going to like it, but it will be the truth. And know you this, Maloren, despite what he's done, I respect and admire and love him."

Bea would have no more secrets, no more hidden

past, no rumors to rise up to plague their future. She would have Maloren understand Ranulf as she did, and forgive him, as she did. Surely Merrick, who had kept a serious secret for fifteen long years, would understand, too, and remain true to his friend. Constance would no doubt agree that Ranulf was a finer, better man than he had been in his youth. He had done wrong and suffered and learned from his mistakes.

Bea told Maloren about the death of Ranulf's brother, and the wager that he'd made. As she'd expected, and to judge by the occasional hiss Maloren made, her former nursemaid was upset to hear these things. But better they should come from me, Bea reasoned, than for Maloren to hear them from another source.

When Bea finished her explanation, Maloren jumped to her feet. "That...that...!"

"You must understand why he did those things," Bea said quickly, determined to calm her. "He was hurt and he—"

"Him?" Maloren retorted. "It's that brother of his, drowning his poor dog! I'd like to get my hands on that lout myself! I'd give him more than a drowning!"

"Then you...you forgive Ranulf?" Bea asked hopefully.

"Are you mad? Forgive him? For seducing all those girls and taking my lamb's virginity without marriage or betrothal? I should say not!"

Maloren's eyes flashed with anger. "I don't blame

you, my lamb. I don't doubt he said some very pretty things and that he's a fine lover, too, with that body and those eyes. He could probably *look* a woman into his bed, that one."

"Maloren, he didn't seduce me. If anybody seduced anybody, *I* seduced *him*—and I'd do it again. I love him, Maloren."

Finally Maloren understood that Bea would not be dissuaded. She sat down again. "What will I say to Lady Constance?" Her eyes widened. "Or Lord Merrick?"

"You won't have to say anything to Constance or Merrick. Ranulf and I will go to them when the time comes and ask to be married. I'm sure Merrick won't object."

Maloren's wrinkled face flushed. "You're right about that! Lord Merrick'll make certain that red-headed devil marries you."

"Maloren, I wish you didn't hate Ranulf," Bea said as she knelt beside the stool and took Maloren's work-worn hands in hers. "If you could have heard the things he said, you'd understand why I'm the happiest woman in England right now, except for one small thing. My dearest, most protective Maloren doesn't like the man I'm going to marry."

Maloren's thin lips trembled. "He's not good enough for you, lambkin. He's a bad, bad man."

Bea sighed. She was never going to be able to change her servant's mind about Ranulf. "I'm sorry you feel that way, Maloren, because I *am* going to marry him. I suppose Constance could find a place for you at Tregellas and you can stay in her household."

"Tregellas?" Maloren cried, aghast. "Are you sending me away?"

Bea rubbed her forehead with agitation. "Well, if you hate the man I'm going to marry—"

"I hate all men, but I'm not about to let that stop me from looking after your children," she declared. "My lamb and her lambkins will need me, especially with such a father. But I promise I'll not say one word against him to you, or them, or anyone, as long as you let me stay with you. Did you ever hear me say one bad thing about your father while he was alive? No, you did not."

This was, Bea realized, quite true.

So while Maloren's acceptance of her marriage to Ranulf wasn't perfect, this would be enough. And yet... "What if our children have red hair?" she asked warily.

"Thank God you'll be their mother, then, and me their nurse. Otherwise..." She shook her head as if to say, without their good influence, Bea's children would be doomed by the heritage of their hair.

In spite of that possibility, Maloren gave Bea a satisfied smile. "So that's decided. I'll tend your babies and keep my mouth shut about your red-haired devil of a husband. At least Lord Merrick will make sure you marry. Sir Jowan couldn't make that son of his do the right thing if *he'd* been the one whose bed you'd shared tonight. I feared you had when I saw him creeping in the corridor in the dark as if he was up to no good." Maloren's expression grew as sour as Bea had ever seen it. "Sneaking around like a tomcat in an alley, he was, so if he wasn't with you, I'd say he was meeting another woman."

Bea found that difficult to believe. "Kiernan isn't the sort to dally with his host's servants."

"Don't tell me you're forgetting that hussy staying here?"

IT WAS ALL Ranulf could do not to start humming during mass that morning. He did hum as he followed his beautiful Bea into the hall to break the fast. It was a rollicking, happy little tune he'd heard Henry sing in the past.

This behavior wasn't exactly dignified, Ranulf realized, and he *was* castellan here, so he should at least attempt to act in a manner befitting a commander.

That proved nearly as difficult as not kissing Bea when he sat beside her at the high table.

"Lady Celeste has sent her regrets that she's unable to join us this morning," Bea remarked after the blessing and sliding him a glance that instantly piqued his curiosity. "Given Kiernan's absence at mass and something Maloren saw last night, I believe she may no longer be pining over you, my lord."

"Really?" Ranulf asked, leaning as close as he dared. Was it possible that Celeste had decided to assuage her disappointment with handsome young Kiernan, whose appearance and friendliness toward Bea had caused him some envious pangs in the past? "You think our other noble guest might be responsible for this change of heart?"

"Maloren's convinced he went to Celeste's chamber during the night."

"I don't suppose she actually asked him where he was going?"

Bea smiled and shook her head. "No."

"Perhaps he was merely on his way to the garderobe."

Bea's smile drifted away. "Oh. I hadn't thought of that."

"On the other hand," Ranulf continued, "it wouldn't surprise me a bit if they'd been together. Celeste knows she has absolutely no chance for me, and we both saw how Kiernan looked at her when they met. Celeste is still a very attractive woman, after all." He found Bea's hand and squeezed it lightly before letting go. "She's not nearly as attractive as my bride-to-be, though."

Lightly brushing her fingers along his thigh, Bea kept a straight face as she whispered, "And here I thought Kiernan was desperately in love with me."

"Just as well if he's not," Ranulf replied with bogus severity as his hand meandered from her knee to her hip. "Otherwise, I might have to challenge him to combat for my lady."

Bea shifted away. "Stop that."

"I like it," he said softly in return. "I think you like it, too. And who has been blatantly caressing my thigh?"

"I suppose we should be a *little* circumspect," she said with a note of real regret, "at least until we have Merrick's permission. I don't want everyone watching us."

"They're watching us right now. They've *been* watching us ever since you arrived. We seem to make a very fascinating couple."

"We may not be able to keep our desire to marry a secret much longer anyway," Bea conceded, finding it too difficult to ignore or prevent his clandestine caresses. "Maloren was awake and waiting when I returned to our chamber. I had to tell her about us."

Ranulf rolled his eyes and, rather to her dismay, took his roving hand away. "Poor little Lady Bea. Is that why she's not here, either? She fell into a fit at your bad news and is lying in bed, one hand to her forehead, moaning and cursing me and my red hair?"

Bea laughed and shook her head. "She's accepted the inevitable and still wants to tend our children, even if they have red hair."

Ranulf looked genuinely shocked. "No!"

"Yes, it's true," Bea said pertly, and with a virtuous expression. "Maloren believes that with my help, we can help them overcome their naturally sinful natures."

"Be careful how you tease me, Bea," he warned, "or I'm liable to forget my position as castellan and kiss you here and now."

"And cause a scandal?" she replied, her eyes sparkling with delight. "Oh, surely not!"

Her voice dropped to such a sultry whisper, he very nearly did forget he was the castellan when she said, "I would prefer to wait until we can be alone."

"God's blood, Bea," he pleaded quietly. "Have mercy, or I'll have to pick you up and carry you to my bed."

"Have mercy on *me,* my lord," she returned. "Surely you know there's nowhere I'd rather be." She rose. "Unfortunately, I have more mundane duties that require my attention."

"As do I," he replied, likewise standing. "And I'd better be about them."

"Until later then, my lord."

He made a deep and formal bow. "Until later, Lady Beatrice."

WHEN RANULF REACHED the courtyard, he was surprised to see Kiernan standing near the stables, finishing what appeared to be the heel of a loaf of bread. Spotting Ranulf heading toward him, the young knight tossed what remained aside, causing several gulls to swoop down from the battlements to fight over the crust.

"Good morning, Kiernan," Ranulf said, barely

managing not to smile, or laugh, or ask him about Celeste. "We missed you at mass."

Kiernan blushed. "I overslept."

I'll wager you did, Ranulf thought.

The young man straightened his shoulders and his expression grew determined. "I've decided there's no need to rush back to Tregellas, after all," he said. "I fear I've wronged both you and Lady Beatrice by implying there was any need for haste. And she may require more time to pack her belongings."

Ranulf's brows rose and it was a struggle not to grin. "Indeed? I'm delighted to hear you don't think me a lascivious lecher."

Kiernan's cheeks reddened still more. "I hope you'll allow me to stay until Lady Beatrice is ready to return to Tregellas."

Ranulf politely inclined his head. "Of course. But there's your lack of baggage to consider."

Kiernan waved his hand dismissively. "I'll send one of my men to the village to purchase what I require."

"Then I see no reason you shouldn't stay."

Kiernan let out his breath, blushing again, as if embarrassed by his relief. "Yes, well, since I am to stay, I was hoping you'd allow me to ride out with you today. I've heard something of the troubles here, and I'd be glad to help in any way I can while I'm here. I have very keen eyesight."

"Do you, indeed? Well, well. I'd be delighted to have you come with us," Ranulf said. In truth, another pair of eyes couldn't hurt when it came to spotting anything amiss or out of the ordinary along the coast.

Together they walked to where Titan waited in a particularly frisky mood. Or perhaps he was empathizing with his master's good humor.

Either way, man and horse were soon leading the patrol out of the gates and toward the shore. They left a small force at the castle, under the command of the sergeant-at-arms. Gareth, the garrison commander, had been born and raised in Penterwell, so Ranulf wanted him in the patrol, too.

It was a mild spring day, with a clear blue sky, and just enough of a breeze to ruffle Ranulf's hair.

They'd ridden some ways in silence before Kiernan spoke. "Tell me, my lord, did you know Lady Celeste's husband well?"

"No," Ranulf answered honestly.

"It seems a pity a woman so young and lovely should be widowed so soon."

Ranulf kept his tone noncommittal. "I'm sure Lady Celeste will find another worthy man eager to marry her."

"I understand she's very wealthy and popular at court."

Celeste *had* been singing her own praises rather loudly last night. He'd been too upset about Bea to pay much attention. "Am I to understand you wouldn't mind making an offer for her yourself?"

Kiernan flushed and stared straight ahead.

"If that's so, I wish you every happiness." Ranulf recalled some of the things Celeste had said to him, and her desperate pleas. "I don't think her life at court has been as happy as she implies."

As a knight and a man, Ranulf felt compelled to be honest with Kiernan. "She's far from poor, but she may not be as rich as you think in terms of landed property. She told me herself she has only movable goods, although as you saw for yourself last night, her jewels alone are quite valuable. However, as you stand to inherit your father's estate, I should think her lack of property is not a serious impediment to your marriage if you were to seek her hand."

"The lady herself would be the prize," Kiernan replied a little stiffly

"Spoken like a man in love," Ranulf remarked. "And here I've been assuming you wanted to marry Lady Beatrice."

Kiernan looked horrified by the very notion. "By the saints, no!"

"Forgive me for upsetting you," Ranulf said, trying not to be offended for Bea's sake, and even if she didn't want Kiernan. "Surely you can't be surprised by my assumption. I thought your concern for her sprang from tender feelings."

"I do *like* Lady Beatrice," Kiernan allowed, "but I'd never want to marry her. She talks far too much and her sense of propriety..." He caught Ranulf's eye. "You must admit it's a little lacking."

"Then why do you care so much about her reputation?" he asked.

"Because I admire and respect Lady Constance. I don't want anyone in the family to suffer because of Beatrice's actions."

"You do know Constance and Lord Merrick agreed to let her come? Beatrice didn't simply grab a horse and ride here on her own."

"I fear Lady Constance loves Beatrice too much to curb her."

"You think Beatrice needs to be restrained?"

"I think, my lord, that sometimes she is heedless and unthinking and forgets to act like the lady she is."

"Yes, sometimes she does," Ranulf agreed. "I find that refreshing."

"A ship, my lord!" one of the soldiers at the front of the column called out. "There, in the cove!"

Ranulf raised himself in his stirrups and saw a two-masted vessel bearing no flags or other marks at the entrance to a nearby cove. Then he spotted something else: a boat full of armed men rowing toward the shore.

Excitement and hope and determination set Ranulf's blood aflame with a different sort of passion. These men could be up to nothing good, or they would have come into the harbor at Penterwell. By God, he'd catch them and find out exactly what they were doing here.

In spite of his resolve, however, it wasn't Ranulf's way to charge into a fight without a plan.

As he dismounted, he called to Gareth to move his men out of sight.

Ranulf crept to the edge of the cliff overlooking the cove and lay on his belly to survey the shore below. He avoided looking at the waves where they washed up upon the sand as he gestured for Gareth to join him. "Do you know those men?"

"No, my lord," Gareth answered. "Never seen them before."

"Or that ship?"

"No, my lord."

By this time Kiernan, too, had crawled up beside Ranulf. "Smugglers," he said, and it wasn't a question. "That's a French ship."

Ranulf looked at him questioningly.

"You can tell by the rigging," Kiernan replied. "What's the plan of attack?"

"This is no fight of yours, Kiernan. Ride back to Penterwell."

"I'm not a coward," the young man replied, obviously offended. "I won't run from a fight."

"And if you're hurt or killed? What am I to say to your father?"

"That I died in battle," Kiernan said with conviction, "as a nobleman should."

Ranulf began to think he'd underestimated the young man, but at the moment, Kiernan's valor was not of prime importance. "We can't come at them from up here. They'll see us and make for their ship before we can stop them. Or are there any caves down there where they could take refuge?"

Gareth shook his head. "No, my lord. None that I know of."

"Why do you think they came here?"

"Could be because the path over there is a wide one," Gareth suggested. "If they plan to steal horses or sheep, they'd need a wide way down to the shore. If that's why they're here, they'll wait till nightfall before leaving the beach."

"Is there another way down?"

Gareth nodded his helmeted head. "Aye, but it's not an easy one."

He pointed at the eastern end of the cove, where a rocky outcrop rose several feet above the water and jutted into the sea. "There's another way to the beach around that point—trickier, that's for certain, but I don't think anybody'd fall into the sea if we was careful. Could be a bit noisy what with rocks falling, though. On the other hand, they won't be expecting anybody to come from there. A bit of rock tumbling down won't alarm 'em."

Looking at the waves crashing against the point, Ranulf pushed back his terror of the churning sea. "Then that way it shall be, for I'm not letting those men get away."

As RANULF AND HIS MEN started making their way toward the point, a smiling, merry Beatrice bustled about the kitchen giving orders for the evening meal, while Lady Celeste contemplated the passionate energy of younger men. In the village, Wenna crooned a lullaby to little Gawan sleeping in his cradle, until a knock sounded on her door.

Wondering who it could be and suspecting it might be Myghal with another small gift, Wenna smiled and hurried to welcome him.

Instead of Myghal, three rough, strong men—one huge, one thin and one missing an eye—charged into her cottage.

"Do not be alarmed, *ma petite fille,*" the one-eyed man said as the thin one closed the door and barred her exit. "We have not come to hurt you."

"Who are you?" Wenna demanded, backing toward the cradle, fighting her terror and swallowing the bile rising in her throat. "Touch me and I'll scream!"

"Scream and we'll kill your baby," the one-eyed man replied, his tone calm, but his expression hard and vicious.

He would do it. He would kill her baby if she screamed.

"There now, that is better," the man said, his hand on the hilt of the sword hanging from his belt. "Now come with us, *ma belle,* and no one will get hurt."

The huge man, who looked more monster than human, started toward her, while the thin one with lanky hair guarded the door.

"My baby!" she gasped, throwing herself over

the cradle, gripping it with all her mother's strength, frantically determined to protect her child. "Don't hurt him!"

"We don't want your baby, *ma belle*. Just you."

"I won't leave him!"

"*Ma petite,* you are making this very difficult."

"I won't leave my baby! You'll have to kill me first!"

The huge man scowled, but the one-eyed man merely shrugged. "Oh, very well. We'll take the baby. He will be worth something, too."

Wenna's eyes widened and a different sort of panic filled her frightened eyes. "Worth something? To who?"

"He should earn enough to cover the cost of his journey to Tangier. You, on the other hand, will fetch a lot more."

Realizing he meant to sell her son as a slave, Wenna scrambled to her feet. "I'll leave him! I'll come with you. I'll leave him here."

The one-eyed man shook his head. "No, *ma petite.* We'll take you both and maybe next time you will do as you're told the first time, eh?"

"No, no please!" she cried, falling on her knees and lifting her clasped hands as she pleaded. "Not my baby! Please, not my baby!"

Sneering, the one-eyed man struck her hard across the face with a backhanded blow. Wenna fell, hitting her head on the side of the cradle with a sickening thud.

Gustaf cursed while Barrabas bent over her prostrate form. "Is she dead?" Pierre asked.

"Still breathing," Gustaf replied.

"Pick her up and bring her."

"And the babe?" Barrabas demanded.

"Him, too, of course," Pierre replied as if that answer was obvious. "She'll do anything we want if she thinks her baby's life depends upon it. And it will."

RANULF FOLLOWED Gareth along the narrow ledge leading down to the cove. They'd tied their horses some distance away, in a small glade in a valley with a babbling brook at the bottom, then they'd returned to make their way along the perilous path.

Below, waves crashed and tumbled against the rocks, throwing frigid salt water over the men until they were drenched, droplets falling from their helmets and chins. They would have been shivering, too, except that the effort of moving along this treacherously narrow trail was more than enough to warm their bodies. Holding on where they could, they crept slowly forward.

Warm or cold, Ranulf would rather have faced a multitude alone than do what he was doing now. But show cowardice of any kind before his men he would not. And he would not turn back or shirk his part in the capture of men who might be responsible for the death of Hedyn and the others.

But oh, God, he prayed, as he inched along behind

the Cornishman, *don't let me fall! Just get me down to the beach and let me fight as I've been trained to do.*

Determined to do just that, Ranulf concentrated on holding on and moving his feet. He wouldn't look at the water raging below, especially when they were near the end of the point and all too close to the crashing waves.

Gareth came to a halt and raised his hand. Ranulf did the same, while Kiernan and the others behind also stopped their slow and careful progress over the rough and slippery rocks.

"Once we get round the point, they might see us, if they're watching," Gareth said to Ranulf. "Chances are they aren't, because God knows I wouldn't be thinking anybody'd be coming 'round this way if I were them. Should we wait until it's dark to go the rest of the way?"

Ranulf simply couldn't imagine either himself or his armed men making their way safely along this path in the dark. "If they see us, how fast can they escape up the cliff or get to their boat?"

"It'd still take them a while, my lord. We should be able to run 'em down before they can reach the top or get the boat off the beach."

If only he had some archers, Ranulf thought, although he didn't want to kill those men. He needed them alive to answer questions, and it could be they were not, after all, the villains that he sought.

"We'll take a moment to catch our breath, then

we'll start around the point. Gareth, I'll take the lead from here, if I can get by you."

"It'll be a tight squeeze, my lord, but I think we can manage," the Cornishman said, flattening himself against the rock to let Ranulf move slowly and cautiously past.

MYGHAL STARED at the overturned cradle in Wenna's empty cottage.

He knew what that meant.

And he knew what he had to do if he was going to get her back.

INTENDING TO RELIEVE himself, one of the smugglers headed for the craggy wall of the bluff a short distance from where the others huddled behind a pile of rock on the beach. Swaying slightly, he yawned and scratched himself. He was tired of waiting and annoyed that they'd been told they could have no fire on the beach. England was a cold, dreary, godforsaken place, and if it hadn't been for the wine they'd brought with them from the barque, he would have been miserable indeed. He hoped Pierre and the rest of the crew weren't late for the rendezvous, either. It was bad enough on this beach in the day; at night, it would be worse.

He muttered a curse as he fumbled with the drawstring of his thick breeches. As he tugged hard on the knot, a stone rolled down from above. Dislodged by the wind, no doubt. He'd be glad to be back at sea, by God, not sitting on this shore without a fire, cold and hungry.

Another rock dropped, clattering to the ground beside his feet.

What if there was about to be an avalanche? the smuggler suddenly wondered, glancing up—to see Ranulf's fierce visage and a sword in his upraised hand as he jumped from on high like an avenging angel bringing destruction from heaven.

The smuggler screamed, but he had no time to unsheathe his sword before Ranulf cut him down. Hearing him, his fellow smugglers jumped to their feet and drew their weapons.

One look was enough to tell the smugglers they were outnumbered, so rather than stand and fight, they made for their boat. They dropped their swords as they ran to have both hands free to shove it into the water.

The tide was against them, and before they could get it deep enough, Ranulf and his men were upon them.

A few left the boat and ran back for their weapons. More abandoned the boat, their weapons and their fellows, and rushed for the path to the top of the bluff. Shouting his commands, Ranulf sent Gareth and five of his men after them, while he and Kiernan and the rest of his soldiers dealt with those at the boat.

Out of the corner of his eye, Ranulf saw Kiernan lunge at one of the smugglers. "Don't kill them," he ordered as he raised his sword. "Catch them but don't kill them!"

Then Kiernan was forgotten as Ranulf attacked a man with a long scar down his neck, wearing motley clothes and swearing in Italian.

"Surrender and you can live," Ranulf told the man who gripped his sword as if it were a club. "There's no need to die."

A slew of foreign words, obviously a denunciation and refusal, issued forth from the man's nearly toothless mouth.

Perhaps he didn't know English, and if so, there'd be no way to get information out of him, Ranulf thought. But just because this fellow swore in those other tongues was no guarantee he didn't speak English. Ranulf still had to try to take the man down while keeping him alive.

Ignoring everything else around him, Ranulf concentrated on his ragged opponent. Patience, boy, patience, he thought, as Sir Leonard had admonished the lads in his care a hundred times. Look for your enemy's weakness. Let him strike first. Watch how he moves, how he holds his weapon. Battles were won not with mere brute strength, but with patience and cunning, with skill and vigilance. Winning was in the head, Sir Leonard used to say. Don't lose yours.

Circling his enemy, Ranulf noted that he not only held his weapon clumsily, he moved like an ox on two legs. Deft Henry would have fairly danced around him.

The man raised his sword, bringing his arms too far back and throwing himself off balance before he brought his weapon slashing downward. Ranulf easily sidestepped the blow and then, as the man stumbled back, he saw his chance. Upending his sword, Ranulf struck the top of the man's head with the base of the hilt as hard as he could.

Splaying his hand upon a pile of rock, the man groaned and staggered, and struggled to stand. Again Ranulf struck him on the head and this time, his opponent collapsed, his face in the sand.

Pleased and only slightly winded, Ranulf turned to go back to the boat. In that same moment, a sword sliced through the side of his tunic. And his flesh.

Holding his left side, the blood flowing between his fingers, Ranulf glared at the one-eyed man who'd struck him. This man knew how to hold to his sword and how to wield it, too.

Nevertheless, and despite his wound, Ranulf planted his feet—firm to the ground, as Sir Leonard used to say—and prepared to defend himself.

CHAPTER SEVENTEEN

CELESTE'S SCREECH OF HORROR echoed against the stone walls of Penterwell. Bea made no sound at all as she ran toward the bloodied, exhausted men riding into the courtyard. She lost all ability to speak when she saw Kiernan mounted on his horse and holding Ranulf in front of him, one arm around her beloved's sagging body.

"Kiernan, are you hurt?" Celeste called out. "What happened?"

Kiernan answered, but it was not to Celeste he spoke. He looked down at the distraught Bea clutching his stirrup as if she was about to fall herself. "We saw some men putting in up the coast and tried to capture them. We were winning the fight until more came to join them. That's when Ranulf was wounded."

Wounded. Wounded, not dead.

As something approaching vitality returned to Bea, she gestured at the grooms who'd come rushing out of the stables when they, too, heard the sentries sound the alarm.

"Take Sir Ranulf to his chamber," she ordered, the words little more than a hoarse croak.

As the men hurried to obey her, Maloren appeared at her elbow. "Oh, my poor lamb! My lady!"

Bea straightened, shoulders back, expression resolute—a lady of power and majesty and strength of purpose. "I'm not the one who's hurt. It's Ranulf and some of these other men who need help. Find me clean linens for bandages and I'll need hot water. Please bring them to Ranulf's bedchamber."

As Maloren rushed to do as she was bidden, Bea walked over to Kiernan. She ignored Celeste, who waited anxiously nearby.

"The smugglers—what happened to them?"

"I don't know, my lady. After Ranulf fell, we retreated because by then, we were outnumbered."

Bea turned next to the garrison commander, who was likewise sweaty and exhausted. "Send a soldier to summon the townsfolk to the market street, Gareth. After I have seen to Sir Ranulf's wounds, I'm going to address them. We've been patient long enough."

Gareth nodded, awed by the determination in Lady Beatrice's face as she turned on her heel and marched into the hall.

THANK GOD THE WOUND WAS not deep, Bea thought as she pulled a needle through Ranulf's ruined flesh. His assailant's blade had slid along the ribs, sparing the vital organs, and although Ranulf was unconscious, she guessed it was more from lack of blood than anything else. He moaned softly as she finished and she spread his own ointment over the stitches, just as Constance had done for Merrick not so long ago.

In some ways, it was fortunate that Merrick had been wounded in his arm by a boar spear; otherwise, she might not have learned what to do now. Fortunately she did, and she tried to concentrate solely on her task, determined to do her best so that Ranulf's wound would heal cleanly, without infection, even if it would leave a scar. At least he was alive. Thank God, he was alive.

As Bea worked and prayed her hope and gratitude, Maloren hovered nearby, anxious but blessedly quiet, handing Bea what she asked for without hesitation or squeamishness.

As Maloren watched her lambkin working with such skilled composure, she saw not the child she had nursed and fussed over and worried about all these years. She saw Bea's mother reborn, only with a competence and capability her dead darling had never possessed.

"There now," Bea said, sitting back and wiping her brow with the back of her hand. "I've done the best I can."

"That's as tidy a stitching as ever I've seen," Maloren assured her. "He'll get better, you'll see."

"I pray God you're right," Bea said, rising. "Stay

with him, Maloren. I doubt he'll wake soon, but if he does, call for Tecca and have her bring him wine and water, and bread and meat, if he can eat it. He must get his strength back."

"Won't you be here?"

"I hope to be, but first, I have to speak to the people of Penterwell."

BEA LOOKED OUT over the villagers gathered in the main street of Penterwell and thought of Ranulf lying pale and wounded in his bed, the same bed where they'd so recently and happily consummated the love they shared.

"People of Penterwell," she announced, her voice strong and carrying down the street lined with curious people. "Your castellan and one of his patrols have been attacked. Even now, Sir Ranulf and several of the men who serve to protect you lie wounded in the castle.

"Ever since he came here, Sir Ranulf has tried to be a fair and just overlord. He's been as horrified as you by the recent murders of at least two good men and poor Gwenbritha. He's tried to find out who is responsible, to no avail. He has overlooked things he need not because he understands your reasons for disregarding the king's law and sympathizes with you. But murder and now an attack upon him and his men mean the time of patience is at an end.

"I ask you, I plead with you," she said with firm

resolve, "if anyone knows anything about the murders, or the men who fought Sir Ranulf's patrol today, tell me. You must no longer think only to protect your own selfish interests, your cache of tin, the coins you've earned by smuggling. Do you think those men who killed Hedyn and Gawan care what happens to you? Do you think they see you as anything other than something to be used to gain more profit for themselves? Will they hold a hall moot and listen to your disagreements and try to render fair judgment? Will they be your voice before Lord Merrick? Will they represent you to the king and try to keep him from making laws that are harsher and taxes more unfair? Or will they cause the king's anger to fall ruthlessly upon you all?

"Help me find out who is responsible for these deaths and the attack today. Let us bring them to justice, before worse befalls us.

"Think about what I've said, people of Penterwell. Think about Sir Ranulf, lying wounded in his bed, and how he waited, hoping that one of you would have the courage and wisdom to come forward before things went this far. Have pity on yourself, if not for him or those already dead and those they left behind, and help us catch the men who seek to do you harm."

Bea fell silent, having said all she had come to say. For a long moment, only the cry of the gulls broke the quiet while she waited, more than half anticipating someone would speak up then and there.

They did not. Instead, the people began to drift away, muttering among themselves.

"My lady?"

She discovered Myghal at her elbow. "Yes?" she asked, wondering if he had something to tell her that could erase her disappointment and despair.

"It's little Gawan, my lady," he said. "I stopped in to see Wenna and he's got a fever. She's frantic, my lady, and begged me to ask you to come."

As concerned as Bea was for little Gawan, she hesitated. What if someone finally decided to come forward and she wasn't at the castle to hear them?

"Please, my lady!" Myghal begged, desperation in his eyes. "He's burning up with it. And he can't keep his milk down, either."

That decided her. And, she told herself, she need not stay long at Wenna's cottage. If little Gawan were seriously sick, she would have Wenna and the baby come back to the castle with her.

Together she and Myghal hurried along the lanes until they came to Wenna's cottage. Myghal stepped back to let Bea open the door and enter.

The moment she did, she sensed that something was wrong. There was no fire and the cottage was not as neat as—

She felt the sharp tip of a sword between her shoulder blades. "Not a sound, my lady," Myghal said quietly behind her. "Not a word."

She whirled around to face him, backing into the

room as he moved forward, the sword now at her throat. "What are you doing?" she demanded. "Have you gone mad? Where's Wenna? Where's the baby?"

"They've been taken and there's only one way to get them back," he replied. "Sit there on the stool, my lady, and don't move, or I might have to hurt you, and that I don't want to do."

Bea could hardly believe what was happening. "Myghal, please! If they've been abducted, we should go to the castle, fetch more men to search—"

"I know who took them and where they went," he said as he gestured with the sword. "Sit *down*, my lady."

She did as he ordered. All those times she'd been uneasy in his presence, she'd been right to worry. How many times had this snake been close to her and she'd convinced herself she had nothing to fear?

As Myghal had convinced Ranulf he was trustworthy, and Hedyn and Sir Frioc, too.

Myghal pulled a piece of rope from his belt and began to tie her wrists.

"Myghal, please," she said as he bound her hands behind her, "how can tying me up here help get Wenna back? We must go to the castle. Even if Ranulf is hurt, there are his soldiers, his garrison commander and Kiernan, too. We'll find her and—"

"No!" Myghal snarled. "The men who have Wenna will kill her if we do that. They'll stop at nothing to get what they want, and what they want, my lady, is *you*."

"Me?" she cried, aghast. "But why? For ransom?"

She was sure Constance and Merrick would pay for her safe return, but that didn't lessen her fear, or her danger. Many things could go wrong between now and then.

Myghal pulled the bindings tighter and she thought she heard him sob.

"Let me go and we'll get Wenna and her baby back," she pleaded, trying not to sound frightened. "Let us help you. I won't hold this against you. You're not thinking clearly because you love her and you're desperate."

"It's because of me they've got her and you, too."

"But they don't have me yet. There's still time to—"

"No!" he snapped. "There isn't. It's now or never for Wenna and little Gawan. Be quiet, my lady. I don't want to hurt you, but if you don't stop talking, I'll have to gag you."

He was going to have to gag her.

"You said you knew these men, Myghal. Who are they? French smugglers? Have you been in league with them all along? Did you help them murder Hedyn and Gwenbritha, and Gawan, too?"

"Stop talking!" Myghal ordered, and this time, he wedged a gag between her teeth. "I've got to get Wenna back the only way I can, and that means trading you for her. You're worth more to them than she is. They only took her to make me bring you."

He grabbed her arm and hauled her to her feet. "I'm sorry, my lady, and I tried to find another way, but there isn't any. I have to take you to them and trade you for Wenna and little Gawan. If I don't, they'll sell them into slavery instead of you."

Instead of her? Bea felt faint when she heard the fate that awaited her. Terror and panic threatened to overwhelm her, especially when she realized Ranulf was hurt and probably not even awake. How could he save her? How long would it be before anyone realized she was missing?

As Myghal started to drag her to the door, she resisted as best she could. While she did, a hope lit the darkness of her fear. Maloren would soon wonder where she was. Others would have seen her leave with Myghal, know in which direction they had gone, realized they must have gone to visit Wenna.

Maloren would tell the garrison commander that she hadn't yet returned, and likely Kiernan, too. Even if Ranulf was not yet awake, they would start to look for her. They would come here.

They must find something to tell them she had been here and taken against her will.

As Myghal opened the door and peered out into the deserted lane, she slipped off one shoe.

Seeing that the way was clear, Myghal pulled her across the threshold, his hold as tight as terror, his expression grim as death.

While her shoe lay on the floor behind her.

Ranulf slowly opened his eyes and blinked in the dim light. He was in his bedchamber at Penterwell. The bed curtains were open, but the room was dark, lit only by the single candle on the table beside the bed. It must be night, or evening at least, and his side hurt as if Titan had kicked him.

Then he remembered. The one-eyed man, the blow, the pain, the blood...

"Oh, Ranulf, you're awake!"

A woman spoke, but it wasn't Bea who came to lean over his bed and regard him with anxious eyes. It was Celeste. "Are you in pain?" she asked solicitously.

"A little," he lied, for it felt as if his side was on fire. "Where's Bea?"

Celeste's alabaster brow furrowed and she turned away to wring out a wet cloth over the basin on the table. "She's gone to the village."

"Why?"

"To demand that the villagers find the men who attacked you, or some such thing. I think she would have been better off looking after you, but no, she marched out of here like a general in a most brazen and unladylike fashion. I said to Kiernan that I'd never act that way in a hundred years."

No, she wouldn't, and Ranulf had to smile—at least a little—at the notion of Bea striding into Penterwell and commanding the villagers to turn over the smugglers who'd attacked his patrol.

On the other hand, maybe they would. "Am I seriously hurt?"

"She had to stitch the wound. I swear, Ranulf, I very nearly fainted when I saw all the bloody linen. I told her that was work for a physician. I think she took a terrible risk doing it herself. What does she know about medicine?"

"A great deal," he answered as he struggled to sit up, gasping when he felt the stitches tugging at his flesh.

"I'm not sure you should do that," Celeste cautioned.

"I've been stitched before." And all things considered, he didn't feel too bad. His side hurt, and he was rather weak—from lack of blood, no doubt—but it could be worse.

He might have been dead. "And the smugglers? Were they captured?"

"You were outnumbered. Kiernan said more came to join the men already on the beach. Since you'd been wounded, he ordered a retreat."

"Kiernan did?"

"Who else? And you were hurt."

"Gareth, the garrison commander, is more than competent to assume the leadership of a patrol. Or was he wounded, too?"

"No," Celeste answered a bit peevishly. "A few of the other foot soldiers were hurt, but none seriously. It was Kiernan who fought off the man who attacked you—a big brute he was, too. I should think you would be grateful."

"I didn't know that, and I *am* grateful," Ranulf replied. "He's clearly a better fighter than I supposed."

Celeste became a little less stiff. "Would you like some wine?"

"Later, please. What of the sheriff? Did anyone go to the village and tell Myghal about the attack?"

"I assume so. I was more concerned about you. Maloren left some bread and butter for you, and some roast chicken. Would you like some?"

He wasn't particularly hungry, but he knew he needed to regain his strength. "Please."

As she went to fetch the tray waiting on the chest, he gingerly felt his bandaged side, noting the scent of his sicklewort ointment. He was quite sure Bea had done a more-than-competent job tending to his wound. God's blood, what he wouldn't give to see and hear her haranguing the people of Penterwell!

The door flew open with a bang and Maloren, her eyes wild, her hair disheveled, came into the room as if propelled by a great gust of wind. "She's gone! My lamb's gone!"

"Sir Ranulf is not to be disturbed," Celeste declared.

Celeste might have been invisible for all the attention Maloren or Ranulf paid to her as he struggled to sit up, ignoring the pain in his side while his heart thudded wildly. A fear more terrible than any he had ever felt—not even when Edmond held him under the water—tore through him.

"There's no need for such excitement," Celeste said with obvious disdain. "She's in the village."

Maloren turned on Celeste as if she'd stabbed her. "She *was* there but now she's *gone!*"

Ranulf climbed out of the bed despite the pain it caused him. He was nearly naked, but he didn't care. "Get me my clothes and my sword."

"You can't get dressed! You're supposed to rest!" Celeste cried as she dragged her attention away from Ranulf's bandaged body to glare at Maloren. "Where would she go?"

"We don't know, you silly slut!" Maloren retorted. "If we knew, she wouldn't be missing!"

Ranulf clutched at the bedpost. There was no time to be lost, no time to get into his mail. "Where are Myghal and Kiernan?"

"Kiernan's already gone to the village to help search for her," Maloren said, wringing her hands. "I don't know where that Myghal is."

"Likely in the village with Kiernan. I'll meet them there."

"You can't!" Celeste protested. "You're hurt."

"I'm going to find Bea," Ranulf replied, speaking not with the red-hot anger of a down-trodden boy, or the fiery passion of a rejected youth, but with the cold-blooded fury of a mature man. He was a warrior in his prime, and he would stop at nothing to rescue the one person in the world who loved him, and whom he loved with all the passion, devotion and determination of his formerly barren heart.

"Bless you, sir!" Maloren cried, sobbing as she rushed to his clothes chest and threw open the lid. "I know you'll find her and my lamb's right to love you, even if you've got red hair!"

"WHY ARE YOU LIMPING?" Myghal demanded as Bea, panting, struggled beside him on the path leading down to the sea.

She glared at him. With her mouth gagged, she could hardly answer his question, and she wouldn't tell him anyway.

Still holding his sword, Myghal impatiently pushed her onto the ground and grabbed her leg, raising her bruised and bloody foot that was only partly covered by her torn stocking. "You've lost your shoe."

As if she hadn't noticed.

Once again he hauled her to her feet. "You're only making this harder, my lady. I'm taking you to Pierre. There's no help for it if I'm to get Wenna and little Gawan back."

Bea tried to say Ranulf would kill him for what he'd done—if he found out what had happened, if he discovered that Myghal was involved, if he found her—but all that came out was garbled noises.

If Wenna were saved and went back to Penterwell, she would tell Ranulf what had happened. Wenna would help her.

Wouldn't she? Would she betray Myghal, who had risked Sir Ranulf's wrath to save her? Oh, please, God, she must!

Myghal started down a narrow path to a small indentation in the coast where a flat-bottomed boat with a single mast, its sail furled, lay beached on the rocks. They were going to set sail in *that?* Above, thick clouds were gathering on the horizon, and she immediately envisioned death by drowning in the cold, cruel sea.

Perhaps that would be better than being sold as a slave in Tangier, into some sultan's harem.

She looked around frantically for any sign of Ranulf's men, although, in her heart, she doubted he would have set a watch here. No ship or boat capable of carrying a group of men could put in anywhere close to these rocks.

She wasn't going to give up yet, so as Myghal pulled her closer to the boat, she abruptly pushed back and sat on the rocky ground. He was going to have to drag her.

"Get up, my lady!" Myghal ordered, trying to tug her to her feet.

She shook her head, determined to make it as hard for him to move her as she could. She kicked her feet, too, hoping to hurt him or delay their progress.

"Get up!" Myghal cried, gripping her hard, but still she fought back, twisting and struggling and refusing to stand.

"I don't want to hurt you!"

He was going to have to if he wanted her to move.

At last he sheathed his sword and grabbed both her arms, tugging her upright.

He was so angry and upset, he didn't notice that her other shoe lay discarded on the ground, especially when she shoved him with her shoulder to distract him.

He grabbed her again, turned her around to face the sea and frog-marched her to the boat. Her nearly bare feet were in agony from the rough rocks, but she would have risked more than sore feet before she got in that boat. Another struggle ensued before Myghal lifted her bodily over the gunwale into the bow and pushed her down upon a thwart. She slipped and fell hard against the side, striking her elbow and ribs, the sudden, blinding pain making tears come to her eyes. Despite that, her mind still sought a way to prevent him from taking her any farther. She considered kicking a hole in the boards with her heel, but feared that might make Myghal notice that both her feet were shoeless now.

Myghal took hold of the bow and shoved the boat into the water, the bottom scraping against rock. Perhaps he'd put a hole in it and they would have to come back, lest he drown, too.

Myghal continued pushing the boat out into the water, then climbed over the left side, making it heel. Bea instinctively leaned her weight on the opposite side to balance it.

No, she didn't want to drown. She would fight and survive, and Ranulf would find her.

Myghal unfurled the sail, then sat in the rear and put an oar over the stern of the boat to make a rudder. The wind caught the sail, and soon they were headed out to sea, skimming over the open water that so frightened Ranulf, to where the whitecaps danced and the dark clouds moved closer.

CHAPTER EIGHTEEN

KEEPING ONE HAND on the handrail so that he wouldn't fall, Ranulf hurried down the stairs as fast as he could, Maloren before him and Celeste coming behind. In the hall, torches flickered in the sconces, the light waxing and waning upon the faces of the worried servants and soldiers gathered there. Kiernan stood in the midst of them, his expression just as anxious and his complexion deathly pale.

The man's visage told Ranulf as plain as words that Bea had not been found.

He let go of the handrail, straightened his shoulders and strode toward Kiernan. The servants and soldiers quickly made way for him, while Maloren and Celeste followed.

"Was there *no* sign of her?" he demanded of the younger man.

Kiernan nodded at something on one of trestle tables left standing after the evening meal. Maloren let out a wail, while Ranulf simply stared at the shoe sitting there. A woman's shoe. One of Bea's shoes, for he'd seen that very shoe peeping out from beneath her gown many times. "Where was it?"

"In the cottage of a woman named Wenna. Some of the villagers saw Lady Beatrice going that way with the sheriff after she spoke to them."

Ranulf gazed steadily at Kiernan. "What does Wenna say?"

"She wasn't there, either. The cottage was empty and no one had seen her, or her child."

Ranulf's brow furrowed as he forced back his fear and his dismay to consider what he was hearing and what he would do next. "All three are missing?"

"I regret to tell you there's more, my lord," Kiernan said. "The sheriff is missing, too."

"Myghal has been taken?"

The garrison commander came forward, looking sick. "Lady Beatrice was last seen in his company, my lord. One of the fishermen tells me Myghal's boat is gone—a small one rigged with a sail. He could travel some ways to make landfall elsewhere, or to meet another vessel."

Ranulf hissed a soldier's earthy curse. He remembered that Bea had felt uneasy when she was with Myghal, at least at first, and he cursed himself for blindly trusting him. Perhaps Myghal had something planned earlier, and Kiernan's arrival had intervened.

But why had he taken Bea, Wenna and the baby? If he had just abducted Bea, he would think it was because Bea was a beautiful woman, and he'd seen the way Myghal had looked at her that first day.

The contemplation or revelation of why Myghal had done this terrible thing could come later, if it was proved he was responsible. First, Ranulf had to find them.

"It's unlikely anybody would risk going far from shore in Myghal's boat with this wind," Gareth said with a hint of optimism. "The waves'd be too high and it'd fill up and sink, or break apart."

"He could have gone to rendezvous with that ship we saw," Kiernan suggested, stepping forward. "I sent other patrols to ride the length of the coast for ten miles in both directions. So far, no one's seen that ship, or the sheriff, Lady Beatrice or Wenna and her child."

"And they would have said so if they had," Gareth added with conviction. "This is different from keeping a bit of money out of the king's coffers. They like Wenna and Lady Beatrice and they want them back as much as you, my lord."

No, they didn't. They couldn't. As concerned as he was for Wenna and her baby, nobody could want Bea back as much as he did. Nobody needed her as much as he did.

Emotions were a weakness.

Except when they gave you strength, as Ranulf's love for Bea strengthened and galvanized him now. His pain, his wound, his despair, were as nothing. "We'll search the roads and moor and all along the coast again," he declared. "There's more than one place to land a boat near here and it could be that something—some sign, some clue—was overlooked."

Kiernan and Gareth exchanged glances and it was Kiernan who reluctantly said, "As much as I want to find them, the sun has set. We'll have to wait until dawn."

Ranulf didn't give a damn if it was dark. "We'll take torches. I want all the men who aren't on watch to join me in the search, half on horses, the other on foot."

"And what if we do find them?" Kiernan asked incredulously. "Would you do battle in the dark?"

"If I had to do battle in hell itself to rescue Bea, I would."

THE LANTERNS on the barque's stern glowed in the darkness like disembodied beings hovering over the rough sea. For the longest time, it seemed that they weren't getting any closer and a shivering Bea dared to hope that the tide or the wind wasn't favorable, and Myghal would have to give up and turn back.

Yet slowly they did get closer, and between the wind, the water sloshing over the gunwales and her nearly bare feet, Bea had never been colder, wetter or more frightened. Yet she was also determined not to lose her head. As long as they were close to the coast of Cornwall, she would have hope.

The boat rose and fell in the waves, while she held on for dear life. She tried to think of some way out of this terrible situation, and about Ranulf. Was he awake? Had he learned that she was gone? Had someone already gone to Wenna's looking for her and found her shoe? How long before they found the other? They probably wouldn't until morning, whenever morning was. When they did, Ranulf might try to ride out to join his men in the search, and that wouldn't be wise. He shouldn't ride or do anything too strenuous. Unfortunately, she doubted he'd be able to sit and wait. Henry had told her how Ranulf had insisted on joining the battle against Henry's enemy, and she could easily envision him insisting on riding out to find her. She prayed he wouldn't injure himself more if he did. It would not be worth her life if he lost his in the attempt to rescue her.

There must be *something* she could do to save herself. If she could get over the side of the boat…she would surely drown. Her hands were bound, her mouth gagged and the weight of her soaking garments would drag her under the water.

As long as she was alive, there was hope she could find a better way to escape, or that Ranulf could rescue her. He would surely search the whole world for her, if he must.

When their smaller craft bumped against the hull of the larger vessel with a thud like a fist striking a coffin, Myghal reached out to push his boat along the side until they were beside it. Standing in their rocking vessel, Myghal grabbed the rope some men on the deck threw down, tying it to his boat. The men on deck—terrible, brutal, evil-looking men—tossed him another rope and laughed harshly when it nearly hit her.

"Over here, my lady," Myghal ordered. He had to shout to be heard above the rising wind. "I'll tie this around you and they'll pull you up."

She shook her head.

"My lady, there's no use not doing what I say. If you don't, some of those men in the ship will come down to get you and they won't be gentle."

The idea of being manhandled by pirates was enough to make her move.

"I'm sorry, my lady, truly," Myghal said again as he tied the rope firmly around her waist and, at last, took the gag out of her mouth. "I've got no choice."

She didn't care what he said, what excuses he made. "Ranulf's going to hunt you down and kill you."

Myghal stared at her as if she'd already struck the deathblow, then stepped back. "Now!" he called, and they pulled her up the side of the ship as if she were so much cargo.

By the time she was hauled over the rail of the ship, more men had come on deck, including one minus an eye. The others made way for him, so she assumed this was the captain, if he deserved that respectable title.

She shook off the crewmen's grasp and found her balance on the heaving deck. As Myghal climbed aboard, she ignored him and the rest of the rough-looking crew to concentrate on the one-eyed man. "I suppose *you* are in charge of this ship?" she asked scornfully.

The man grinned like a gargoyle. "*Oui,* my lady. I am the captain, Pierre de Lessette." He made a sweeping bow. "Welcome aboard."

"If I am welcome, cut these bindings. They're hurting me."

"We don't want that," the captain mockingly agreed, taking a very slender dagger out of his wide belt.

She swallowed hard. She had heard that the knife that had killed Hedyn had been narrower than most.

Stinking of wine and fish and tar, of dirt and sweat and tallow, the smuggler came close and slipped the dagger between the ropes and her hands and sliced the bindings off. He leered as he did it, and she felt the bile rising in her throat until he moved back.

"If you have an ounce of intelligence in that thick skull of yours," she said as she rubbed her bruised and aching wrists, "you'll give me Wenna and her child and return us to the shore. Otherwise, Sir Ranulf of Penterwell, Sir Henry of Ecclesford and Lord Merrick of Tregellas will hunt you down and kill you and all your crew."

Pierre laughed, the sound as coarse as a crow's caw. "*Mon Dieu,* beauty and spirit, too. What a pity I can't keep you for myself. But I must point out, my lady, that it is not wise to threaten me." His broad gesture encompassed the ship. "This is my ship and I command here. As for these men you name, they do not frighten me. Once I've sold you and that other sobbing, pathetic woman and her child, I will be rich enough to give up the sea and live in comfort in Marseilles for the rest of my life."

"You're to give Wenna and Gawan back to me!" Myghal exclaimed, starting forward. "That was the bargain! That was why I brought Lady Beatrice to you!"

Pierre regarded Myghal without the least pity or concern and shrugged. "I lied."

Myghal didn't even draw his sword before he lunged at Pierre. His attack was hopeless and doomed, and the men of the crew wrestled him to the deck in the blink of an eye.

Bea moved back toward the rail of the ship, and the small boat rocking below. With her hands free and the gag gone, she could perhaps get down to the boat... And leave Wenna and little Gawan here to be sold into slavery?

No, she could not.

The men tugged Myghal, his head bleeding, his cheek scraped, to his feet. Passing his dagger from hand to hand, Pierre approached the sheriff. "Like I told my lady, I rule here. And since we shall not be coming back this way again, your usefulness is done."

With that, he shoved the dagger into Myghal's stomach. As Bea quickly looked away, the sheriff screamed in agony, then gasped as Pierre twisted the terrible knife. Myghal made a horrible choking sound and his body fell onto the deck with a sickening thud.

Despite what Myghal had done, tears started in Bea's eyes and she could scarcely breathe.

"Throw that dog over the side," Pierre ordered as he roughly grabbed Bea's arm. "Now come, my lady, and join me in my cabin."

"THIS IS MADNESS, Kiernan, madness!" Celeste cried as she watched him adjust the girth of the saddle on one of the garrison's horses in the courtyard, now lit with several flickering flambeaux. "You won't be able to see anything in the dark, and there are bogs and quicksand and all sorts of dangers out there."

"Would you have me stay here?" he asked, turning to look at her. "I don't love Beatrice, but I value her as a friend, and her cousin loves her dearly. When I think of what Constance will feel if her cousin is never found…" He could only shake his head as he went back to his task.

"You care about Lady Constance more than me? How will I feel if something happens to you? I can tell you—my heart will break."

Kiernan glanced over at Ranulf a short distance away, then answered her plea quietly, although it was unlikely that Ranulf could hear what was said over the noise of his men preparing to ride out. "I do care about you, Celeste, very much. You gave me the best night of my life."

His voice grew resolute, and so did the look in his eyes. "But I must help find Beatrice."

"Will you at least promise me that you'll be careful?"

"I do. I will," he vowed, looking down into the lovely Celeste's anxious face and seeing the fear she had for him in her eyes. He remembered the passion, the laughter, and the sense that more than mere desire had bloomed between them last night. She was not Constance, the serenely unattainable. She was certainly not the loquacious, unladylike Bea. She was a woman who'd suffered, who longed to have a home. Who needed him, as he needed her warmth, her desire, her admiration and respect.

Unable to resist, wanting to reassure her and to tell her that what they had shared was no mere brief, meaningless encounter, he pulled her into his arms and kissed her passionately, regardless of who was watching.

BEA STUMBLED and nearly fell as Pierre shoved her into his dimly lit cabin. She sprawled upon the table bolted to the floor, then immediately rose and turned, leaning against it, ready to kick and bite and scratch if he so much as touched her.

"My lady!" Wenna gasped. She was huddled on the floor in the corner, her face scratched, the shoulder of her gown torn, her child cradled against her breasts.

Bea didn't dare do more than glance at her as Pierre, who still held that terrible dagger, kicked the door shut. She quickly surveyed the rest of the cabin, seeking any kind of weapon.

There was nothing obvious—no knives lying unguarded, no mace, no spear, no arrow, no stick, no piece of metal, not even a cup or plate.

There was only the table, a chair, a cot against the wall and likely attached to it, and a lantern reeking of sheep's tallow hanging by a chain from the ceiling. She might be able to reach the lantern and pull that down. The chair shifted a little every time the ship rocked; maybe she could pick that up and hit him with it.

Holding to the edge of the table, she began to sidle toward the chair.

"What are you doing, my lady?" Pierre asked silkily. "Do you think to put that table between me and you? Or to strike me down with that chair?"

She froze.

"You see how I anticipate you? You are not so clever after all."

"Or perhaps you've been hit on the head with a chair before."

He chuckled, the sound as monstrous as the rest of him. "Other women have tried to stop me from doing what I wish, but like them, you will not succeed."

He raised his dagger, as if he were admiring it in the lantern's feeble light. "You really ought to cooperate, my lady, unless you want that woman to lose her child, and possibly her life."

Wenna groaned aloud and little Gawan began to wail.

"Shut that brat up or I'll throw him over the side," Pierre ordered with a harshness at odds with his former tone and more in keeping with his ugly face.

Trembling, Wenna opened her bodice and put her babe to suck.

Had Wenna been hurt? Or raped? Bea didn't know, but at least she was no longer alone. Perhaps together they could somehow overpower Pierre and escape. As long as Myghal's boat was still tied to this ship, there was a chance.

"Now, my lady, I think it is time we came to terms," Pierre said.

"Terms?" Bea replied, forcing herself to look at him. "I don't talk terms with murderers and pirates."

"You should. Otherwise your journey will be very unpleasant. If you do as I say, it should be…better."

"How can any voyage taking me to slavery be made *better?*"

Pierre sat on the edge of the table and tapped the tip of his blade lightly on the top. "You could have this cabin for your accommodation. Otherwise, I'll put you below with the rest of my men. I'm sure they'll be very glad to have your company, and by the time we reach Tangier, all the fight will have been raped out of you."

Even though her stomach turned with revulsion,

Bea's mind worked quickly. There was no point appealing to this man's mercy or kindness—he had none. What he appreciated was money and profit. "What sort of worth will I have if you do that?" she charged. "Very little, I think.

"At present, I'm a virgin," she lied without compunction. "How much more will a virgin be worth to a man who has a harem?"

Pierre's brow furrowed, and she pressed on. "Treat me well, and you will get more for me. Treat Wenna and the child well, and the same holds true for them. Wenna's pretty, and the child strong—any man of intelligence could see he'll grow into a strong boy and a strong man. But abuse and starve us and you might as well let us go home."

Pierre sniffed derisively. "You talk like a slaver yourself, my lady."

"I've seen the difference between well-treated servants and those who are not."

Pierre rose and sauntered toward her. Despite her wish to appear brave, she couldn't help backing away, until her head hit the sloping cabin wall. "Clever as well as pretty, eh? Perhaps I should forget selling you and keep you for myself."

"And what will you tell your crew? That you put them at great risk to get me and then changed your mind? Won't they demand some sort of compensation?"

Pierre laughed harshly and shook his head. "*Sacre*

coeur, you know men!" He tilted his head. "How did you come by this knowledge, I wonder, if you are a virgin as you claim?"

"A woman doesn't gain wisdom by spreading her legs," she retorted. "Indeed, one could argue that in some cases, she becomes a fool if she gives her heart, as well. I can guess what your crew is likely thinking because my father was one of the greediest, most clever schemers in England. He planned for years to get what he wanted, and he couldn't gain his ends alone. He needed men like you and your crew, mercenaries who care only for the number of coins in their purse. I was brought up listening to his talk of plans and deceptions—what one man would want to help him and what would satisfy another, who he would discard easily and why, and who he must keep close. I sat like a dutiful daughter and learned duplicity at his knee."

Pierre's suspicious gaze searched her face. She saw his doubts and uncertainty, and a little flame of triumph flickered into life. "And there is something else you've obviously failed to consider. If you sell me as you plan, the man who buys me will be rich, and rich men have power. I'm a beautiful woman, and beautiful women have been getting men to do what they want for centuries. I'll find a way to make that man turn against you. I'll make the man who owns me your enemy."

"I will be in Marseilles," Pierre scoffed. "What harm could he do to me there?"

"Rich men can't hire assassins? Rest assured,

Pierre, I'll make you sound like evil incarnate. I'll tell my master a pitiful tale of the indignities you forced upon me and the things you made me do."

She spoke with firm conviction, as if these things would surely come to pass, and gave free rein to her imagination. "Do you doubt that if I tried, I could charm a man into doing whatever I wanted? That in his bed I could pour such a tale of sorrow and mistreatment, and make you sound so terrible, that he would feel he was doing mankind a favor by killing you?

"Nor would I stop there. I'll tell him you're not just a smuggler, you're a spy, one being paid to overthrow his country's rulers. What might happen to my rich master if that happens? He would foresee disaster and do everything to stop you."

"I'm a smuggler, not a spy! I have never worked for kings or noblemen!" Pierre struggled to regain his self-control. "Besides, I would be far away."

"But who can say what schemes you set in motion before you sailed? I'll tell him you're a spider sitting in a web of intrigue in Marseilles, the center of a vast conspiracy against his country. I'll tell him things I heard you say aboard your ship—of the money you were going to get, how you laughed at his people and made sport of his religion."

"You wouldn't!"

"Wouldn't I? What would I have to lose? I'll tell my master I've fallen in love with him, that his prowess in bed has won my heart, and I'm trying to save him from your schemes. Rich men are often vain, and what man wouldn't believe his skill between the sheets has made a woman love him?"

Staring at her incredulously, Pierre backed toward the door. "You're…you're mad!"

Bea walked toward him, the prey having become the predator. "I'm a woman you're going to sell to a rich man. I'm a woman who'll do everything in her power to bring you to your death."

"Stop talking or I'll kill you!" Pierre roared, raising his dagger as if he would truly strike her down.

"What then would you tell your crew? Where would their profit be? And do you think my death would stop Sir Ranulf, Sir Henry and Lord Merrick from seeking you out and bringing you to justice?"

"Aye!" Wenna said suddenly from her place on the floor. "The folk of Penterwell will be after you, too. They've guessed it's you been doing all those terrible things. They know your name, your ship, your men. They'll tell Sir Ranulf everything if you kill her—by God, they've probably told him everything already. You took their lady, you stupid oaf, and they'll want you dead just as much as he will!"

His face full of fear, Pierre reached around and fumbled for the latch of the door.

"You're already a dead man, Pierre!" Bea cried as he slammed the door shut behind him.

CHAPTER NINETEEN

RANULF STAYED IN HIS SADDLE by willpower alone as Titan walked along the coast in the dim light of dawn. He would have preferred to be on foot, as were the men in his patrol who checked the ground carefully, but he dared not dismount. He feared he'd faint; otherwise, he'd be on his hands and knees if necessary, examining every rock, every pebble, every patch of mud and blade of grass, for any evidence that Bea, Wenna or Myghal had passed that way.

"*Ranulf!*"

He turned to see Kiernan riding toward him at a breakneck pace from farther up the coastal path. "We found her other shoe!" he shouted.

"Where?" Ranulf demanded when Kiernan reached him and pulled his horse to a snorting halt.

"Three miles from here on some rocks near the shore. Your men tell me that no one uses that place to bring in a boat because it's too rocky for a landing, but it could be done. And one of the farmers who had his flock near the shore saw the

French barque last evening. It's probably heading back to France, judging by the direction it was sailing."

"My lord!" Gareth called out, waving to get his attention. "There's something down here on the rocks! It looks like a body, my lord."

Dear God, don't let it be Bea! Ranulf fervently prayed as he called for one of his men to help him dismount. He didn't care if asking for help made him look weak, as long as it wasn't Bea lying drowned and battered on those rocks.

As he drew near, Gareth and three of his soldiers gingerly made their way out onto the water-soaked rocks. "It's Myghal, my lord!" Gareth called out. He bent closer to examine him. "And by all the saints and angels, he's alive!"

"Bring him here!" Ranulf ordered, although they would hardly leave him lying on the rocks. The four men lifted Myghal up, two holding his shoulders, the others his legs, and they carefully made their way back to Ranulf with their sodden burden.

When they laid Myghal at Ranulf's feet, he went down carefully on one knee, taking in the unconscious man's pale face and dripping hair and clothes. How long he'd been in the water, Ranulf couldn't begin to guess.

"Myghal!" he shouted, slapping the face of the former sheriff to bring him to. "Myghal!"

The man's eyelids fluttered open.

"Where's Lady Beatrice? And Wenna and her baby?"

Myghal coughed, spitting up seawater, before he moaned and closed his eyes, his hand moving to his stomach and his torn clothes. Ranulf spread open the garments to see a small hole in Myghal's flesh. Blood trickled out of it, and he didn't doubt Myghal had lost much more.

He'd been stabbed and thrown into the sea. Whoever had done it had likely believed he was already dead when he went over the side, or would drown. Even so, it was a gruesome end—but perhaps not gruesome enough, if Bea was gone forever because of Myghal's treachery.

He slapped Myghal again to wake him. "Where is Lady Beatrice?"

Kiernan knelt across from Ranulf and produced a wineskin. "Try this."

Ranulf opened the stopper and poured some wine down Myghal's throat. He coughed and spluttered and his eyes slowly opened.

"Where is Lady Beatrice?" Ranulf repeated.

Myghal's lips moved and Ranulf leaned closer to hear. He didn't care that it strained the stitches in his side. He didn't notice his own pain as he listened to Myghal whisper, "On Pierre's ship."

A knowing murmur started among the men, until Ranulf held up his hand for silence.

"Forgive me," Myghal gasped. "I had to take her to

him. He had Wenna." Myghal closed his eyes and a tear slid out of the corner. "He killed Gawan, too. And Hedyn and Gwen…" He drew in a deep, ragged breath.

"Where's he taken Bea? France?"

"No…" His eyes closed and his head started to loll back like a doll's.

Ranulf grabbed Myghal's tunic, lifting him and shaking him in his distress. *"Where?"*

"Tangier… Slave market."

Oh, God.

Myghal took hold of Ranulf's tunic and heaved himself up. "He killed Gawan. I paid him to. I wanted Wenna so much. I loved her, but she chose *him*." He gasped and started to sink back to the ground. "Forgive me."

Ranulf knew the pain of rejection, knew it all too well. He could understand the heartache, the rage, the wounded pride, and the desperation that could compel a man to do murder. "I do."

"God…forgive me."

"In His mercy, He will," Ranulf said as Myghal's eyes rolled back and he let out his last breath in one long sigh.

Ranulf slowly and painfully got to his feet. He couldn't think about Myghal now, or his own mistake in trusting him. He had to save Bea. He *must* save her. He would, and nothing—no man, no ocean, no fear— was going to stop him. He would go to the ends of the earth for Bea. He would brave the surging, restless sea.

"I need a ship," he said, looking steadily at Gareth.

"There's a merchant's vessel in Penterwell harbor that ought to be fast enough to catch a French barque," his garrison commander replied.

With a nod, Ranulf started toward Titan.

"A storm's blowing in," Gareth warned.

Ranulf glanced at the man over his shoulder and the look on his face said everything.

"I'm coming with you," Kiernan said, following.

"And storm or no storm, me and your men," Gareth declared.

RANULF'S STOMACH HEAVED with every plunge of the ship through the six-foot waves. He clung to the rigging on the foredeck of the merchant's ship with desperate strength, his face and body lashed by rain, wind and water. The waves frothed and surged, and the deck bucked beneath his unsteady feet.

This was the stuff of nightmares. To be out at sea in a storm, on a ship that seemed no more than a child's fragile toy, at the mercy of the sea and wind, while below the water waited to swallow him up like a malicious god.

Kiernan made his way along the shifting deck to join Ranulf. "The captain said only a smuggler, or a madmen bent on catching one, would be out in this gale."

Ranulf didn't answer as he fought his fear and the sickness roiling in his belly.

Kiernan regarded him with sympathy. "At least we're running before the wind, or I think the captain would have refused your request, despite what the owner of this vessel had to say."

"If he had, neither he nor his master would have been welcome in Penterwell again, or any port Lord Merrick commands."

Fortunately, it hadn't come to threats. It would have taken more bravery than most men possessed to refuse Ranulf when he came seeking aid that day, so the merchant who owned the vessel had swiftly acquiesced.

"How long before we reach them?" he asked.

Kiernan grabbed for the gunwale as the ship dipped and rose again. "I don't know, but the captain's doing his best and this is a fine ship."

And then, as if God Himself had heard his question, a cry went up from one of the men on lookout up in the rigging. "There! Off the port bow!"

His heart soaring with hope, Ranulf peered through the rain. "I'm coming, Bea," he whispered as new vitality and strength filled him. "I'm coming."

"MORE SAIL!" Pierre shouted to the men up on the yards as he stood at the wheel of his ship. "Let the sails out full!"

"They'll be torn from the masts!" Barrabas bellowed over the howling wind. "Reef them or we'll lose them! Bring us closer to shore."

"And let that ship catch us?" Pierre demanded, looking once more over his shoulder at the vessel nearing them. "We are already too close to the shore. There could be rocks."

"I told you those women would bring us bad luck!" Barrabas shouted, the rain running down his fiercely angry face. "You're going to kill us all, you bastard!"

Pierre gripped the wheel more tightly as he swayed with the motion of the ship. "I'm still captain here!"

Above the moan of the wailing wind, a shriek pierced the air and Gustaf fell from the shrouds into the heaving sea.

"You see, damn it?" Barrabas roared as he swiped the water from his face. "We're cursed! Cursed, you bastard! Give me the wheel!"

"Do as I say or go below!"

Barrabus shoved Pierre away from the wheel and turned the ship toward land. "I'm not letting you kill us and all for a woman!"

"Fool, you don't know this coast the way I do. There are rocks—"

"There's a cove, isn't there?" Barrabas called to one of the men clinging to the rain-soaked rigging.

With his arm wrapped around the yard, the man pointed up the coast.

"We can't put in there," Pierre protested as he swayed with the bucking deck. "They'll find us, and then they'll hang us."

"Not if we kill them first," Barrabas said, his eyes on the sea ahead and the coast beyond.

He didn't see the flash of the dagger that killed him, slitting his throat so that the only sound he made when he died was that of his body falling on the deck. Nor did he hear the terrible crunch of splintering wood, nor feel the lurch of the ship as it struck a rock lurking below the surface of the ruthless, surging sea.

BEA AND WENNA HEARD the cracking wood and the rush of water as the ship shuddered to a halt, throwing them to their hands and knees.

"We've run aground," Wenna cried as the ship rocked with the slap of the waves.

Like Bea, she was still clutching one leg of the chair Bea had smashed against the table and she held tight to it as she crawled to check Gawan in the nest she'd made for him in the cot.

"Pierre and the others will have even more to worry about now," Bea said. "They won't be thinking about us."

She struggled to her feet and, with renewed determination as well as all her might, threw her shoulder against the door.

"THEY'VE RUN AGROUND!" Kiernan cried.

Knowing what that meant, Ranulf stared at the wrecked craft. The smugglers' ship had hit a rock or reef. Yet although it had stopped moving forward, if help didn't reach the damaged vessel soon, it would be dashed to pieces by the waves, and everyone in it hurled into the sea to drown.

No, he silently vowed. He would save Bea, and Wenna and her baby, too. As long as he lived, he would not give up hope. They would reach the ship and he would find them before the hull cracked and parted and the frigid water poured in to kill her.

Once more he shouted at the captain to bring his vessel as close as possible to the listing ship and ordered his archers to nock their arrows.

The captain made no protest. He'd never seen such ferocious determination as had been in the eyes of Sir Ranulf when he told him to catch that ship, and he called on every lesson, every technique, every trick he'd ever used or heard of, to coax some extra speed from his ship without having the sails torn asunder, the ribs cracked, or the rudder ripped away.

Ranulf kept his eyes on the smuggler's barque, praying to God to keep it safe and in one piece until they could reach it and rescue his Bea, and Wenna and her baby, too. Closer they came, and closer and, mercifully, the ship stayed together.

Soon they were in range, and after his men assured him they saw no women on the deck, he ordered his archers to fire. A volley flew across the water, aided by the wind, and he heard screams as some hit their targets.

They drew nearer still and the captain shouted to

Ranulf to get ready to board. His heart pounding, Ranulf picked up a grappling hook with a long rope, one of several he'd had brought from the castle before they boarded the merchant's ship. Usually they were for scaling enemy walls, but they would do to get hold of the ship and bring the merchant's larger vessel near enough to leap the distance between.

He would not fall between the ships and be crushed. No, nor Kiernan nor any of his men. Not if God was just.

As if God had heard his fervent prayers, or perhaps it was their proximity to the shore—for Ranulf was not schooled enough in the ways of wind and water to know—the fierce wind began to abate. The waves grew smaller, although they were still enough to push the injured ship against the rocks and do more damage.

By now those aboard the merchant's ship could see the smuggling crew on the deck of their wrecked vessel. They were armed and waiting, their faces and shouts fierce, their weapons raised. No doubt they would prefer a fast death from the blow of a sword to a watery grave or a hangman's noose.

There was no sign of the women. They were likely locked inside a cabin or down in the hold, probably bound, maybe even chained. They would be the first to drown if they weren't rescued before the ship broke apart.

Gritting his teeth, his jaw clenched, Ranulf threw

his hook. But for once in his life, Ranulf had been impatient, and the hook landed in the sea. Quickly he hauled it back up and prepared to throw again. In the meantime, Kiernan let fly with his hook, and it caught on the ship's rail at the stern.

"Let it go!" the captain of the merchant ship bellowed. "We don't want to be at the stern, man!"

Kiernan dropped the rope, which lashed about like a whip, striking Ranulf hard in the face.

He ignored the pain as he waited for the captain to bring his ship in nearer before he threw his hook again.

"Now, sir!" the captain shouted. "Throw now!"

Ranulf did, with all his strength and skill and desperation. It fell on the deck and caught on the rail as he pulled it back. In the next moment, three more hooks went flying from the midship of Ranulf's vessel. As some of the brigands rushed to cut the ropes, one hook fell into the water.

Ranulf cursed his wound that he couldn't help pull their craft in closer. But others could and did, including Kiernan. Working with strength and unity, they brought the merchant ship alongside the wounded vessel.

Ranulf had no concern about the danger facing him on that wet and slippery deck; no fear hindered him as he prepared to leap onto the smugglers' ship, and as soon as he could jump, he did.

Once on the ship, he scrambled to his feet and round himself surrounded by three savage, equally desperate and determined smugglers. They knew there could be no surrender. If they survived this, they would be hanged.

Even so, they didn't stand a chance, for Ranulf was filled with burning, righteous rage. He fought without care for his own life, the wound at his side, the blood dripping from his cheek, or his form and stance. This was no place for finesse. This was a place where he *must* triumph, so he struck hard and fast, slicing through the shoulder of the first man, who staggered backward and fell. The two others facing him jumped away as Kiernan and more men from Penterwell's garrison leapt onto the ship beside him.

Ranulf lashed out again, and his two opponents moved farther from his reach. And then, as Ranulf's attention was on the foes before him, another man rushed in at him from the side.

Unfortunately for the one-eyed man, he had never been trained by Sir Leonard de Brissy. Otherwise, he would have realized that the training Ranulf and his fellows had undergone ensured their instincts were as finely honed as it was possible to be.

Those instincts came to Ranulf's aid now, and without conscious thought, he lunged at the blur of motion near him—and ran his sword through Pierre's chest.

With a grunt, the smuggler stumbled forward. He hit the rail of his ship and, with a shriek, tumbled over it into the frothing sea. Ranulf saw his terrified face and one upraised hand desperately seeking something to grasp before a wave rolled over him and he disappeared.

Gasping as if he were drowning, too, Ranulf turned back. The rest of the smugglers were either engaged in fighting with his men and Kiernan, or were already dead on the deck.

His side burning, the pain intense, Ranulf saw two men blocking a door as if they were on guard. Or protecting something precious.

Bellowing his war cry, Ranulf rushed forward. Kiernan joined him and the two smugglers stood no chance at all.

When they were dead, Ranulf ran to the door. "Bea! Bea!" he shouted, throwing his shoulder against it as the ship gave another great shudder and heaved upward before crashing down again.

He broke through that door, to find himself in a narrow passage with another door at the end.

"Ranulf! We're here, Ranulf!" Bea cried from the other side of that door, banging on it with her fists.

Thank God, oh thank God!

Ranulf ran at the door and hit it with the full weight of his entire body.

It shattered.

And there was Bea, desperately pulling away the broken wood from the inside of the cabin. You're hurt!"

'tt's nothing," he answered as he, too, started to

make the hole large enough for her and Wenna to climb through.

Once more, the ship lurched before shuddering and settling against the rock.

Kiernan appeared and joined the effort, until Bea pushed her way through, regardless of any shattered wood still attached to the frame.

She threw herself into Ranulf's arms, saying nothing, for her heart was too full to speak. Nor did he, because he could find no words. Yet they hugged for only a brief moment before he let go and gently pushed her toward Kiernan, who moved her along to Gareth, as if there were a fire and she a bucket full of water to put it out. Meanwhile, Ranulf helped Wenna through the door, her baby in her arms. They, too, were passed along until they all stood at the side of the ship, Bea and Wenna trying not to look at the bodies on the blood-soaked deck.

Some of Ranulf's men laid a plank from the smugglers' barque to the merchant's ship, and it was across that perilous bridge that they would have to make their way to safety.

"Crawl across, Bea," Ranulf said. "Or lie on your belly and drag yourself."

Crawling would be faster, she thought. But…

"Wenna or her child should go first," she declared in a tone as commanding as Ranulf's.

He wisely made no protest. "Gareth," he ordered, "sit on the plank and I'll hand you the baby. Then you turn and hand it over to one of the men on the merchant vessel."

He ordered two of his soldiers to hold the plank, then shouted across the space to one of the archers watching on the deck. "Come onto the plank and sit down, and be ready to receive the child."

Gareth made his way a short distance along the plank and sat with his legs dangling over the sides to keep his balance. With trembling arms but hopeful eyes, Wenna held out her child to him. He took it and, twisting, handed it back to the archer, who was seated facing the same direction. Slowly, cradling the baby in one arm, using the other hand to push himself, the archer inched his way back to the merchant's ship.

The smugglers' ship groaned and the plank shifted. Bea gasped and Wenna cried out, but mercifully the plank didn't fall.

Once he was close to the merchant's ship, the archer turned and handed Gawan to one of the crew who was leaning down to take him.

"Oh, thank God!" Wenna fervently sighed when Gawan was safely on board, echoing Bea's own thoughts and, she was sure, that of everyone else on the smugglers' ship.

Gareth, meanwhile, came back to the smugglers' ship, ready to help the women. "You next, my lady," he said.

"Wenna," she resolutely replied, reaching out to take Ranulf's hand in hers.

Grasping her hand tightly, Ranulf nodded, so Gareth helped Wenna onto the plank. She chose to crawl, holding to the sides and going carefully toward the other ship, and her child.

"Your turn, Bea," Ranulf said once Wenna was safely across and taking her baby from the seaman's arms.

She didn't refuse. Instead, she let go of his strong hand, took a deep breath and crawled as Wenna had, trying not to look at the turbulent water below, or think about the plank tipping, or the ship behind her breaking into pieces and sending all aboard into the sea.

Two men grabbed her arms and lifted her up until she was standing, shaky but alive, on the deck of the merchant's vessel.

And then came the most terrible wait of all as the other men came off the smugglers' ship. Ranulf wouldn't leave until all the others had made it safely across the narrow plank, including the men who'd been holding it steady. She could expect no less, and yet she thought her heart would beat right out of her chest as he began to crawl across the plank the way she had. She thought of his fear and prayed to God to give him courage. She saw his bloody cheek and remembered the worse wound in his side, and prayed that he would have the strength to hold on.

His face pale as a corpse, his expression grimly resolute, he kept his gaze on either his hands, or her, the entire time. Never once did he look down.

Then—oh, and then!—he was on the deck and in her arms.

She held him tight for one glorious, relieved moment before she felt his body relax against her and realized he had fainted.

CHAPTER TWENTY

WHEN RANULF NEXT OPENED his eyes, he was back in his bedchamber in Penterwell. Bea wasn't sitting solicitously by his bedside, though. Nor was Celeste. Instead, the lord of Tregellas regarded him gravely.

"So, you're awake at last," Merrick observed in his low, deep growl of a voice. "About time, too."

A little dizzy, Ranulf struggled to sit up, hissing at the sharp pain in his side as he moved and the stitched flesh protested. "Where's Bea?"

Merrick raised a brow. "You mean my ward, Lady Beatrice?"

"Yes. Where is she? Was she hurt?"

"Beatrice is fine," Merrick replied, to Ranulf's vast relief. "A little bruised, perhaps, and her feet were cut, but otherwise, she is quite well. Indeed, her capacity to talk at length remains undiminished."

"Where is she?"

"I thought you'd appreciate some peace and quiet, although it took quite an effort to make her leave your chamber. She didn't want to go even after Constance had seen to your side—you tore the stitches open—

and the cut on your cheek and assured her about fifty times you weren't going to die. Meanwhile, so my wife informs me, Maloren kept moaning in the corner about how wrong she'd been about you and if you died, it would be some sort of judgment on her. How she reached that remarkable conclusion, neither Constance nor I can fathom."

Why did Merrick have to pick such a time to be loquacious? *"Where is Bea?"*

"Sleeping, I hope. The poor girl was completely exhausted. I suspect Constance gave her something to *make* her sleep, or she likely would have kept talking until she dropped, telling us about the murders and the smugglers and who was guilty and what happened." He tilted his head to study Ranulf. "You look very happy for a man who's got to be in considerable pain."

Ranulf hoisted himself a bit more upright, in spite of the agony. "What of Wenna and her baby?"

"They are well, too. Apparently Wenna might not have been had Beatrice not been brought aboard that ship when she was."

Merrick shifted, grimaced and glanced down at his left leg, which Ranulf realized was still splinted and wrapped.

"Aren't we a fine pair?" the lord of Tregellas observed with a roguish gleam in his dark eyes. "All we need is Henry with his ruined face to complete the picture."

"How did you get here? Bea said you weren't supposed to ride."

"I came in a wagon and, please God, never again. I felt like a feeble old man."

"At least you haven't made the mistakes I have. God's blood, I was a fool, Merrick. I trusted Myghal and—"

"We can discuss your shortcomings as castellan later. I'm sure Sir Leonard will have a few things to say, as well."

"You're going to write to him about this?"

"No need, since he's sitting in your hall."

"No, I'm not," a familiar voice growled from the doorway.

Sir Leonard himself stood on the threshold. His back was still straight as a lance and his expression not unlike the one Ranulf well remembered from the day he'd demanded to train with Sir Leonard de Brissy. The only noticeable change was that their mentor's hair was now snow-white.

"And a fine thing I discover when I travel here," Sir Leonard declared as he strode into the bedchamber. "You fighting a sea battle? Good God Almighty, I thought young Merrick here had lost his mind when he told me."

"I had to rescue Lady Beatrice," Ranulf answered, knowing Sir Leonard would have done the same thing. He struggled to sit up straighter. "Have you met her?"

"Couldn't help it. She jumped me like an assassin

when she found out who I was." He smirked, but there was laughter lurking in the wise old eyes. "Affectionate girl, I must say."

"She's wonderful and I love her and if Merrick will give us his permission, we want to be married," Ranulf replied, speaking nearly as breathlessly as Bea at her most enthused.

Sir Leonard's bushy white brows rose as he looked from Ranulf to Merrick.

"I gathered from certain cryptic remarks the lady made to my wife that something like that was in the offing," Merrick observed. Then he smiled, and a very satisfied smile it was. "About bloody time, I must say. Constance was beginning to fear you'd never ask for her. I've had to listen to her expound on the subject several times when I'd much rather we were doing other things."

Ranulf flushed. "How did she know—?"

"Women's intuition, I suppose, or some other mysterious process known only to their sex." Merrick shrugged. "She's been convinced you and Beatrice should marry for months. Why else do you think we sent Beatrice here?"

Sir Leonard chuckled and crossed his still powerful arms. "A conspiracy, eh?"

"Before you get angry, Ranulf," Merrick said, although in truth, Ranulf looked more stunned than annoyed, "it wasn't *my* conspiracy. Constance convinced me that Beatrice ought to help you, although

Beatrice was most insistent about coming to your aid, too. She feared you were living in squalor, and since Constance couldn't come because of the baby, she had to. I thought the plan most unseemly, but Constance believed otherwise, and so..." Again he shrugged his broad shoulders. "What else could I do? And no doubt Beatrice would have been grumbling and pouting all over Tregellas if we didn't."

"She rarely does either," Ranulf said, compelled to defend his beloved.

"She might have started, since it was you she was worried about. At any rate, Constance was more than half hoping you'd both finally stop beating about the bush and admit that you love each other."

"You always were a proud and stubborn boy," Sir Leonard noted.

"It wasn't my pride or stubbornness that held me back," Ranulf said, compelled to defend himself now. "I'm a poor man and Beatrice can do better."

"The daughter of a traitor?" Sir Leonard inquired. "I doubt it."

"You don't know her. She's good and clever, as well as beautiful. She knows much of medicine and how to run a household. What can I give her? Nothing except my love and devotion, my training and my sword. She could do a hundred times better than me when it comes to marriage. Ask Merrick if you don't believe me."

Merrick held up his hand. "Save your declarations of unworthiness for Beatrice. I believe women like that sort of thing, or are at least flattered by it. As for me, why the devil wouldn't I want my closest friend related to me by marriage? And regarding your fortune—or lack of it—if you're willing to remain in command of Penterwell, I see no troubles there. I hope you will, or I'm liable to have a revolt on my hands. There's been a crowd of people waiting to hear word of your health ever since the ship returned and they saw you carried ashore. I knew Beatrice could talk, but I must say, I never realized how loud she could shout. I could hear her calling to clear the road all the way from the wharf."

Sir Leonard nodded, chuckling. "She's got lungs, I'll say that. And she could do worse herself. You two and Henry were the best I ever taught, in every way, and I couldn't be prouder of you than if you were my own son."

As Ranulf's throat tightened, Sir Leonard cleared his own and his cheeks were conspicuously pinker as he turned toward the door. "Yes, well, I'd best be going back to the hall. Your garrison commander's going to show me what the masons have been up to."

"Not that I'm not happy to see him," Ranulf said as the door closed behind Sir Leonard, "but why did he come here?"

"Can't you guess?"

Ranulf shook his head.

"You're his favorite, Ranulf. You always have

been and likely always will be. When we sent word you'd been wounded, he came right away. He rode all night, in fact, and most of the day. I think he loves you as the son he never had—although," Merrick added with a grin lurking at the corner of his full lips, "Henry and I are damned if we know why."

Ranulf knew. In a way, he realized, he'd always known Sir Leonard's concern for him was more than that of a teacher for a pupil. "He knew my mother when she was young. I think he loved her, but she was married to another."

Merrick frowned. "Henry sometimes wondered if you might be his natural son."

Ranulf shook his head. "No, although I would be delighted if I were. After my mother married my brute of a father, she never saw Sir Leonard again. My father made sure of that. He kept her all but imprisoned, and if you ever met my vicious sire, you'd see his features mirrored in mine. But enough talk of that unpleasant subject. When can I see Bea?"

Merrick continued to look grave as he leaned forward. "Because I'm one of your oldest friends, I'm going to be frank with you. Are you *quite* sure you want to marry her? Granted she's pretty and a more competent chatelaine than I ever would have guessed she could be, but you may never have a moment's peace and quiet with her for your wife."

Ranulf's lips curved up in a winsome smile as he remembered the night he'd made love to Bea.

Never in his life had he known such peace and contentment as when he lay in her arms afterward. "Oh, I daresay I'll manage. As for quiet, I think that quality in a woman is vastly overrated. Your own lady wife never struck me as a pliant, demure and silent young woman."

Merrick laughed ruefully. "No, she is not," he agreed. "So, how soon do you want the wedding to be?"

"It cannot be soon enough for me," Ranulf replied, and rarely had he ever been so frankly honest.

WHEN BEA'S EYES OPENED a short time later, she expected to find Constance or Maloren sitting beside her bed. Instead, there was a man. A clean-shaven, redheaded, youthful-looking man with a scabbed cut on his smooth cheek. A rather familiar looking man whose hazel eyes seemed to fairly shine with—

"Ranulf?" Concern quickly replaced her joy as she scrambled to sit up. "What are you doing here? You should be in bed! You're wounded. You could have died! You absolutely must rest and I'm shocked Constance let you get up. How long have I been sleeping? I'm going to call—"

"Bea—"

"She gave me something to sleep, I know she did! And she's let you get out of bed and come here when you're wounded. She shouldn't—"

"Bea—"

"I was sure she'd take better care of you. I was so

happy to see her, and Merrick, too, when we came ashore, and oh! Did you know Sir Leonard has come?"

Before he could answer, she reverted to her former subject, which was obviously uppermost in her mind. "If this is Constance's idea of taking care of somebody who's saved her cousin's life, I've been seriously misled and I'll tell her—"

"*Bea!*"

At his explosive declaration, her eyes widened and all thoughts of Constance, Merrick, Sir Leonard and everything else fled her mind. "I knew it!" she exclaimed. "You're in agony! We must call someone. Maloren or—"

"God's blood, no!" he commanded. Then he smiled in the sudden silence and took her hand in his. "I don't want anyone else here, and I'm fine, Bea. A little sore, to be sure, and likely to be weak as a kitten for a few days, but they would have had to tie me down to keep me away from you another moment longer, and as you can see, they thought better of it. So here we are. Alone."

Her eyes lit up as she glanced over his shoulder and realized he was right. And then her shapely brows lowered in puzzlement. "Merrick is letting us be alone together?"

"Since he's also allowing us to marry, apparently he saw no harm in it."

Beatrice let out a whoop that was most certainly neither dignified nor ladylike. She threw back her covers and was about to embrace him when thoughts of his wound halted her. "How's your side? You pulled out the stitches."

"So Merrick informed me. To be perfectly honest, my beloved, my side is *quite* sore. However, I note that my lips are unaffected, so a kiss should not cause me pain. In fact," he said, tugging her down onto his lap, "I think a kiss from you would make me feel much better and quite possibly speed my healing."

"When you put it like that, my lord, I'm delighted to help any way I can," she murmured, lifting her face to kiss him.

He responded with enthusiastic fervor, and in a few moments, when she broke the kiss to repeat the wonderful news, she was breathless. "Merrick and Constance are going to let us marry? They have no objections at all?"

"Not a one, and it seems, my love, that Constance had our marriage in her mind all along. That's why they let you come here and save me from my squalor."

Bea frowned as she took in that revelation. "She was trying to bring us together?"

"Apparently."

Bea's brilliant, delighted smile reappeared. "Whatever reason they had for allowing me to come here, I'm thankful they did, and I always will be."

"So will I," he solemnly and sincerely agreed.

She wound her arms about his neck and laid her

cheek upon his shoulder. "I think that right now, I'm as happy as it's possible to be."

"As am I," he replied as he kissed her smooth cheek. He couldn't resist teasing her a little. "But I fear you might miss the excitement of unrequited love."

She regarded him gravely as she caressed his smooth jaw. "It *was* rather thrilling when I wasn't sure how you felt about me and I hoped that you might come to love me eventually, but it was very difficult to be patient. The rest of the time, when I feared you didn't love me and never would, was misery."

"I shall have to ensure you are never miserable or doubt my love again," he murmured as he brought his lips to hers. "Never as long as I live."

"As I'll do *my* best to see that you're never lonely again, my love," she whispered before she kissed him.

EPILOGUE

RANULF AND BEA ADHERED to the vows they made that morning and as time went on, the castellan of Penterwell and his wife became famous for the happiness, merriment and contentment to be found in their hall. Guests often clamored to hear the lady tell of the daring rescue at sea by her husband and Lord Kiernan of Penderston, whom Bea forgave for any past offense when she learned he'd saved Ranulf's life in the fight on the beach. Sir Ranulf preferred to regale their company with his wife's "clever strategy of the shoes" and tell them how she'd talked her captor into fleeing his own cabin.

Kiernan married the Lady Celeste and fathered several very beautiful daughters with his equally devoted wife. One of these young ladies eventually married Sir Gawan, a most famous and valiant knight who began his career as page, then squire, to Sir Ranulf of Penterwell.

Wenna wed Gareth, the garrison commander, and started an inn that became famous for its meat pies. Their children prospered, although neither they, nor their parents, ever condoned or participated in any smuggling, despite the temptation and the king's unjust taxation of Cornish tin.

The lord and lady of Penterwell had children, too—a merry, boisterous band of offspring with reddish golden hair. At first, Maloren was there to nurse them, but then she married the cook, to the shock of everyone in the castle, although perhaps none so much as Much.

Some of Ranulf and Beatrice's children had blue eyes, others hazel, and all were quick-witted and clever. The boys became knights renowned for their skill in battle, their cutting sarcasm and, among the ladies, their fine physiques, handsome faces and passionate natures. Their equally passionate sisters, declared beauties by all who met them, were famous for their wit, their laughter and, truth be told, their tendency to talk.

For little Lady Bea never did become quiet and demure.

Her husband wouldn't have had it any other way.

From #1 *New York Times*
bestselling author Nora Roberts

When you've surrendered your heart, and the
one you love is involved in murder, it can be...

⚰ANGEROUS

This collection contains three unforgettable classics:
Risky Business, Storm Warning and *The Welcoming.*

Available in bookstores in August.

Silhouette®
Where love comes alive™

Visit Silhouette Books at www.eHarlequin.com PSNR5?s

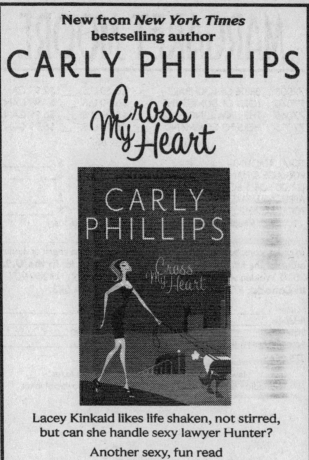

MARGARET MOORE

77003	BRIDE OF LOCHBARR	___ $6.50 U.S.	___ $7.99 CAN.
77040	LORD OF DUNKEATHE	___ $6.50 U.S.	___ $7.99 CAN.
77065	THE UNWILLING BRIDE	___ $5.99 U.S.	___ $6.99 CAN.
77095	HERS TO COMMAND	___ $5.99 U.S.	___ $6.99 CAN.

(limited quantities available)

TOTAL AMOUNT $ _____
POSTAGE & HANDLING $ _____
($1.00 FOR 1 BOOK, 50¢ for each additional)
APPLICABLE TAXES* $ _____
TOTAL PAYABLE $ _____

(check or money order—please do not send cash)

To order, complete this form and send it, along with a check or money order for the total above, payable to HQN Books, to: **In the U.S.:** 3010 Walden Avenue, P.O. Box 9077, Buffalo, NY 14269-9077; **In Canada:** P.O. Box 636, Fort Erie, Ontario, L2A 5X3.

Name: _____
Address: _____ City: _____
State/Prov.: _____ Zip/Postal Code: _____
Account Number (if applicable): _____

075 CSAS

*New York residents remit applicable sales taxes.
*Canadian residents remit applicable GST and provincial taxes.

HQN™

We *are* romance™

www.HQNBooks.com

PHMM0806BL